Praise for

"**Ms. Krentz** has deservedly won the hearts
of readers everywhere with her unique blend of
fiery passion and romantic adventure.... One
of the greatest pleasures of reading Ms. Krentz is
the marvelous symmetry between characters and
plot.... It is this gratifying intricacy that makes each
and every Krentz book something to be savored."
—*Rave Reviews*

"Jayne Ann Krentz is one of the hottest writers
in romance today."
—*USA TODAY*

"Jayne Ann Krentz entertains to the hilt...."
—Catherine Coulter

"**Amanda Stevens** always delivers what I want most
in a book—excitement, romance, adventure—but
she adds something special to the mix. Her stories
are filled with a tenderness that keeps the reader
emotionally involved to the very end."
—Susan Wiggs

"**Rebecca York** delivers page-turning suspense."
—Nora Roberts

JAYNE ANN KRENTZ
is one of today's best-loved authors of women's fiction. With multiple *New York Times* bestselling novels to her credit, she is a prolific and innovative writer—much to the delight of her legions of fans around the world. She has delved into psychic elements, intrigue, fantasy, historical and even futuristic romances. Jayne lives in Seattle with her husband.

AMANDA STEVENS
knew at an early age that she wanted to be a writer, and began her first novel at the age of thirteen. While majoring in English at Houston Community College and the University of Houston, she was encouraged to write a romance novel by one of her instructors, who was himself writing a historical. Her first romance was sold to Silhouette Intimate Moments in 1985. Amanda lives in Houston, Texas, with her husband of sixteen years and their twins.

REBECCA YORK
is the pseudonym of Ruth Glick and Eileen Buckholtz, who started Harlequin Intrigue's popular 43 LIGHT STREET series together. Recently Ruth has been writing the series on her own as Rebecca York. Her book *Shattered Vows* was honored as Intrigue's 500th book. *Nowhere Man* was honored by *Romantic Times* as the Best Intrigue of 1998 and by *Affaire de Coeur* as Best Contemporary Novel. Eileen Buckholtz is a master computer scientist and Internet consultant. Taking a break from writing fiction, she fulfilled a lifelong dream to work on Capitol Hill, published a bestselling business e-book and developed several popular worldwide community service Web sites.

JAYNE ANN KRENTZ

WITCHCRAFT

HARLEQUIN®

TORONTO • NEW YORK • LONDON
AMSTERDAM • PARIS • SYDNEY • HAMBURG
STOCKHOLM • ATHENS • TOKYO • MILAN • MADRID
PRAGUE • WARSAW • BUDAPEST • AUCKLAND

ISBN 0-373-83542-6

WITCHCRAFT

Copyright © 2003 by Harlequin Books S.A.

The publisher acknowledges the copyright holders of the individual titles as follows:

WITCHCRAFT
Copyright © 1985 by Jayne Ann Krentz

LAST CHANCE CAFÉ
Copyright © 2000 by Harlequin Books S.A.

BAYOU REUNION
Copyright © 2001 by Harlequin Books S.A.

This edition published by arrangement with Harlequin Books S.A.

® and TM are trademarks of the publisher. Trademarks indicated with ® are registered in the United States Patent and Trademark Office, the Canadian Trade Marks Office and in other countries.

Visit us at www.eHarlequin.com

Printed in U.S.A.

CONTENTS

WITCHCRAFT

Jayne Ann Krentz

CHAPTER ONE

THE ROSE with the needle thrust into its heart arrived on Kimberly Sawyer's doorstep that morning. Darius Cavenaugh, the man with the emerald eyes, arrived that evening. Both events shook her to the core.

There was nothing unusual at first about the rose, other than the fact it had been left without a note. Kimberly discovered it as she opened the door to walk down to the beach. Startled and then mildly intrigued, as any woman would have been, she picked up the bloodred flower and cheerfully stuck it into an old wine bottle. It would look nice sitting on the windowsill in front of her typewriter.

Not until midmorning, when the petals began to open, did Kimberly look up from her work and see the vicious shaft of the steel needle spearing the center of the rose. It had been carefully insinuated between the folded petals so that it would be revealed only when they gradually opened.

Kimberly froze at the subtle, deliberate violence. She sat very still, staring at the wicked needle, and tried to chase away the frisson of fear that flashed down her spine.

Then she remembered Darius Cavenaugh.

The image of his savagely hewn features and the gleaming emerald depths of his strangely compelling eyes appeared with shattering intensity in her mind. Her gaze never leaving the needle in the rose, Kimberly reached out a trembling hand and picked up the receiver of her chromium-yellow telephone.

She found herself searching blindly for the little card Darius Cavenaugh had given her two months ago, her fingers shuffling awkwardly through the file on her desk. And then she was dialing the number without even pausing to think.

Halfway through the process, Kimberly suddenly realized how foolishly she was behaving. This was ridiculous. Someone was playing a joke on her, nothing more. But the phone had already started to ring. Before she could slam down the receiver a woman's voice answered.

"Hello?"

Frantically Kimberly tried to retreat. "I'm…I'm sorry, I have the wrong number."

"This phone is unlisted," the woman said coolly. "May I ask who's calling and where you got the number?"

"I'm sorry, I misdialed." Kimberly hastily replaced the receiver. Stupid. What on earth was she thinking of to call Cavenaugh's residence just because she'd had a small, but rather jolting experience?

She was back under control now. Kimberly frowned at the offending rose and tried to imagine which of her few neighbors might have played such a bizarre trick on her. There was gruff and dour Mr. Wilcox who lived farther down the beach. Then there was Elvira Eden, the aging flower child who had never quite evolved mentally beyond the era of the 1960s. She had a huge garden, Kimberly reminded herself. But it was hard to picture the perpetually serene and smiling Elvira doing something like this. And old Wilcox, while admittedly not possessed of a charming personality wasn't really the type, either.

Restlessly, Kimberly got to her feet, shoving her hands into the rear pockets of her snug, faded jeans and went to stand in front of the huge window that faced the ocean.

This was a particularly desolate and rugged stretch of

California's northern coast. Few people lived here year-round, although the tourists would be pouring in from San Francisco and the Bay area when summer arrived. But it was early spring right now and there was only a handful of residents strung along the craggy coastline this far north of Fort Bragg.

None of the ones whom she'd met seemed the type to pull this little stunt with the rose.

"You're going soft in the brain, Kim," she lectured herself as she filled a teakettle and set it on the stove. "It's got to be someone's crazy idea of a joke."

Once again Cavenaugh's image flashed through her mind. She couldn't help wondering about the woman who had answered his phone. It could have been any one of his relatives or someone who worked on the estate. The Cavenaugh winery undoubtedly employed several people. As far as relatives went, there was his sister, Julia, Julia's son Scott, an aunt whom Kimberly vaguely remembered being named Millicent and who knew how many others?

Kimberly shuddered at the notion of so many people intimately involved in one's daily world. Extended families were not high on her list of life's pleasures. In fact, families of any size tended to make her wary.

That thought made Kimberly remember the buff-colored envelope that had arrived in her mailbox yesterday. It was still lying, unopened, on the kitchen counter. That envelope wasn't the first she had received, bearing the discreet address of a Los Angeles law firm. After opening the first several months ago, Kimberly had determined not to open any more. Still, for some obscure reason, it was difficult for her to just toss it in the garbage.

The kettle came to a boil and Kimberly poured herself a huge mug of tea. She needed to get back to work. Her fictional characters were making more pressing demands on her than the silly incident with the rose. With a frown of concentration, she sat down to finish chapter three.

She worked for an hour before thinking again of the pierced rose. Kimberly looked up, gazing absently into the middle distance beyond her window, and found herself staring at the crimson flower instead of untangling the intricacies of her current plot.

That needle had been placed inside the petals deliberately. There was no point telling herself it had happened accidentally. And no mere accident had brought the flower to her doorstep.

A spark of sunlight glinted on the needle, illuminating it harshly. Then one of the storm clouds rolling in from the ocean blotted out the brief ray of light. The steel needle continued to gleam dully.

She ought to throw the rose into the garbage along with that letter from the lawyer, Kimberly told herself uneasily. But the unanswered questions surrounding the rose's presence on her doorstep seemed to make it impossible to just dismiss the incident.

Thoughts of Darius Cavenaugh brushed through her mind again, and before they had disappeared she found her eyes sliding toward the yellow telephone. Without stopping to think she picked up the receiver, dialing the number on the small card quickly, as though something beyond her own will drove her to do so.

"This is ridiculous," Kimberly muttered as she listened to the phone ringing a hundred miles away on the estate in the Napa Valley. She took a deep breath and hurriedly disconnected herself before anyone could pick up the receiver.

But all afternoon as the storm began to gather itself out at sea for the assault on the coast, Kimberly's thoughts kept ricocheting back and forth between the rose on her windowsill and the image of Darius Cavenaugh. Twice more she found herself reaching for the phone as though an outside force were prompting her. Twice more she slammed the receiver back into the cradle with an exclamation of disgust. She could not call Cavenaugh. Not over something as trivial as this damned rose business.

Chapter three grudgingly ended shortly before five o'clock. With a feeling of relief Kimberly covered the typewriter. It had been terribly difficult to keep her mind on her work. Outside, the sky was already quite dark and the wind was beginning to howl demandingly around the small beachfront cottage.

Turning on a few more lights to ward off the pressing, storm-driven darkness, Kimberly built a small fire on the old stone hearth. It was not uncommon for the electricity to go off during a storm, and she didn't want to find herself without heat or light later on this evening.

A feeling of tension, real restless uneasiness, began to work on her nervous system as she lit the fire and went into the kitchen to see about dinner.

Long accustomed to eating alone, Kimberly normally viewed the prospect with a certain quiet pleasure. She poured herself a glass of Cavenaugh Merlot wine and sipped it slowly as she prepared a baked potato and a green salad. This evening would be a good time to finish that wonderfully trashy adventure novel she had started reading last night.

As usual she set a neat table for herself, preparing the baked potato exactly as she liked it with loads of sour cream and salad dressing, grated cheese, chopped black olives, a sprinkling of peanuts and some sliced hot peppers. Setting out the bottle of hot sauce to which she was pleasantly addicted, she poured a bit more of the Merlot into her glass.

Kimberly had bought the Cavenaugh wine on a whim earlier that week when it showed up on the shelves of the tiny market in the nearby town. It had been an expensive whim, and not one she would indulge frequently. Writers living from one royalty statement to the next tended to become connoisseurs of wines that came in large bottles with screw tops. She'd actually had to dig out a genuine corkscrew for the Cavenaugh Vineyards bottle. The wine inside had proven to be excellent, but that didn't really surprise her. Anything Darius Cavenaugh did would be done well. No, she thought absently, more than just well. It would be done *right*. With all the loose ends tied up. She wasn't certain why she knew that on the basis of only having spent a few hours with him, but she didn't question the knowledge.

She had been hoping the extra half glass of wine that she'd allowed herself tonight might dispel some of the strange tension she was experiencing, but it didn't seem to be working.

Kimberly was just about to sink a fork into the elaborately decorated baked potato when the lights flickered and went out.

"Well, damn. There goes my chance to finish that novel tonight," she murmured with a sigh. Across the room the fire crackled. Picking up her plate, the hot sauce and the remaining glass of wine, Kimberly started toward it, intending to finish her meal while sitting in front of the hearth.

The purr of a sophisticated car's engine in her driveway captured her attention when she was halfway across the small room. The sound rose briefly above the increasing howl of the wind and rain and then suddenly fell silent. Someone had chosen a miserable night to come visiting.

A moment later came the knock on her door. Kimberly

had already set down her dinner and was peering through the tiny window set in the door panel. It was impossible to see who stood on the step because the porch light was not working.

"Who is it?" she called with a trace of unease. Except for that incident two months ago, crime was not a real problem around here. Nevertheless, Kimberly was instinctively wary tonight. That business with the rose had unsettled her more than she had realized.

There was no answer. Perhaps whoever it was couldn't hear her over the roar of the storm. Taking a deep breath and telling herself not to be so skittish, Kimberly unlocked the door, leaving the chain on, and opened it a couple of inches.

"Who's there?" she inquired coolly, peering through the small opening.

The man on her front step turned his head in that moment, and the faint light from the fire flared briefly on his roughly etched features. His gaze flicked over her shadowed face; a gaze that Kimberly knew would be emerald green in the full light of day.

"Cavenaugh," he said.

Kimberly closed her eyes with an odd sense of relief at the succinct answer. "Cavenaugh," she repeated. The rough texture of his voice brought back memories of the last time she had seen him. It also brought an indescribable wariness that she had never been able to properly identify or understand.

As she stared up at him the wind screamed eerily, just as it had that night two months ago when she had gotten herself involved in the incredible situation that had led to her meeting Darius Cavenaugh. She realized abruptly that he must be getting chilled out on her porch.

Without another word she closed the door, undid the

chain lock and then allowed him inside. She stepped back as he moved into the firelit room, her eyes moving over him, trying to accept the fact he was here.

"What a coincidence that you should show up tonight," she finally managed politely as she motioned him to a comfortably overstuffed chair in front of the fire. "I was thinking about you today. What are you doing here? Have you come on business regarding that mess two months ago? Let me have your jacket. The electricity went off but the fire should keep the place warm. I was just about to eat. Have you had dinner?"

When he simply looked at her as he shrugged off the suede jacket he was wearing, Kimberly realized belatedly that she was babbling and wondered why. It wasn't at all like her. Annoyed with herself she hastily closed her mouth and silently accepted his jacket. It was still warm from the heat of his strong, lean body and the leather seemed to carry a trace of his scent. As soon as she caught the hint of the unique masculine essence, Kimberly knew she had never forgotten it.

How odd to have that surprisingly intimate realization about a man whom she barely knew; someone whom she'd had no relationship beyond the quite limited association brought on by the events of two months ago.

"I think," Cavenaugh said calmly as he sank down into the old chair, "that you did more than think about me today."

Startled, Kimberly finished hanging up his jacket and then started back across the room. "What on earth are you talking about?"

"That was you on the phone this morning, wasn't it? When Julia mentioned that a woman had called and then claimed to have misdialed I had a feeling—" He broke off with a faintly slanting smile. "And later on the phone rang again but the person on the other end of the line had gotten cold feet by the time I picked up the receiver. That was you too, wasn't it?''

Slowly, her amber brows knit together in a small frown, Kimberly walked over to the kitchen and poured another glass of the Cavenaugh Merlot wine. ''How did you know?''

''A hunch. The number's unlisted and people rarely misdial it. Two or three such hangups in one day were a little suspicious. Something told me it had to be you. Offhand I can't think of anyone else I know who would have hesitated to make the call.'' His mouth moved briefly, wryly. ''Everyone else seems to have no qualms at all about contacting me for just about any reason.''

''You didn't even call me back to make certain,'' she pointed out quietly as she walked back to her chair in front of the fire.

He reached up to accept the glass of wine she offered. Almost idly Cavenaugh held the glass so that the deep ruby liquid was lit by firelight. He perused the color with an expert's eye and then took a cautious taste.

''Very good,'' he pronounced, watching Kimberly over the rim.

''It should be. It's a Cavenaugh wine,'' she murmured dryly. ''Cost me half a royalty check.''

''I know.'' He swirled the wine in the glass and smiled faintly. ''You must have known I was arriving tonight.''

She blinked, mildly surprised. ''How could I know that?''

''Beats me. The same way I realized it was you on the phone today, I suppose.'' He took another sip of the wine and continued to watch her.

''Coincidence,'' she assured him roundly. Kimberly found herself having to quash an unsettling sensation of intimacy caused by his words. She'd had that bottle of wine in the kitchen cupboard for several days along with a few others. It was odd that she'd opened it tonight. Then again… "Well, maybe it was more than sheer coincidence," she admitted. "I did think about you several times today and you're right. It was me on the phone. I suppose I had Cavenaugh on the brain, and when I chose a wine tonight it was automatic to reach for the name."

"Automatic," he agreed blandly. "Subliminal advertising. I'll have to talk to my public relations consulting firm about the technique."

"That doesn't explain why you didn't try to phone me back to find out whether or not I was the mysterious caller," she pointed out. Kimberly reached for her plate. "And did you get any dinner?"

"No, I didn't get any dinner. I drove straight through."

"Want to split a baked potato and salad?"

"Is that what that is?" He eyed the heavily decorated baked potato as if it were some alien life form. "Well, I'm hungry enough to risk it."

She got up again to find another plate and then she carefully divided the still hot potato. "So?"

"So what?" He took the plate and fork from her and then watched, fascinated as Kimberly sprinkled hot sauce liberally over her own share of the food.

"Why didn't you call to find out if it had been me on the phone?"

"Because I'd been planning to drive over here for a week. Deciding it had probably been you on the phone just pushed me into making the trip tonight instead of this coming weekend." He forked up a chunk of potato warily. "What all have you got on this thing?"

"Everything I could think of."

"Well, it's interesting."

"A highly personalized baked potato," she said with a grin. "One of the many advantages of living alone. You can eat anything you want and have it fixed any way you like. Want some hot sauce?"

He considered the matter for a few seconds and then accepted the bottle. "Why not? In for a penny, in for a pound." Cavenaugh gave her an assessing glance. "You're very content living by yourself, aren't you? I realized that when I met you two months ago. You're quite self-contained. Have you always been alone?"

Kimberly shook her head with a small smile of amusement. "I don't really think of myself as being isolated. I'm just independent and used to doing things exactly as I like to do them; that's the way I was raised. When I was growing up there were only my mother and me. It must seem strange to you because you're always surrounded by family and all those people who work at the winery. From my point of view that kind of constant pressure would drive me crazy!"

"Pressure?"

She nodded. "Where there is a lot of family, there are a lot of demands. And in your case, you have the additional pressure and responsibility of supervising the winery staff. Many of them must be almost like family by now. You told me that the Cavenaugh winery had been around for a long time so I imagine many of the workers have, too."

Cavenaugh nodded slowly, emerald eyes appraising her features in the firelight. "You're right. There are certain demands in my situation."

"Well," Kimberly pointed out thoughtfully, "at least you're at the top of the pile instead of at the bottom. If one is going to have to live with so many other people it's probably best to be the one in charge."

"It has its moments," he agreed coolly. "But I get the feeling you wouldn't want to trade places with me."

Kimberly gave a mock shudder. "Not for the world. I'm afraid I've grown very accustomed to the freedom of being alone."

"But perhaps you wouldn't mind sharing your life with one other loner?"

Kimberly hesitated. "What makes you say that?"

"I've read the first two books in the Amy Solitaire series. *Vicious Circle* and *Unfinished Business*."

She smiled slowly. "You surprise me. I wouldn't have thought they would appeal to you."

"Being in the author's debt is bound to give me a certain curiosity about the author herself," Cavenaugh said sardonically. "Reading your books is a natural extension of that curiosity."

"Did you learn anything?" she quipped, wishing he wouldn't bring up the subject of being in her debt. Yet if she were perfectly honest with herself his promise of repayment had been on her mind today. She had thought of it the moment she had seen the petals of the rose unfolding to reveal the needle.

Kimberly could remember very clearly Darius Cavenaugh's last words to her two months ago. They had flickered in and out of her head along with his image all day long. *I want your word of honor that if there is ever anything I can do to repay you, you will call me. Anytime, anywhere. Do you understand, Kimberly Sawyer? I'll come to you wherever you are.*

She'd understood the shattering intensity of his gaze two months ago. Understood that he meant every word. But it had never occurred to her then that she might actually call on him. In fact, a part of her had warned that it would be very dangerous to call on Darius Cavenaugh for repayment of the debt. That warning had caused her to hang up the phone repeatedly today.

"I learned in *Unfinished Business* that Miss Solitaire is quite capable of passion even while she's got her hands full trying to defeat a homicidal corporate executive. And since you didn't kill off her lover, Josh Valerian, at the end of the book I presume he's going to reappear in the next one?"

Kimberly's mouth twisted in rueful humor as she finished her potato and put aside her plate. "I rather liked him."

"So did Amy Solitaire."

"Umm." Deliberately she kept her answer noncommittal.

"Because he's so much like Amy herself? Another loner? You're going to make him your heroine's soul mate, aren't you? Two lovers united against the world, completely self-contained, independent and totally in tune with each other. They will live life on their own terms, having various and assorted adventures together, saving each other's necks occasionally. And they will not be bogged down with the demands and pressures of families, of real life."

"A perfect relationship, don't you think?" Kimberly retorted, thrusting her jeaned legs out toward the fire and leaning back into her chair. "The way I see it Amy Solitaire and Josh Valerian will have a rare degree of mutual understanding. Two people who know each other so intimately that they're aware of what the other is thinking without having to put it into words."

"Do you really believe that kind of perfect communication is possible between a man and a woman?" Cavenaugh asked quietly.

"Why not?"

"Men and women are fundamentally different, in case you haven't noticed. And I'm not talking about just the obvious biological differences. We…well, we *think* differently."

She slid him a sharp glance, wondering at the certainty in his words. "Perhaps in real life it's unrealistic to expect that kind of total understanding. But that's the great thing about being a writer of fiction, isn't it? I'm free to work out my fantasy of total intimacy with a member of the opposite sex to my own satisfaction."

Cavenaugh's hard mouth lifted in mocking amusement. "You see? There's a good example of why there can't be perfect communication between a man and woman in real life. You say the words 'total intimacy' and the first image that comes into my head is being in bed with you—having you completely nude and lost in passion. But that's not what you meant at all, is it?"

"No," she snapped, annoyed at the feeling of warmth that was flowing into her cheeks. She concentrated intently on the fire. "That's not what I meant."

"By total intimacy you mean something resembling telepathy, don't you? Being able to read each other's minds. And more than that; being in perfect agreement with what the other is thinking."

"I admit it's an ideal, not a realistic goal. As I said, I'm lucky to be a writer of fiction."

"Aren't you afraid of missing something good in real life while you pursue your fictional love affairs?"

"I choose to live alone, Cavenaugh. That does not mean I spend every moment alone," she informed him coldly.

"But until you find your soul mate, you don't intend to allow a man into your life on a permanent basis, right?"

She'd had enough of this insane conversation. "I think it's time we changed the subject. Why are you here?"

2

2

 1. JAYNE ANN KRENTZ 23

"Because you almost sent for me today," he said. "And because I want to be here. A week ago I decided I wouldn't delay matters much longer."

Kimberly shifted uneasily. "What matters?"

"You and me," he told her simply. "I've thought about you a great deal during the past two months, Kim." His eyes never left her face. The message in those emerald depths was very plain to read.

Kimberly stared at him, fiercely aware of the primitive light flickering on his coal-black hair. It illuminated the silver at his temples, making her think of moonlight on a dark ocean. Darius Cavenaugh was somewhere in his late thirties, and the years were heavily etched on his harsh features.

His body was lean, toughened by hard work in the Cavenaugh Vineyards, Kimberly imagined. But there was more to him than physical strength. The toughness went all the way through him, was a part of his emotional and intellectual makeup as well as the physical side of his nature. Briefly she wondered why a man who had made his living creating fine wines should have developed such a thoroughgoing, almost arrogant strength.

The white shirt, jeans and well-worn boots in which he was dressed tonight gave no indication of the financial resources she suspected he commanded, but the clothes did emphasize the fundamental impact he made on her senses.

"What are you thinking?" he asked when she didn't say anything for a moment.

"That somehow you don't come across as a jolly little old wine maker," she remarked dryly.

His eyes narrowed for an instant. "Maybe that's because I haven't always been a wine maker. But that's another matter. Let's get the business side of this out of the way first. What happened to make you think of calling me today?''

She sighed, unable to see the rose hidden in shadows on her windowsill when she automatically glanced in that direction. ''It was silly, really.''

''I doubt that. You may have some weird notions about the basic relationship between a man and a woman, but you're not silly. My family owes you more than it can ever repay, and I am more than willing to give you anything I can against that debt.''

Kimberly stirred uneasily again. ''I wish you wouldn't talk about it in such terms. I only did what seemed logical in the circumstances.''

''You saved my nephew's life. He sends his best, by the way. When I told Scott I was going over to the coast to see you he asked me to tell you he'd like to play the 'escape' game again some dark night.''

Kimberly groaned and lifted her gaze heavenward in mocking supplication. ''You can tell him he'll have to play it alone next time. I was scared to death!''

She remembered all too vividly that night two months ago when she had looked out her window and seen the lights in the normally closed cottage a few hundred yards from her own. The old, two-story house on the bluff above her cottage was used primarily as a summer rental so the fact that it was occupied in winter had mildly interested Kimberly.

Other things had interested Kimberly about that house for three days preceding that fateful night. She had seen the car arrive with the woman and the small, dark-haired child. The little boy had been wearing a bright orange windbreaker. But after they had disappeared inside the old house they had not emerged again. It made no sense to come to the coast and stay locked inside a shack of a cottage for three solid days. People who came to this part of the country wanted to walk on the beach, hunt for shells and generally immerse themselves in the stark drama of winter on the coast.

On the third day, Kimberly had decided to pay a visit to her neighbors. She had been rudely turned away at the door by a strikingly beautiful woman who had made it quite clear that the family did not want to be bothered. It was as she was walking back to her own cottage that Kimberly had happened to glance up at the second-story window and seen the face of the seven-year-old boy staring down at her.

In that moment she realized she had never seen such an expression of emptiness on any human's face, young or old. It had stunned her. As she had stood there looking up at the boy he had abruptly been yanked away from the window, presumably by one of the adults inside the cottage.

Instinctively alarmed but at a loss as to what might be happening, Kimberly had gone back to her own place and located the phone number of the real estate firm that handled rentals in the area. When she asked the agent if he had rented the house he told her that he hadn't.

Kimberly had explained there was someone staying there and the agent had agreed to check with the owners to see if they had rented it out on their own. When the word came back that the owners were in Jamaica and couldn't be reached, the agent had said he'd drive by his client's property the following day when he got a chance and see what was happening. Possibly some freeloaders had broken in to use the facilities.

That evening Kimberly had found herself watching the other cottage almost constantly. Something was wrong and she wasn't sure how to handle it. After all, she had no real evidence of any sort of criminal activity taking place.

The only thing she had to go on at all was the strange look on the face of the child in the window and the fact that she was almost certain there should be no one staying in the cottage at this time of year.

And then she had turned on the radio to catch the evening news and heard the bulletin about the kidnapping. It had taken place three days earlier but the family had tried to keep it quiet while they handled the situation. Someone had leaked the news to the press.

As she listened to the description of the missing boy, Kimberly had gone very, very still. He had dark hair and he had last been seen wearing a bright orange windbreaker. By the end of the news broadcast she knew that the child she'd seen in the upstairs window was little Scott Emery whose wealthy uncle, Darius Cavenaugh, had just received a ransom note.

There had been a storm brewing that night, just as there was tonight, Kimberly recalled. When she'd tried to call the local law-enforcement authorities she'd found her phone was out of order because of the high winds.

Her next thought had been to take her car and drive into the nearest town, which was several miles away. She'd pulled on a waterproof jacket and a pair of boots and stepped outside, keys in her hand. Instinctively she'd glanced over at the other cottage and seen the lights in the upstairs window go out. Perhaps, she remembered thinking, the boy had just been put to bed for the night.

She decided to take the risk of climbing up onto the porch roof of the old cottage. It wasn't such an outrageous idea. After all, the storm would muffle any noise she might make as she approached the house under cover of darkness and climbed up on the shaky railing of the porch.

It was easy enough to swing herself up onto the porch roof, and from there she made her way to the darkened window where she had last seen the child.

Peering through the window she was able to make out the shape of a small boy lying quietly on the bed. He was alone in the room.

He'd been startled by Kimberly's soft knock on the window but he didn't cry out. Instead he simply stared at what must have been only a dark, shadowed face. Gently Kimberly knocked again.

With a bravery that exceeded his years, Scott Emery came slowly toward the window until he could see Kimberly smiling encouragingly at him. And then he recognized the lady he'd seen earlier that day.

Once the recognition was established Kimberly had no trouble at all getting Scott to cooperate. Together they raised the old window. The child's movements were slow and unusually awkward. It wasn't until the window had been forced open and Kimberly had gotten a whiff of the strange odor in the room that she realized he might be drugged. The penetrating fragrance of a burning herb stung her nostrils and she held her breath as she guided Scott out the window. He crawled out wearing a pair of cheap pajamas and nothing else. There wasn't time to search for the orange windbreaker. Following Kimberly's whispered instructions he kept very quiet as they made their way over the porch. Kimberly balanced precariously on the railing, lifting Scott down and then they ran through the storm toward her car. For once the temperamental vehicle started relatively easily and Kimberly drove straight to the local authorities.

During the drive Scott Emery told her how his kidnappers were really witches. One good thing about the drugging effects of the herbs, Kimberly had reflected privately, was that they seemed to have mitigated the emotional trauma most kidnap victims suffered. Scott didn't appear to realize just how much time had elapsed since he'd been taken. He simply looked forward to seeing his uncle.

After that there was a time of confusion and chaos capped by the appearance of Darius Cavenaugh when he arrived to claim his nephew.

Whatever drugging influence Scott had been under evaporated quickly in the fresh air. He began to perk up almost at once and started chattering quite cheerfully about the "witches" who had held him captive. His uncle listened intently. The authorities arrived at the cottage to find it abandoned with virtually no clues as to the identity of the kidnappers.

Scott's tale of being held prisoner by witches had been dismissed as a child's fantasy, possibly induced by the drug. Only Darius Cavenaugh refused to dismiss Scott's story as an embroidery of the facts. He'd held his own counsel on the subject.

Kimberly had spent several hours with Cavenaugh that night. The paperwork and the questions had gone on seemingly forever. Cavenaugh had handled it all with a cool, relentless patience and efficiency that said a great deal about him. During that time she had sensed the strength, the total reliability of the man. No wonder little Scott was convinced his uncle would ultimately take care of things. Cavenaugh was the kind of man who fulfilled his responsibilities, regardless of what it took to do so.

The kidnappers, as far as Kimberly knew, were still at large.

"Why did you almost send for me today, Kim?" Cavenaugh asked again.

She took a deep breath. "You won't believe this, but I tried to call you because someone gave me a rose."

He was silent for a moment. "A rose?"

Without a word Kimberly got to her feet and went over to the windowsill. Gingerly she picked up the wine bottle and brought the flower over to where Cavenaugh sat watching her.

"Remember what Scott kept saying about being held captive by witches?" she whispered.

Cavenaugh contemplated the needle in the rose. "I remember."

Kimberly sat down again, her fingers lacing together tensely between her knees. "Do you think I'm letting my imagination run away with me?"

Cavenaugh met her eyes across the short distance separating them. "No. I think this little gift could quite properly be interpreted as a threat." He considered the rose once more. "That's why you called me, wasn't it? Or rather why you considered calling me. You're scared."

"Yes." It was a relief to admit it aloud. Then something struck her about the way he had asked the question. She gave him an uncertain glance. "Why else would I have gotten in touch with you?"

He smiled whimsically in the firelight. "It occurred to me that you might want to see me again for the same reason that I wanted to see you."

Kimberly felt the electrical charge that seemed to be coiling around her. It was a culmination of the growing tension she had been experiencing all day. "Why did you want to see me again, Cavenaugh?"

"I've never been sure how much of Scott's story I should take at face value," Cavenaugh said slowly. "But I do know one thing for certain. I did meet a real live witch that night I came to collect him from the local sheriff's office. I haven't been able to get her out of my head for nearly two months. But I told myself it would be wise to wait until she called in the debt I owe her. I was just about to give up and come to see you, anyway, Kim. Our timing was just about perfect, wasn't it? Almost like telepathy.''

CHAPTER TWO

CAVENAUGH HAD ANTICIPATED a variety of circumstances under which Kimberly Sawyer might conceivably ask him for help. Most of the scenarios he had imagined involved money. He was used to people asking him for money.

It wouldn't have mattered to him if she'd needed money. After seeing the rather battered old Chevy in the drive and noting the general condition of the worn furniture, he would certainly have understood such a request. And since he had only been looking for an angle that would bring her to him, he'd decided that money was as good as any other reason.

After all, Cavenaugh acknowledged, the main goal was to bring her back into his life long enough for him to explore the strange attraction he'd experienced the first time he'd met her. He was thirty-eight years old and he knew damn well the curious hunger to see her again should have faded rapidly after he'd returned to the Napa Valley. But it hadn't. Something in her called to him and he wasn't going to be able to get her completely out of his mind until he'd satisfied the need to see her again.

It hadn't occurred to him that what Kim might ultimately ask for in repayment of the debt he owed her would be something as basic as protection. Now that she was tentatively raising the issue, Cavenaugh was startled at the rush of fiercely protective instincts he felt.

By now he had freely admitted to himself that he wanted

her. He just hadn't been expecting the force of that desire to spill over into other areas of his basic instincts. The sudden, compelling need to protect her put a new light on what should have been an essentially simple situation.

After all, Cavenaugh reminded himself, he knew what it was to want a woman. He also knew how quickly superficial desire could burn itself out. Sexual attraction was a compelling, if frequently short-lived drive. That was something he could handle. But when the attraction became enmeshed with other emotions and instincts such as this strange protectiveness, it threatened to metamorphose into something much stronger and infinitely more dangerous.

Watching Kim now in the firelight, Cavenaugh admitted to himself that he wasn't quite certain why this particular woman held such fascination. He hadn't really been joking when he called her a witch.

Amber was the word that came into his head whenever he had conjured up her image in his mind. For example, there were the warm amber curls that she wore in a delightfully straggly knot at the back of her head. It was understandable that several of the twisting tendrils had been loose the night he had met her. She had been through a hectic adventure in a storm. But tonight the suggestion of disarray was present again and he sensed the style was simply part of her personality. All Cavenaugh knew for certain was that he felt a strong urge to unpin the amber knot and watch her hair tumble around her shoulders.

Amber described her eyes, too. Golden brown and quick to reflect emotion. More than once during the past two months Cavenaugh had wondered what that gaze would look like shadowed with passion.

There was nothing extraordinary about the rest of her features. There was strength in her face, intelligence in her glance. Cavenaugh sensed the willpower beneath the surface as well as an innate wariness, and wondered idly what had caused the latter. He guessed that she was in her late twenties, perhaps twenty-seven or twenty-eight.

Her body was pleasantly rounded and softly shaped with breasts that would perfectly fit the palm of his hand. He could see the outline of them beneath the butterscotch-and-black plaid sweater she wore. And that sweetly curved derriere so nicely revealed in the snug jeans made him want to reach out and squeeze.

While everything went together in a reasonably attractive package it didn't explain the compulsion he had been experiencing to see Kimberly Sawyer again. Something else was at work.

"Witchcraft," he murmured.

"Ridiculous," Kimberly declared, assuring herself that Cavenaugh was no longer alluding to the glimmering tension that had sprung up between them. "I overreacted to that damn rose. I'm sure it's someone's idea of a sick joke."

"But you called me today."

"I almost called you," she corrected firmly. "I kept changing my mind because I kept realizing how foolish it was to take that thing too seriously."

He sent her an assessing glance. "I'm here now."

"I told you two months ago that there was absolutely no need for you to feel you owed me anything!"

"I rather thought it would be money," he said musingly.

She glared at him. "I beg your pardon?"

"I somehow assumed that when you decided to collect on the debt, it would be money you'd want."

"I certainly don't need any of your money!" she exploded tightly.

"The Amy Solitaire books do all right?"

"They do just fine, thank you."

"I couldn't be sure," he explained gently, examining the inside of the beach cottage. "After all, you live way out here in the middle of nowhere, drive a ten-year-old car, dress in jeans that look about as ancient as the car—" He broke off with a shrug. "How was I to know your financial status?"

"I live out here because it suits me. Writers need lots of privacy and quiet, in case you didn't know. As for the car, well, I realize it's not exactly a late model Cadillac, but then I never did like Cadillacs. And the jeans happen to be very comfortable. Writers like comfortable clothes," she added far too sweetly.

"You're getting annoyed, aren't you?"

"Sharp of you to notice."

"You're also scared," he reminded her flatly. "Which brings us back to the issue at hand." He lifted the rose to examine it once again. "They haven't found the kidnappers, you know."

Kimberly licked her lower lip a bit nervously. "I'd been rather hoping something had turned up."

"Not a thing. No leads, no clues, no descriptions other than that one you gave of the woman and Scott's insistence that he was being held by witches. Nothing."

She heard the hint of controlled savagery in his voice and drew in her breath. "It must be very frustrating," she suggested uneasily.

The emerald eyes lifted from contemplation of the rose, and Kimberly found herself staring into the remorseless gaze of a predator. In that moment she almost pitied the kidnappers. The realization of just how implacable this man would be when the people who had dared to threaten a member of his family were found was almost frightening.

"Frustrating is a mild term for what I feel whenever I

consider the matter," Cavenaugh informed her very evenly.

Kimberly swallowed. "Yes. I can see that."

"Sooner or later I'll have them."

"The kidnappers? I certainly hope so. But if the authorities have nothing to go on…"

"I have my own people working on it."

"Your own people! What on earth do you mean?" she asked, startled.

"Never mind." He set down the wine bottle with the rose and reached for the glass of Merlot he had been drinking. "At the moment we should be discussing your situation. I don't think we'll take any chances. Someone may be out to punish you for having gotten involved. It's possible they know or have figured out who it was who rescued Scott that night. Regardless of what's going on you'll be safest at the estate. Can you be packed and ready to go early in the morning?"

Dumbfounded at the suggestion, Kimberly nearly choked on her own sip of wine. "Ready to go? That's impossible. I'm not going anywhere. I have eight chapters left to write on *Vendetta* and a deadline to meet. Furthermore, this is my home. I'm not about to leave it. I can't just pack up and move in with you until the kidnappers are found! For heaven's sake, this business with the rose is probably a totally unrelated incident."

"You can't be sure of that. If you had been sure you wouldn't have almost called me today. Even if the rose isn't related to the kidnapping, it's still quite deliberately vicious. You'll be safest at the estate."

"No," Kimberly answered with absolute conviction. "It's kind of you to offer, but—"

"This is hardly a matter of kindness. I owe you, remember?" he shot back harshly.

"Well, consider the debt canceled!"

"That's not possible. I always pay my debts."

"I haven't asked that you pay this one," she protested violently.

"You no longer have any choice in the matter."

"What on earth are you saying?" Kimberly leaped to her feet to confront him. "No one invited you here tonight. And no one is going to tell me what to do. I've been on my own a long time, Cavenaugh, and I like it that way. I like it very much. The last thing I intend to do is move into a crowded, busy household such as yours and stay indefinitely. It would drive me crazy and I'd never get any work done."

He stood up slowly, the light from the fire playing over the bluntly carved planes of his face. The shifting, golden shadows alternately revealed and veiled the visible signs of the force of his determination, but Kimberly could feel the impact of it on another level altogether and it made her shiver. She wished with all her heart she hadn't made that phone call today.

"It made little difference. I would have been here within a day or two, anyway," he assured her calmly as if he could read her mind.

Kimberly didn't care for the ease with which he seemed able to interpret her thoughts. "Look, Cavenaugh, don't you understand that what you're suggesting just isn't practical?"

"You can bring your typewriter and anything else you need. There's plenty of room."

She gritted her teeth. "I don't want to go with you."

"I can see that." He reached out a hand to touch one of the curling tendrils of hair that had escaped the amber knot. "Are you more afraid of me than you are of whoever sent the rose?" he asked very softly.

Mutely Kimberly stared up at him, aware of the controlled desire lying just below the surface of that green gaze. She felt the answering response in her own body and shook her head wonderingly. "You want me, don't you?" she asked very carefully.

"Is that why you're afraid of me?" Cavenaugh released the curl of amber hair to let his fingertips gently graze the line of her throat.

Kimberly flinched at the intimate touch. "Yes."

His gaze narrowed. "You're an adult, self-confident woman. Why does my wanting you make you afraid?"

She answered starkly as the fundamental truth came into her head. "Because you can't have me. And I think you could be very dangerous, Cavenaugh, in a situation where you can't have something you want."

His hand fell away but even though he was no longer touching her, Kimberly could feel the faint menace in him. It was controlled but nonetheless formidable. It made her want to flee. Until today she had never known such an instinctive desire to run, least of all from a man.

"Why can't I have you, Kim?" The words were spoken with a deceptively silky edge.

She tried to keep her own voice calm and very matter-of-fact in an attempt to diffuse the stalking threat in him. "How about the trite, but true reason that you and I live in two different worlds?" Kimberly swung away from him, turning to face the hearth. "You are a man of property, community status, family responsibilities, commitments. You are tied to that winery and the people who live and work there just as much as they're tied to you. I understand how the demands of family and status and business all have to mesh for a man in your situation. I operate differently. I'm free. You're not. Whatever we might have together would, of necessity, have to be short-lived and unsatisfying. At least from my point of view. Of course, from your angle a brief, passionate little affair with no future might be just what you'd like. But I'm not willing to play the role of casual mistress for any man.''

She could feel the intensity of his gaze burning into her as he moved silently up behind her. His nearness made her tremble faintly. The knowledge annoyed her.

''You *are* afraid of me, aren't you? And you have the nerve to call yourself *free?* I don't think you know the meaning of the word.''

Nervously Kimberly stepped away from him. ''Please, Cavenaugh, this has gone far enough.''

He hesitated and then shrugged. ''Perhaps you're right. For now. We have a more pressing issue at hand.''

''The rose?''

''I was referring to the little matter of where I'm going to sleep tonight,'' he retorted dryly. ''Or did you intend to send me out into the storm?''

The wind howled with increased ferocity, and rain hammered against the windows as if to impress upon Kimberly what a cruel female she would be if she actually drove Darius Cavenaugh from her home on a night such as this. He gave her a small, crooked smile and all of a sudden her sense of perspective returned.

''I wouldn't throw my worst enemy out on a night like this and you're hardly in that category, are you?''

He shook his head, but the faint expression of amusement disappeared and he gave her a surprisingly serious look. ''No. I'm not your enemy. Never that. We're bound together in some way, you and I.''

''Because you feel you owe me something because of what I did for Scott.''

''That's part of it. But who can always say why a man

and a woman find themselves linked? There are other ties that bind,'' he reminded her softly.

"Uh-huh. Ties of family and responsibility and status. I've already mentioned them. And none of those ties exist between you and me."

Cavenaugh raised heavy black brows in sudden enlightenment. "You're looking for a real life Josh Valerian, aren't you? Another self-sufficient, self-contained loner with no emotional ties or responsibilities to anyone other than you and himself."

Kimberly was silent for a moment, mildly astonished at his perception, then she inclined her head austerely. "Every woman has a right to her fantasies."

"And your particular fantasy is of a man who will need and want only you," Cavenaugh hazarded roughly.

"A man whose loyalties are always one hundred percent with me," she agreed simply. "A man who is free to give me as much as I can give him." Kimberly shook off the assessing intent of his gaze and summoned a brisk smile. "And now about this little matter of where you will sleep tonight."

Cavenaugh looked as though he was going to pursue the discussion of her "fantasy" man but the forbidding expression in her amber eyes must have stopped him. He bit back whatever words had been poised to attack and nodded once. "As we've already decided, I don't fall into the category of enemy. And as I'm not yet your lover—"

Kimberly flushed at the easy way he began that last sentence and found herself rushing to interrupt. "I'll get some blankets from the closet. You can use the couch. I'll want your word of honor, however, that I'm not going to have to kick you out of my bedroom at any time during the night."

"Your hospitality overwhelms me."

"Sorry, but you're a little overwhelming, yourself," she confessed wryly. "And I've had an unsettling day."

Humor flashed in the green eyes. "I take it you don't have many unsettling days?"

"Hardly. Another advantage to living alone, Cavenaugh. My days usually go exactly as I wish them to go."

"I think you're really quite spoiled, Kim."

"*Thoroughly* spoiled," she said with a quick laugh. "Believe me, I treasure the luxury of my independence. Now, back to your word of honor. Do I have it?"

"About not invading your bedroom? I would much prefer to be invited."

She let that pass, assuming it was as close to a promise as she was going to get and fully aware of the fact that she wasn't about to force him back out into the storm tonight. He was not her enemy even though he represented a very ancient form of danger. Walking to the hall closet she opened it and began pulling down sheets and blankets.

"One pillow or two?"

"One will do." He caught the pillow she tossed at him, his hand moving in an almost negligent gesture that betrayed an easy sense of coordination. "Kim, about your coming home with me in the morning," he began quietly.

"In the morning you'll be on your way back to the Cavenaugh Vineyards. Alone. How many quilts do you want?"

"One," he ordered, sounding irritated. "Kim, you were right to be nervous about that damn rose. We're going to take precautions."

"I'll take them."

"You called on me to protect you," he reminded her grimly.

"No, I did not call on you. I considered calling you, and at a few points during the day I almost did call you. But in the end I never actually asked for any help, did I, Cavenaugh? You keep forgetting that. You're here because you decided all on your own to drive over to the coast, not because I yelled for help.''

"You're being unreasonable about this and with any luck by morning you'll have calmed down enough to realize it." Cavenaugh shoved his hands into the back pockets of his jeans and regarded her with ominous warning.

Kim refused to be browbeaten. She had been taking care of herself too long to allow herself to be intimidated by any man.

"That expression may be very effective on little Scott or on one of your employees who is late for work, but that's the limit of its usefulness, I'm afraid. It doesn't have any effect on me at all."

"I keep asking myself how Josh Valerian would handle this," Cavenaugh murmured just as Kimberly swept past the counter where the buff-colored envelope from the Los Angeles law office had been lying.

"He'd know when to stop pushing," Kimberly advised. The trailing corner of the quilt she was carrying in her arms caught the envelope and nudged it over the counter edge.

"He'd know when to stop because of this uncanny communication he shares with Amy Solitaire, I take it." Cavenaugh watched the envelope drop to the floor and moved forward to retrieve it.

"You don't have to sound so scornful. The relationship between Amy and Josh is going to help sell a lot of books."

"Not to men," Cavenaugh predicted as he studied the return address on the envelope.

"Women are the largest segment of my readers," Kimberly informed him grandly. "And I'll tell you right now they're going to love the sense of complete emotional and mental intimacy I'm building between Josh and Amy."

"Well, if you put enough sexual intimacy in the books, maybe you'll hang on to your male readership, too."

"I use the violence to keep my male readers interested," Kim gritted. "Men are really big on violence. Maybe it's a substitute for genuine intimacy for them. What are you doing with that letter?" She glanced up from preparing the couch and frowned as she saw the envelope in his hand.

"Wondering why you haven't opened it. Most people open letters from lawyers fast."

Kimberly's mouth curved grimly. "Not in my case. I've already had two letters from that law office. I know what's inside."

Cavenaugh eyed her intently. "Trouble, Kim?" he finally asked softly, tossing the envelope gently into the air and catching it absently. "Have you got other problems besides receiving roses impaled with needles?"

"No. The folks who employ those fancy lawyers are the ones with the problem. They created it themselves, however, and I have no intention of helping them solve it." She stepped back from the couch, examining her work. "There, that should do for tonight. It's going to be a bit cramped but it's better than sleeping on the floor."

"The floor is the only alternative you're offering?"

"I'm afraid so," she said cheerfully. "And since you're sleeping out here, you're in charge of the fire. I don't know how long the electricity will be off and it could get quite chilly by morning."

"I'll take care of the fire," he agreed, glancing down at the letter in his hand. "Are you sure this isn't something I can help you with, Kim?"

"What's inside that letter has nothing to do with you. It has nothing to do with me, either. That's what I told the lawyers after they sent the first one. You can toss that envelope into the garbage."

He set it back down on the counter instead. "You can be amazingly stubborn at times."

"Something tells me you can be just as stubborn," she retorted humorously. "But I think stubbornness in men is generally referred to as willpower."

"In the morning we'll have to see whether my willpower is stronger than your feminine stubbornness, won't we?" he queried easily. "Thanks for the bed, Kim."

"You're welcome. I'm sorry I don't have any extra toothbrushes or razors or whatever it is men need when they stay overnight."

"It's all right. I've got everything I need in the car."

"I see. You came prepared?" she asked a bit caustically.

"Going to hold it against me?" he challenged gently.

"Good night, Cavenaugh. Don't forget to keep an eye on the fire." Head held regally high, Kimberly swept past him to her small, comfortable bedroom. Damned if she was going to get into a useless argument about where he had originally intended to spend the night.

Half an hour later the house was quiet and Kimberly lay in bed under her huge feather quilt studying the ceiling. This had definitely not been one of her normal, pleasantly predictable days. She wasn't quite certain how to react to today.

No doubt about it, she was accustomed to having the unpredictable and the potentially dangerous confined within the pages of her manuscripts.

She turned over on her side, fluffed her pillow and considered the man in her living room. It was strange that he had shown up on her doorstep even though she had never actually summoned him. Darius Cavenaugh must be very anxious to pay off his debt to her.

Or else he was very anxious to get her into bed.

Kimberly glowered into the darkness. Men, in her experience, rarely pursued women quite this far, at least not ordinary women such as herself. She couldn't help wondering what it was that had brought Cavenaugh all the way from his vineyards to her front door.

She could understand that a man such as Darius Cavenaugh would be very conscious of the bonds of the debt he felt he was under. After all, he had undoubtedly grown up imbued with the notion of obligation and loyalty and family honor. The noble-sounding virtues were stamped all over his hard face. Kimberly remembered little Scott solemnly telling her all about the generations of Cavenaughs who had been in the wine business. The boy had chatted quite freely while they had waited together in the sheriff's offices for the arrival of his uncle. Scott was, even at his young age, quite aware of the importance of family heritage.

"That's why the witches kidnapped me," he had explained with a touch of pride. "They knew my uncle would pay anything he had to, to get me back. Uncle Dare wouldn't let anyone keep me."

"Dare?" Kimberly had questioned, wondering about the mysterious uncle who was on his way to collect his nephew.

"His real name is Darius. But we all call him Dare."

For some reason Kimberly had not felt sufficiently at ease with the tough, powerful man who had arrived later to call him by the shortened version of his first name. He had remained Cavenaugh in her mind. And after tonight, that hadn't changed.

"Do you have an uncle who would pay lots of money to get you back?" Scott had demanded interestedly, kicking his feet as he sat on the wooden chair beside her. One of the men in the sheriff's office had bundled him up in an old leather flight jacket, which Scott had loved on sight.

"No, I'm afraid I don't have anyone who would shell out cold cash to get me back," Kimberly had told the boy, unprepared for the way it had upset him.

"How about your mom and dad?" he'd pressed anxiously.

"I never knew my father," Kimberly had said carefully, "and my mother died a few years ago."

"And you don't even have an uncle like mine?"

Kimberly had gently denied the existence of any such useful uncle in her life. Later, after meeting Darius Cavenaugh she'd privately decided there were very few little kids in the world with uncles like Cavenaugh.

She had thought the topic of who might pay her ransom should she ever be kidnapped had been closed. Certainly Scott's attention had been totally diverted the moment Darious Cavenaugh had walked through the door. The child had rushed forward with excitement and confidence in his greeting. Cavenaugh had swept him up and examined every inch of him with eyes of green ice. At last, satisfied that the boy was all right, he'd allowed Scott to make the introductions.

Eagerly Scott had explained who Kimberly Sawyer was and how she had come to his window that night.

"We went across the top of the porch and down the side and the witch never even knew we were gone, did she, Kim?"

"No," she agreed, smiling affectionately at the youngster. "She never even knew. Rather like Hansel and Gretel."

"I told Kim you would have paid anything to get me back, isn't that right, Uncle Dare?" Holding the hand of the green-eyed man with happy possessiveness, Scott looked up at his uncle for confirmation.

"Anything," Cavenaugh had agreed.

Kimberly had seen the grim protectiveness in the depth of the man's gaze and had known he spoke the truth. Cavenaugh would have done more than pay a ransom to get Scott back. He would have killed to save the boy. The stark realization of just how far this man would go to fulfill his obligations had sent an odd shiver down her spine.

"Kim doesn't have anyone who would pay to get her back if someone took her away," Scott went on before Kimberly realized what he was going to say. "But we would pay, wouldn't we, Uncle Dare?"

Cavenaugh had looked straight into Kimberly's embarrassed gaze and had said with absolute conviction, "We would do anything we could for Miss Sawyer. She has only to ask."

Later, after the long talk with the authorities, Cavenaugh had taken Kim aside and reiterated that vow.

Recognizing the powerful sense of obligation by which Cavenaugh had felt himself bound, Kimberly had quickly promised to call on him should she ever need help. At the time, of course, she had never anticipated such an occasion.

Yet his face was the first thing she had thought of when the arrival of the rose sent a shaft of fear through her. And now he was here.

But there was a new element in the situation. In addition to the sense of obligation he felt toward her, there was no mistaking the fact that Cavenaugh wanted her physically.

When it came to dealing with the sensual tension he evoked in her, Kimberly knew she was trying to handle something just as strong as any witchcraft. But it was a comfort to know he was out there in her living room tonight. Normally she did not mind spending the nights alone. Tonight, she realized, would have been an exception. The knowledge that Cavenaugh was close by soothed the lingering fear the arrival of the rose had caused. She soon fell asleep.

When she awoke several hours later the storm had slackened somewhat but the wind continued to hurl rain against the windows behind the drawn shades.

Kimberly heard the sounds of the storm only vaguely. Her main awareness was of being thirsty. Too many salty black olives on the potato tonight. Hovering in that floating region between wakefulness and dreams, she wondered if she could get back to sleep without making a trip out to the kitchen for a glass of water.

But the growing thirst finally had its way. Still half asleep, Kimberly pushed back the quilt and padded barefoot to her bedroom door. Dimly she wondered why she had closed it tonight. She never closed her door. After all, there was hardly any need. She was always alone in the house.

Wrenching it open in annoyance, she continued on down the hall to the open kitchen. There was a faint flow of light from the fireplace and Kimberly vaguely remembered that the electricity was off.

It was getting cold, she realized. The oversized man's cotton T-shirt she habitually wore to bed barely covered her derriere. One of these days she was going to remember to buy some real pajamas. There was a robe hanging in her closet but it had seemed too much bother to drag it out just for a short trip to the kitchen.

With comfortable familiarity she found the cabinet door in the darkness and groped inside for a glass. Then she shuffled over to the sink and ran the water. The shade on the kitchen window had been left up this evening, and as she stood barefoot in front of the sink, drinking her water, Kimberly stared disinterestedly out into the darkness. If she was careful she could stay in this half-asleep state until she crawled back into bed.

She had almost finished the contents of the glass when something moved outside the window.

Startled by shifting shadows where there should be nothing but open expanse between her and the view of the ocean, Kimberly belatedly began to come awake.

As her eyes widened, lightning crackled across the sky, obligingly illuminating the scene in front of the kitchen window. In that split second of atmospheric brilliance Kimberly stared in horror at the figure in a cowled robe who stood outside staring back at her.

She had no time to discern a face in the shadowy depths of the cowl. Kimberly's entire attention was riveted on the silver dagger the figure was holding upright in front of himself.

In that moment she knew the dagger was meant for her.

Although the scream that echoed through the small house was hers, Kimberly felt dissociated from the sound of unadulterated terror in her voice. She was more conscious of the glass sliding from her fingers and crashing into the sink.

"Kim!"

Cavenaugh. She had forgotten all about him. Half turning she saw him as he leaped over the back of the couch, rushing toward her.

"What the hell…?"

"Outside the window," she managed to gasp. "Someone outside the window with a knife. I, oh, my God!"

"Get down."

The command cracked violently through the air. He was right, Kimberly realized, stunned. She was standing silhouetted against the kitchen window. But she couldn't seem to move.

Then movement on her part became unnecessary. Cavenaugh reached her a second later, driving into her with the full weight of his half-naked body. He dragged her violently down onto the floor behind the protection of the counters and out of sight of anyone who might still be standing at the kitchen window.

CHAPTER THREE

"STAY DOWN," Cavenaugh gritted, sprawling along the length of Kimberly's body.

Crushed against the cold vinyl tile of the kitchen floor, Kimberly gasped for breath. "I can't do much else with you on top of me like this. You weigh a ton, Cavenaugh!"

He ignored that, his features a rigid mask of concern in the shadowy light. "Tell me exactly what you saw out there," he whispered roughly. He lifted his head so that he could meet her wide-eyed gaze.

"I told you. There was a man, at least I think it was a man. He was wearing a hooded robe or something. I couldn't see his face. But when the lightning flashed I saw a knife. A big silver dagger. It was horrible. I had the awful feeling he meant me to see it."

"Given the fact that the bastard was outside your window and not someone else's on the block, that's a fair guess," Cavenaugh mocked grimly. He shifted his weight and she realized he was going to get up off the floor. "Lie still. Don't move until I get back, understand? No one can see you down here behind the kitchen counters."

"Until you get back!" Kimberly repeated, horrified. "What's that supposed to mean? Where on earth do you think you're going?"

"I'm going to have a look around outside." He rolled off her, uncoiling easily to his feet.

"No, you can't go out there!" She grabbed for his jean-clad leg. It was like trying to hold on to a breaking wave. He slipped from her grasp as if he hadn't even been aware of it. "Cavenaugh, this is stupid," she hissed as she watched him stride across the room to find his boots. "You can't go out there. Who knows what might be waiting? For Pete's sake, come back here."

He didn't bother to answer. The golden afterglow of the fire flickered on the sleek planes of his bare back as he bent over briefly to shove his feet into the boots. And then he was at the door, slipping off the chain.

"Don't move," he ordered once again as he stepped cautiously outside. He shut the door softly behind himself.

"Cavenaugh, wait!"

She was appealing to an empty room. Angrily Kimberly sat up on the chilly floor, hugging her bare knees to her chest as she stared at the door. For what seemed an unbearably long time she continued to sit where she was, visions of the cowled figure holding the knife repeating themselves endlessly in her head. Suddenly, startlingly aware of her own near nudity as the icy vinyl finally made its presence known against her backside, she started to get to her feet. Halfway up she remembered Cavenaugh's injunction to stay where she was.

Astonished that she had allowed the force of his command to keep her there on the floor for even a few seconds, Kimberly stood up completely and peered cautiously out the kitchen window. She could see nothing, and the thought that Cavenaugh was out there somewhere, facing who knew what on her behalf, finally jolted her into action.

Turning away from the window, Kimberly started toward the hall to her bedroom. She needed to find her jeans and some shoes and a shirt before following her guest out into the stormy night.

She was nearly across the room when the door opened

again and Cavenaugh stepped back inside. Whirling, she halted to demand anxiously, "Are you all right? I was terrified!"

He stood staring at her, eyes deep and unreadable in the dim glow of the firelight. The rain had dampened his shoulders and hair and the jeans rode low on his hips. Kimberly saw the glistening drops of moisture caught in the curling dark hair on his chest and was violently aware of the lingering hint of anger emanating from him.

"I told you to stay down on the floor." Cavenaugh fastened the catch on the door and then started toward her.

"I decided sitting on a cold vinyl floor wasn't doing anyone much good," Kimberly retorted, injecting a measure of irritation into her words. She found herself increasingly uneasy now and the sense of anxiety wasn't caused by what she had just seen through the window. "You didn't answer my question. I take it you're all right?"

"I'm fine." He stopped beside the couch and pried off his wet boots. "Got a towel? I'm soaked."

"Of course." Grateful for the small diversion, Kimberly reached into the hall closet nearby and yanked down a towel. She stepped forward to hand it to him and then remembered the short T-shirt she was wearing. "Here," she said quickly, tossing him the towel. "I'll go find my robe." She hurried to her bedroom door. "Did you see anything out there?" Opening the closet she pulled out the red terry cloth robe.

"No, I couldn't find a trace of anything or anyone. Hardly surprising with this rain and wind."

His voice came from her bedroom doorway. Startled that he had followed her down the hall, Kimberly fumbled with the robe. The darkness wasn't providing much privacy. She knew the pale length of her legs must be quite visible beneath the incredibly short hem of the T-shirt. Cavenaugh stood watching her as though he had a right, idly drying his hair and the back of his neck.

"Perhaps in the morning we'll be able to find some signs," she suggested hesitantly, wondering why it was proving so difficult to get into the robe. Her fingers didn't seem to want to function properly. Although she had been quite chilled a few minutes ago her whole body now seemed unnaturally warm.

"I doubt it." He didn't move from her doorway and the vividness of his gaze seemed to burn over her. "Who owned that T-shirt originally?"

"I beg your pardon?"

"I just wondered what man left that T-shirt behind for you to wear to bed. Will he be coming back to collect it or you in the near future?"

Kimberly felt herself flushing and was glad he couldn't see the change in her skin color here in the darkness. Distractedly she managed to knot the red robe around her waist. "I always sleep in T-shirts. I buy them myself in packages of three. No one left it behind. Now, if you've finished commenting on my lingerie, I suggest we go back to the living room and talk over this situation."

He didn't move. Kimberly drew in a deep breath and decided on a firmly aggressive approach. She walked straight toward the door, giving every indication that she fully expected him to step aside. When he didn't, she was forced to halt a foot away.

"Excuse me," she said very politely. "You seem to be blocking the door."

Cavenaugh slowly lowered the hand holding the towel. "Why didn't you stay on the floor in the kitchen?"

"Because the floor was damn cold!" she exploded. "And because I didn't know what you were doing outside.

I was worried, Cavenaugh. I've had something of a shock this evening.''

He searched her face in the darkness, his own gaze brooding and watchful.

''Pardon me, Cavenaugh, but you really are in the way.'' She put out a palm, flattened it boldly against his chest and shoved with all her strength. The situation was slipping out of control, and she was woman enough to know it.

She might as well have been pushing against a granite wall for all the good it did. Realizing belatedly that the forceful approach wasn't going to have much effect, Kimberly hastily tried to pull back her hand. She didn't move quickly enough; he managed to snag her wrist.

''You realize, of course, that what happened tonight clinches tomorrow's plans.'' He didn't move, just stood there chaining her wrist. ''You're coming back to the estate with me in the morning.''

Kimberly swallowed, violently aware of his strength and the absolute certainty with which he spoke. Her need to rebel was more of an instinct than a reasoned act. After all, she had been literally terrified tonight. Staying alone here in this house was about the last thing she wanted to do at the moment. But giving in to Darius Cavenaugh seemed almost as dangerous.

''I make my own decisions, Cavenaugh. Don't ever forget that,'' she asserted, lifting her chin defiantly. ''I've been doing it a long time and I'm quite good at it.''

''From now on,'' he grated softly as he pulled her closer, ''you're going to get used to having a little help in the decision-making department. I'm responsible for you because of what you did for Scott two months ago. I have every intention of carrying out my duty.''

''I'm sure you do. You're the kind of man who would always do what was expected of him, aren't you? And you're accustomed to being in charge of other people. But I don't expect you to protect me, Cavenaugh, and I most certainly don't intend to take orders from you. I'll handle this in my own way." She was trembling now and not just from anger. Cavenaugh was too close, too big, too overwhelming dressed in nothing but a pair of jeans. Her earlier fears of the robed figure holding the dagger were being swamped with a new and altogether different type of trepidation.

"Don't be afraid of me, Kim," he said quietly.

She narrowed her eyes, angry that he had perceived her new nervousness. "If you don't want to frighten me any more than I've already been frightened this evening, I suggest you release my hand," she ordered coolly.

"I might be more willing to do that if I hadn't seen you running around in the firelight dressed in that skimpy little T-shirt," Cavenaugh told her in a husky voice as he dragged her half an inch closer. "And if I hadn't felt you lying half-naked under me out there on the floor. And if I hadn't just gone hunting for that bastard with the knife." He tugged her another half inch toward him. "Or if I hadn't been wondering off and on for two months what it would be like to take you to bed—"

"No!" But her protest was a breathless squeak of denial that held no real power. Mesmerized by the sensual tension crackling in the air around them, she found herself crushed against his bare chest, her fingers splayed wildly on his shoulders.

"Come here, witch," Cavenaugh growled softly as he lowered his head to find her mouth. "Let's find out just how strong your spells are."

Kimberly had an impression of emeralds that gleamed with a thoroughly dangerous fire and then her own eyes closed beneath the impact of Cavenaugh's mouth. The kiss was not a gentle, tasting caress. Her lips were captured and parted; her inner warmth exploded with a hunger that astounded her.

As his hands slid down her back, sensing the shape of her through the robe, Kimberly felt a tantalizing heat flare to life in her body. She had been honest with herself earlier this evening when she'd privately admitted the effect his politely controlled desire had on her. She would be less than honest with herself now if she tried to deny that Cavenaugh's unleashed passion was devastating.

She heard the soft, feral groan deep in his throat and her pulse raced. His mouth was warm and marauding, unbelievably exciting. Kimberly cried out with stifled regret when he finally freed her lips. But almost immediately he was searching out the delicate skin of her throat and his hands slipped around her waist to find the sash of the red robe.

"Do you have any idea what you look like in that T-shirt?" Cavenaugh demanded hoarsely as he untwisted the knot of the sash. "What you felt like out there on the floor?"

"I felt cold," she tried to say, struggling for some self-control.

"You felt soft and warm and silky. Not cold at all. And you feel even warmer now. I knew it was going to be like this. For two months I've known—"

"Cavenaugh, wait," she managed on a thread of sound and then she caught her breath as his hands moved inside the parted edges of the robe.

"Why should I wait? You want this as much as I do."

The classic male reasoning provoked her as nothing else could have done. Kimberly slapped at his hand, trying to step away from his compelling touch.

"No, I'm not at all sure I want it. Everything's happening much too fast. I've been through a great deal this evening. I want time to think.''

"If I give you time to think, you'll come up with a thousand reasons why you shouldn't get involved with me."

Kimberly gasped, both at the accuracy of his muttered analysis and at the feel of his palm as he pushed his hand up under the T-shirt to find her breast.

"Ah, Cavenaugh, please…" But the words were on a fine line between surrender and resistance and she knew instinctively that he realized it.

Dimly she tried to tell herself that her strong physical reaction to this man was the result of the scare she'd had. Heaven knew she'd used that rationale often enough to introduce a sex scene in her novels. After a scene of action or violence adrenaline and excitement were flooding the nervous systems of her characters. It seemed natural to channel it into sex on occasion.

But only within the confines of a book, she thought frantically. Surely that sort of thing didn't happen in real life! But how else could she explain her explosive reaction to Cavenaugh's touch?

And then the electricity was restored without any warning. Cavenaugh lifted his head abruptly as lights blazed around him. Kimberly saw the flash of impatience and irritation in his gaze.

"You must have had every light in the house on before you lost the electricity," he complained brusquely.

"Another advantage to living alone," Kimberly tossed back a little breathlessly. "There's no one around to lecture me about my electricity bills. Or anything else."

But the mood had been broken and they both knew it. Reluctantly, Cavenaugh let her slide from his grasp, the emerald fire of his eyes lingering on her flushed face. Kimberly busied herself retying the sash of the robe.

He studied her trembling fingers and understood how shaken she was. After hesitating a moment he decided to give her the out she needed. If he didn't, matters were going to be a lot more difficult in the morning.

"I shouldn't have assaulted you like that," he told her quietly. "Hell, I was supposed to be the one protecting you, wasn't I?"

"These things happen," she surprised him by saying in a very distant tone.

"Do they?" He controlled the flicker of amusement her words caused.

"Oh, yes. I use this sort of scenario all the time in my books. Scenes of action often precipitate scenes of...of..."

"Passion?"

"Exactly. All that pent-up adrenaline and stuff. Very useful. I just hadn't realized it worked that way in real life, too." Her smile was rather forced but it was there as she faced him with casual challenge.

Cavenaugh felt a little stunned. "You've already got the whole thing neatly rationalized, haven't you?"

"As I said, it was just one of those things. Chalk it up to an odd quirk in human nature."

He struggled to restrain himself from taking hold of her and tossing her down on the bed. Cavenaugh was astonished at the force of the urge he felt to do exactly that. He'd show her the difference between one of her books and real life! Almost immediately, he realized the stupidity of that course of action. He had other, more immediate goals to work toward, he reminded himself grimly. After all, the most important matter at hand was to get her into the car without opposition in the morning. Humoring her now might make that task simpler. He smiled crookedly.

"I'll accept your analysis of the situation. From my point of view, I can only apologize for my actions. I appreciate your understanding."

There was an odd look of relief in her eyes as if she knew she had just come perilously close to an infinitely dangerous confrontation. A confrontation with herself or with him, Cavenaugh wondered fleetingly.

"Yes, well, it's been a hectic evening, hasn't it?" she remarked condescendingly.

Cavenaugh wanted to shake her. He'd like to show her just how "hectic" he could make her neat, self-contained world. Instead he said politely, "Yes, it has. I think I'll recheck all your locks before I go back to bed. And it might be a good idea if you left the door of your bedroom open."

"So that you can hear me if I get carried off by witches?"

"It's not really all that funny," he murmured.

"I know," she said with a sigh, toying nervously with the end of her red sash. "I was scared to death earlier. I'm glad you were here, Cavenaugh. Very glad."

Wisely he decided to let that ride without following it up with a demand that she let him continue to protect her. Given a few more hours alone in her room to think about the situation, she would come to her senses.

"Get some sleep, Kim. Everything will be fine. Whoever was out there knows you're not alone now."

"Good night, Cavenaugh," she nodded, sounding vaguely wistful.

He looked down at her, aware of the fierce restlessness in his body. She looked so intriguing with her amber hair in tumbled disarray. Her bare feet beneath the hem of the robe made her somehow charmingly vulnerable and he found himself wanting to pull her nervous fingers away from the sash that kept the old terry cloth robe close to her body. Taking a resolute grip on his senses, Cavenaugh stepped out into the hall. Then he thought of something.

"There's just one thing, Kim."

"What's that?" She frowned curiously.

"The next time I give you an order in a situation like the one we had tonight, I'll expect you to obey it."

Instantly he knew he'd made a mistake. The small frown on her face turned into a mask of feminine hauteur. "Since I don't expect too many more situations such as the one we experienced tonight, I don't see that as a problem. Good night, Cavenaugh."

He decided he'd better get out of her room before he said anything further to annoy her. Without a word he stalked down the hall, turning off lights as he went. Stopping in front of the fire, he poked at the embers, listening as Kimberly turned off the light in her own room and climbed into bed. A moment later the house was silent again.

There was one more light still blazing, the one in the kitchen area. Cavenaugh walked over to flip the switch and his eyes fell on the buff-colored envelope from the Los Angeles law firm. Idly he picked it up, wondering why Kim hadn't opened it. Perhaps she had trouble on her hands from another source besides Scott's "witches."

Long accustomed to dealing with trouble, Cavenaugh made his decision. He unsealed the envelope and lifted out the stiff, formal stationery. Then standing barefoot in Kimberly's kitchen, he read the letter without any compunction whatsoever. When he was finished he had even more questions about Kimberly Sawyer.

Thoughtfully Cavenaugh refolded the letter and stuffed it back into the envelope. Then he turned off the kitchen light and walked to the uncomfortable couch. In front of the fire he stepped out of the slightly damp jeans and spread them out so that they would dry by morning. As he slid under the blanket Kim had given him earlier he propped himself on his elbow and stared intently into the glowing coals of the fire.

Kimberly Sawyer was an intriguing woman. She was also proving to be something of a mystery. Above all, Cavenaugh reminded himself, he had an obligation to protect her. He owed her that much in return for what she had done two months ago. But it wasn't the sense of responsibility he felt that stayed on his mind as he allowed himself to go back to sleep. Nor was it the questions engendered by that letter in the kitchen.

The last, disturbing thought he had of Kimberly was a memory of the way she had begun to respond to him when he'd held her in his arms. If he'd had a little more time or a more appropriate set of circumstances, he decided, he could have had her in bed. That realization was deeply satisfying.

KIMBERLY AWOKE the next morning with a decidedly grim realization of her own. She knew she didn't want to face another night alone in this isolated house. Someone was deliberately trying to terrorize her. The man in the living room was offering shelter. She really had no logical choice but to accompany him back to the wine country until this business was all cleared up.

No sense fooling herself, she thought as she climbed out of bed and headed toward the bathroom. It wasn't going to be easy living in a house full of strangers. But handling figures in hooded robes who walked around carrying large silver daggers wasn't much more inviting. She could just imagine what the authorities would say if she tried to tell them what had happened last night. They would think she'd gone off her rocker. At least Cavenaugh hadn't questioned her story of what she'd seen through the window.

The closed door of her bathroom and the sound of running water inside brought her up short.

"Cavenaugh, are you in there?"

"Were you expecting anyone else?" he called back provokingly.

"Don't dawdle," she warned.

The door opened a minute later and he stood in front of her wiping the last of the shaving cream off his neck. He was naked from the waist up and it was obvious he had made himself quite at home. Emerald eyes glinted as he took in the disapproving way she peered around him into the interior of the bathroom.

"Your trouble is that you're simply not used to having a man in the house. Or anyone else for that matter. Don't worry, I'm fully trained. I won't leave my towels lying on the floor."

"Are you finished?" she demanded frostily, wondering if there would be any hot water left.

"Just about."

"Good. Then you can start breakfast," she informed him triumphantly, sweeping past him to commandeer the small bathroom. He allowed himself to be pushed out into the hall, but not before she'd caught sight of the half-amused twist of his mouth.

"A man would have his hands full teaching you the fine art of household compromise," he observed.

"When it comes to having enough hot water for my morning shower, I don't believe in compromise. Go start the eggs, Cavenaugh. I like them on the well-done side." She started to close the door and then stopped. "Oh, by the way, I've decided to take you up on your offer. At least for a few days."

He raised one dark brow. "No more arguments about returning to the estate with me this morning?"

"Is the offer still open?"

"It was never an offer, Kim," he explained gently. "It was more of a requirement. I can't stay here with you because I have too many other responsibilities at home. But I can't leave you alone here, either—not after what's been happening. The only alternative is for you to go home with me."

She tilted her head to one side, studying him coolly through narrowed lashes. "If I have a few things to learn about sharing the bathroom, allow me to inform you that you have a hell of a lot to learn about diplomacy."

"Meaning I ought to learn how to make commands sound like requests?" he drawled.

Disdaining to answer that before she'd even had her morning coffee, Kimberly slammed the door in his face.

Half an hour later when she strode into the kitchen dressed in a fresh pair of jeans and a peach-colored shirt, she sniffed appreciatively at the aroma that greeted her.

"Not bad, Cavenaugh. Not bad at all." She examined the eggs he was scrambling at the stove. A stack of toast was keeping warm in the oven.

"I do my best to please," he murmured.

Kimberly grinned. "Something tells me you just happened to be hungry yourself. Not that I'm complaining. I can't even remember the last time someone cooked breakfast for me. I'll enjoy it while I can." She opened the refrigerator. "What do you want on your eggs?"

"Anything but hot sauce."

She tossed him a disapproving glance. "You don't know what you're missing. I love it on my eggs." Pulling the huge bottle of pepper sauce from the refrigerator she carried it toward the counter. Actually, having Darius Cavenaugh around was rather interesting, she decided privately. What would it be like living in his house for a few days?

Setting down the hot sauce, Kimberly leaned across the counter to collect a couple of napkins. It was then her eyes fell on the opened envelope from the lawyers. Instantly the good mood she had been indulging evaporated as she realized that Cavenaugh must have read the letter.

"What's this all about?" she demanded softly, holding up the opened envelope.

Cavenaugh didn't pause in the act of dishing out the eggs. "That's what I was going to ask you."

"You opened this!"

He nodded, putting the frying pan into the sink and picking up the two plates.

She stared at him in stunned amazement. He didn't even appear mildly embarrassed. "You deliberately opened a private letter!"

"I was curious."

"Curious! My God, Cavenaugh, what gives you the right to be curious about my personal correspondence?" she flung furiously.

He still appeared unperturbed. "In my experience letters from lawyers often spell trouble. Since you didn't seem interested in opening it I thought I'd better."

She sat down weakly on the stool beside him, feeling more amazement than anything else. "I can't believe you had the nerve to do something like this."

He slanted her a glance. "Who are the Marlands, Kim?"

"To blithely open someone else's private mail. It's incredible. There are laws against that sort of thing," she went on, ignoring his question.

"Kim, who are the Marlands? Why have they hired that

law firm to contact you? Why are they asking you to meet with them?''

"Are you this high-handed with all those people you have working for you and living with you? If so, I don't see how you keep your employees. Your relatives must find you absolutely infuriating."

"Kim," he interrupted patiently. "Just answer my questions."

"Why should I?"

He muttered something short and explicit under his breath. "Because if you don't answer my questions, I'm liable to contact that law firm myself and find out what's going on."

"First invasion of privacy and now threats," she gritted.

"Kim, just be reasonable about this, all right? I'm only trying to find out if you've got real trouble. Maybe it's got something to do with that character at the window last night. Maybe we're way off base thinking he was connected with the kidnapping."

Kimberly was too startled at his conclusions to restrain her answer. "Good Lord, no! I assure you that Mr. and Mrs. Wesley Marland would never dirty their well-manicured hands in something as nasty as kidnapping."

"So who are they?" he persisted gently. "Why do they want you to get in touch with them?"

Kimberly decided it really wasn't worth the battle. Besides, she reasoned, it wouldn't do any harm to tell him the truth. "My father's parents."

"Your grandparents?"

"Technically." She shrugged and began lacing her eggs with hot sauce. "I don't really think of myself as being related to them except in a strictly biological sense. I've never even met them."

"From the sound of that letter they want to meet you."

"It's a little late for them to play the role of loving grandparents."

"What happened?" Cavenaugh asked quietly.

"Breakfast is hardly the time to drag family skeletons out of the closet," Kimberly parried brightly.

"I've learned there aren't any good times to do it. Might as well be over breakfast," he retorted dryly.

Something in his tone caused her to send him a questioning glance. Whatever lay beneath the surface of the remark was destined to remain a mystery for now, however. Cavenaugh was on the trail of her secrets and had no intention of being sidetracked into revealing any of his own. Still, she found herself wondering suddenly about his past. What was it he had said last night? There had been some remark about him not always having made his living making wine.

"Tell me, Kim," he broke into her reverie to prod softly.

"It's short and sordid. Actually, given your own family background, you'll probably understand the Marlands' position completely. My father was their only son and heir. The Marlands own a big chunk of Pasadena, California, and have sizable investments throughout the state. The family goes back for generations. All the way back to Spanish land grant days. Lots of pride of heritage and lots of money. They had raised my father to be a worthy inheritor of the money and the name. He had been perfectly groomed for his role in life, as I understand it. Private schools, the best of everything money could buy. And then one day the noble son and heir committed a serious judgmental error. He felt in love with my mother."

"Let me guess," Cavenaugh inserted coolly. "Your mother didn't come from the right background?"

"My mother was an underpaid, overworked nurse. She lacked any sort of background at all, let alone the right one. She was an orphan. She met my father when he went into the hospital for some minor surgery. You know what they say about men falling in love with their nurses.''

"No. What do they say?" Cavenaugh inquired.

"Never mind. Apparently it's a regular nursing syndrome. It usually wears off as soon as the man is discharged from the hospital. Only in my father's case, it didn't. He knew he'd never get his parents' approval to marry my mother so one night in the heat of passion he ran off with her to Las Vegas.''

"Hoping to present his parents with a fait accompli?"

"Umm," Kimberly said, nodding. "It didn't quite work out that way. The Marlands were infuriated and demanded an immediate divorce. I gather my father tried to resist at first but they worked on him, pointing out his responsibility to the family name and fortune, forcing him to consider where his true loyalties lay. And then they cut off the money. My parents were divorced shortly thereafter," Kimberly concluded dryly.

"What happened when you were born?"

"Absolutely nothing. There was no contact from the Marlands.''

"You don't even bear your father's name?"

"I refuse. I took my mother's."

"Scott said your mother died a few years ago," Cavenaugh said gently.

"She was killed in a car accident on an L.A. freeway," Kimberly explained bleakly.

Cavenaugh was silent for a while as he thoughtfully munched toast. Kimberly decided he had abandoned the topic but a moment later he asked, "Why do the Marlands want to contact you now after all these years?"

Kimberly allowed herself a savage little smile. "Because the noble son and heir, my father, never had any more children. He married well, mind you, but his wife proved unable to have children. My father was killed in a sailing accident a year after my mother died, according to those lawyers.'' Fleetingly she remembered the odd sensation of loss she'd had when she'd learned that the father she'd never known had died.

"So now the Marlands have no one except you."

"They don't have me," Kimberly said with cool finality. "As far as I'm concerned they made their bed twenty-eight years ago. Now they can sleep in it. They chose to wield all that family power and pressure then and they can damn well live with the results. I'll never forgive them for what they did to my mother."

"That letter from their lawyer implies there would be a large settlement for you if you'll agree to a meeting with the Marlands."

"I don't need or want their money."

"How about the sense of having family ties?" Cavenaugh pointed out. "You're just as alone now as your grandparents are."

"I'm not a big fan of strong family ties," Kimberly told him wryly. "Not after what family ties did to my mother."

"Is that why you're so intent on finding a man who's as free as you are?"

Kimberly blinked. "Full marks for analysis. You've got it in one. If I ever decide to marry it will be to a man whose loyalty is one hundred percent with me. I won't share him with several generations of responsibility and clout and money."

"And of course he must share this deep sense of non-verbal communication with you, too."

"You find it humorous?" she asked coldly.

"I think you're living in a fantasy world. You want a

man who will materialize out of nowhere with no ties to anyone but you, and who will think the same way you do.''

''It's a pleasant enough fantasy,'' she returned negligently.

''You might like the real world just as well,'' he suggested.

''Not a chance.''

''Are you sure there won't come a time when you'll need a real flesh-and-blood man?''

''Not on a permanent basis,'' she tossed back caustically. ''Would you please pass the jam?''

''Is that a way of telling me you want to change the topic?'' He handed her the jar of strawberry jam.

''I am continually amazed at your perceptive abilities.'' She gave him a brilliant smile.

''I have a few other abilities, too, but you have so many built-in prejudices against men in my position that you're not going to give yourself a chance to test them, are you?''

''If you're talking about the way you seemed to read my mind yesterday…''

He shook his head impatiently. ''There was no telepathy involved yesterday. I just put a few facts together and realized it must be you calling the house. Since I had intended to drive over to the coast to see you soon, anyway, I decided to arrive sooner rather than later. No, Kim, I'm not referring to any supernatural abilities. I'm talking about more concrete ones. I'd like a chance to prove my ability to satisfy you in bed, for example.''

Kimberly drained her coffee in a single, hot swallow and set the cup down with a sharp clatter. ''Don't hold your breath. If you think that I'll sleep with you in exchange for your offer of protection, you might as well leave now. I'll take care of myself.''

Cavenaugh's emerald eyes glittered with sudden proud

fury. "When I decide to sleep with you, witch, it will be on my terms, not yours. And you can bet my terms won't include exchanging sex for protection. You're not the only one who has a few ironclad rules regarding relationships. I may choose to be generous in a relationship but I definitely will not resort to buying a woman, with either money or protection or anything else. Do we understand each other?"

Kimberly caught her lower lip briefly between her teeth as she considered the arrogant anger in him. "I didn't mean to insult you, Cavenaugh," she apologized aloofly. And it was the truth. She hadn't meant to antagonize him. It was just that he had pushed her a little too far.

"Terrific," he growled sardonically as he reached for the coffeepot. "Maybe we do share some mystical channel of communication. At least you understand me well enough to know when to back down."

CHAPTER FOUR

THE CAVENAUGH VINEYARDS and winery could have served as a picture postcard of a Napa Valley wine estate. Gently rolling hills of neatly trimmed vines surrounded the chateau-style buildings in the center. A tree-lined drive led from the highway through the vineyards to the winery.

Kimberly sat in the passenger seat of Darius Cavenaugh's well-bred Jaguar as he turned off the highway and headed toward the main house. She was feeling very wary as she approached his home—more so than she had expected to feel.

"It looks as though it's all been here a couple of hundred years," she finally remarked, studying the vaguely French country house architecture of the two main buildings.

"Not quite," Cavenaugh said. "My father had the winery building constructed in the 1960s. It's open to the public three days a week. I had the main house built two years ago. So much for family history."

"But your family has been in the wine business here in California for several generations, hasn't it?"

"Off and on," Cavenaugh said cryptically.

Kimberly's brows came together in a small line. "Well, right now it looks like it's definitely on." The grounds appeared sleek and prosperous, well cared for and undoubtedly quite profitable.

Cavenaugh allowed himself a remote expression of satisfaction. "Yes. Right now, it's on."

The Cavenaugh home was set on a hill above the winery building, protected from tourists by a gated drive and a deceptively casual-looking low rock wall.

"I've had electronic equipment installed along the entire perimeter of the wall," Cavenaugh explained as he used a small gadget to open the gate automatically. "No one can get past without Starke knowing."

"Who's Starke?"

"A friend of mine. He's in charge of security around here. With all the tourists we get on weekends we've always had to exercise some controls. After what happened to Scott, we've really tightened things up." He threw her a grimly compelling glance as he halted the Jaguar in front of the house. "As long as you stay on the house grounds you'll be safe, Kim. I don't want you going beyond that wall without someone accompanying you. Is that very clear?"

Kimberly glanced uneasily around at the perimeter of her new jail and wondered what she'd gotten herself into. A trapped sensation began to nibble at her awareness. She wasn't certain how she should respond to Cavenaugh's orders and was therefore grateful for the distraction that came barreling through the main door of the house.

"Uncle Dare, Uncle Dare, you brought her! I knew you would!" Scott Emery's delighted face appeared at the window of the car on Cavenaugh's side. He looked past his uncle to examine Kimberly. "Hi, Miss Sawyer," he said, his voice lowering under a sudden attack of shyness. "Do you remember me?"

Kimberly grinned. "Believe me, Scott, I will never forget you!"

"Kim's going to be staying with us for a while," Cavenaugh began, opening his car door and pushing a hand affectionately through the youngster's shaggy black hair.

"Oh boy, I can show her my new train setup!"

"Miss Sawyer, we're so glad to have you. I told Dare he wasn't to return without you!"

Kimberly was sliding out of the Jaguar, not waiting for Cavenaugh to open the door for her when the new voice interrupted Scott's excited chatter. She looked up to see an attractive, black-haired woman with Cavenaugh-green eyes coming down the front steps. There was no doubt about who she was.

"Julia?" Kimberly held out her hand politely to Darius Cavenaugh's sister.

"I've been wanting to meet you since the night Dare brought Scott home and told us what happened. I'm sure he told you how very, very grateful we all are for what you did. I'm delighted he was able to talk you into visiting us!"

"Thank you," Kim began awkwardly, wondering how long she would be welcome when Cavenaugh's household discovered that she was there for an unspecified duration. Before she could think of anything else to say to the pretty young woman who was Scott's mother, Kimberly became aware of yet another person standing at the top of the steps.

"Hello, Starke," Cavenaugh said calmly as he nodded at the newcomer. "I'd like you to meet Kimberly Sawyer. We'll be looking after her for a while."

Kimberly managed a polite smile as the man came slowly down the steps. It wasn't the easiest task she had ever set herself. The man they called Starke suited his name. A forbidding face that Kimberly guessed rarely knew the tug of a smile was outlined in awesomely blunt planes and angles. There was a sense of restrained menace about the man, as if the layer of civilization was rather thin. Kimberly could see a raw, potentially violent intelligence deep in the dark pools of the brooding gaze under which he pinned her. She hid a shudder and wondered where on earth Cavenaugh had found him.

"It's about time you got here, Miss Sawyer," Starke said in a graveled riverbed voice as he inclined his iron-gray head austerely. "Cavenaugh needs you."

Before Kim could find a response to the outrageous remark, Starke had already turned and stalked back into the house.

"Don't mind Starke," Julia Emery exclaimed cheerfully as she urged Kimberly up the steps. "He's a little weird but he's nice."

"And no one will ever get past him to get at Scott again," Cavenaugh observed softly as he carried Kimberly's suitcase inside the house.

"You can say that again," Julia whispered confidentially to Kimberly. "Poor Starke took it very hard when Scott got kidnapped. I think he felt it was his fault, which of course it wasn't. Whoever took Scott got him on the way home from school. We used to let him ride his bike, you see. Not anymore, naturally. Starke drives him back and forth now."

"I see," Kimberly said, glad that everyone was going to let Starke's nutty remark about Cavenaugh needing her slide by without comment. To make certain nothing more was said on the subject she hurried to exclaim over the beautiful interior of the house. "What a lovely home, Julia. It looks like an elegant old chateau."

"But fortunately has all the modern conveniences," Julia said, chuckling. "Including plenty of room. I'll take you upstairs to the bedroom you'll be using. We had it prepared just in case Dare succeeded in getting you to agree to stay with us for a while."

Another figure bustled forward as Julia guided Kimberly through the wide hall toward a large, curving staircase. "This is Mrs. Lawson. She takes care of us. Don't know what we'd do without her. The house would probably fall apart. Mrs. Lawson, this is Kimberly Sawyer."

The plump housekeeper held out her hand with a cheerful smile and a crinkle of genuine humor in her gray eyes. She was probably in her late fifties, Kimberly estimated, as she greeted the woman. Privately she wondered how many other people there were in the household. The sense of being surrounded grew.

She and Julia had reached the second floor of the house and were halfway down the hall toward the bedroom Kimberly was to use when two other figures popped out of a sunny sitting room with loud exclamations of pleasure.

"Ah, this must be Kim," the first declared. "So glad you could come, dear! I'm Dare's aunt, Milly Cavenaugh."

Kimberly smiled at the charmingly stately woman in her midsixties who swept up to her. Milly Cavenaugh had the now-familiar green eyes of the family but her once-black hair had silvered quite elegantly. She wore it in a regal bun at the back of her head. The queenly style suited the woman. Milly was tall and proudly built. Her eyes sparkled with animation and an unquenchable curiosity. Cavenaugh had mentioned that his aunt had lost her husband years ago and now divided her time between whatever projects happened to take her fancy.

Kimberly knew she was going to like the older woman, but she also knew she was going to thoroughly enjoy the creature in the purple turban and lime-green dress who stood behind her. For an instant she just stared at the brightly dressed woman. The robust, vividly attired lady was about the same age as Milly, but where Cavenaugh's aunt had an air of elegance about her, her companion appeared wonderfully eccentric and not a little scatterbrained. A good character for a book, Kimberly found herself thinking.

"Kim, this is my aunt's friend, Ariel Llewellyn," Julia said, making the introductions quickly. "Ariel and my aunt are inseparable."

"Rubbish," Ariel announced grandly, shaking Kimberly's hand with brisk enthusiasm. "Milly and I amuse each other and spend a good many afternoons together but we certainly aren't inseparable, are we, Milly?"

"Vile slander," Milly agreed lightly. "How long will you be staying, dear?"

"A few days, I think." Kimberly felt decidedly uneasy under the questioning. It was anyone's guess how long she could bring herself to stay in this energetic, well-populated household, even under the best of circumstances. Already she felt a wave of panic at the notion of having so little privacy. She realized she had become accustomed to privacy, living by herself most of her adult life. Vaguely she wondered how Cavenaugh stood having so many lively people surrounding him. But then, he had grown up in this environment, she reminded herself. And he was a man who carried out his responsibilities.

"Is that everyone in the house?" Kimberly asked Julia hesitantly as Scott's mother swept her on down the hall to the room assigned to her.

"For the moment," Julia assured her breezily. "We get a lot of people in and out during the day, of course. Mostly employees who come to see Dare or visit with Mrs. Lawson. Then there are the visits from Scott's friends. And Milly and Ariel are very fond of tea parties so they frequently entertain."

"It sounds rather, uh, hectic," Kimberly noted cautiously.

"You get used to it.'

"Oh." Kimberly said nothing more as Julia ushered her into a warm, sunny room that looked out over the vineyards. She headed at once for the window, peering out at the view.

"I hope you'll like this room," Julia remarked. "Dare will bring your suitcase up soon. He's busy talking to Starke down in the study at the moment."

Kimberly suddenly realized that Cavenaugh had not followed his sister and Kimberly up the stairs. "That's fine. I'm in no rush. I'll need to get my typewriter out of the car, too, and my supplies."

"Don't worry. Starke will take care of it." Julia smiled warmly. "You know, we really are glad you decided to come and visit for a while. We'll never be able to thank you enough for what you did two months ago."

"Please, don't keep mentioning that," Kimberly begged. "It really wasn't that big a deal."

"You'd feel differently if it were your son who had been taken," Julia assured her in heartfelt tones. "I was a nervous wreck during those three days. When the ransom note arrived I really went to pieces. Up until that point I had been telling myself that the kidnapper was probably Scott's father, and at least, being his father, Tony wouldn't have hurt Scott. After the note arrived we knew it had to be a real kidnapping. It was terrifying."

"You thought Scott's father might have taken him?" Kimberly asked in disbelief and then realized the full implications. "Oh, I see. A…a custody dispute?"

"Not really," Julia said wryly. "The last thing Tony would want is to be burdened with a child. He was furious when I got pregnant. But he was also furious when he left.''

''He divorced you?''

''Not willingly.'' Julia's gentle mouth curved bleakly. ''He wasn't about to divorce the tie to the Cavenaugh money. Then Dare informed him that there really wasn't any money except what Dare personally controlled.''

Kimberly stirred uneasily as Julia confided the information. She wasn't at all sure she wanted to know too much about the Cavenaughs. ''I see,'' she said again, a bit weakly, but Julia plowed on without any sign of hesitation.

''My father filed for bankruptcy three years ago. Then he and mother were killed in a light-plane crash on the way home from Tahoe. A few months later Dare came home and rescued the winery and the family.''

''Came home from where?'' Kimberly asked blankly. She had assumed Cavenaugh had always lived here.

''He had a business of his own. An import-export company that he operated out of San Diego. He spent a lot of time traveling abroad in connection with the business and we saw very little of him for a long time. But when he finally showed up in our lives again he was quite successful in his own right. He had the capital it took to get the Cavenaugh Vineyards back on its feet. He also sized up the situation with Tony, my husband, and kicked him out.''

Kimberly stared at her. ''Did you love Tony?''

''By the time he left I was more than glad to get rid of him,'' Julia admitted calmly. ''He had been using me for years, hoping to inherit my father's money. I thought he cared about me, though. That's how completely he had me fooled. It took Dare to see through him. Dare and Starke are very good judges of human nature, by the way,'' Julia added lightly. ''They've been together for years and they seem to have an instinct for people like Tony Emery. It was all very traumatic but I'm glad it's over.''

Kimberly considered the absent Tony and wondered what had really happened. She couldn't help wondering if Tony Emery had found himself in the same situation in which her mother had found herself so many years ago. Kimberly wouldn't put it past Darius Cavenaugh to get rid of someone he deemed no more than a conniving gigolo who was unworthy of a member of the Cavenaugh family.

But even as she accepted the fact that Cavenaugh could probably be quite ruthless, she also found herself realizing that he must have had legitimate grounds for his actions. She didn't want to believe Darius Cavenaugh would have done something as traumatic as throwing out Julia's husband unless there were real reasons. Julia herself seemed content with the situation, Kimberly had to admit.

The remainder of the afternoon was a hubbub of unfamiliar activity for Kimberly. She was taken on a tour of Scott's train land, introduced to Julia's new fiancé, Mark Taylor, the owner of a small winery nearby, shown around the grounds by Milly and Ariel and generally kept in constant motion by one member or another of the Cavenaugh household. A number of winery employees came and went from the study Cavenaugh used for an office on the first floor of the house.

She didn't see Cavenaugh himself until dinner. By then she was so tired she could barely hold up her end of the conversation. Ariel Llewellyn stayed for dinner, as did Mark Taylor. Scott was wound up with excitement and managed to dominate the conversation. By the time Mrs. Lawson had cleared away dessert, Kimberly was frantic for an excuse to escape. There seemed to be no letup of activity or conversation in the house and she simply wasn't used to being surrounded by so many people.

And there had been no hot sauce on the table at dinner. Depressing.

When she pleaded a headache and tiredness, she was allowed to flee up the stairs to the privacy of her own room. But not before Ariel had produced a special herb tea and given her strict instructions on drinking it before going to bed. Kimberly's sense of relief as she closed the door was overwhelming. In that moment she decided she would willingly accept a few more glimpses of people in cowled robes carrying silver daggers if it meant she could be alone again with unlimited quantities of hot sauce.

Wearing one of her comfortable T-shirts, Kimberly sank wearily onto the bed and sipped the tea Ariel had prescribed for her headache. It was bitter and unpleasant but for some reason she felt obliged to finish it. Ariel had been so anxious to help her. The knock on her door startled her so much she nearly spilled the contents of the cup.

Sighing, Kimberly pulled on her robe and went to answer the summons, half expecting Scott or Julia to be standing on the other side of the door. But it was Cavenaugh who stood there.

"Think you'll survive?" he asked wryly, stepping into her room without waiting for an invitation. He turned to run his eyes over her tousled figure.

She drew a breath and said carefully, "Cavenaugh, I'm not used to so many people and so much activity."

"I know. How do you think it was for me when I came back two years ago? I thought I'd go nuts."

Kimberly blinked in amazement at the unexpected confession. "You did?"

"All I can say is, you get used to it."

"That's what Julia says." She smiled.

"Well, personally I'm looking forward to the day Julia marries Mark and she and Scott move in with him," Cavenaugh said firmly. "And Aunt Milly and that wacky Ariel travel a bit. They're often gone for several days at a time. I'm more than happy to foot the bills for those trips, believe me." He hesitated and then said deliberately, "But even when a few of them are gone, it's never really *quiet* around here. The business side of things alone keeps everything in motion."

"I can imagine." She had the strangest impression he was trying to tell her something else, something oblique, but she was too tired to figure it out.

He prowled around the room, absently checking the windows. "I suppose you're tired..."

"Very," she mumbled in forceful tones. "Scott seems to have my entire day planned out for tomorrow. I suppose I'd better get prepared for it."

Cavenaugh stopped his restless prowling, coming to a halt in front of her. "You realize they all assume we're sleeping together."

"What!"

He nodded. "I'm afraid so. Except for Scott, of course, who hasn't gotten around to thinking about things like that in great detail yet."

"But...I...you...we hardly even know each other." Kimberly exploded. "How could anyone assume..." Words failed her.

"They know I've been planning on seeing you again. I didn't make any secret of it. There have been occasional business trips I've made during the past couple of months that I think they've interpreted as slipping away to find you. And since they know we spent last night together, it's natural for them to think we slept together. I just thought I'd warn you."

"Oh, gee, thanks," she said furiously. "Did you know

everyone was going to assume that when you came over to the coast to collect me?''

He dismissed the question as unimportant. ''There's no harm done, Kim. Relax. Is it really so terrible? The whole family is very anxious to see me married, I'm afraid. It's just harmless fantasizing on their part.''

''Harmless for whom? I'm going to look like a fool!''

His mouth hardened and the green eyes flared dangerously for an instant. ''Why should you look like a fool?''

''How else can you describe a woman who appears to be sleeping with a wealthy man in hopes of marrying him?''

''But you don't have any wish to marry someone like me, do you, Kim?'' He moved toward her, catching her chin with his palm and studying her infuriated features broodingly.

''Just as you wouldn't wish to marry someone like me,'' she flung back tightly. ''But in a situation like this, I'm the one who will look foolish, not you.''

''Because you're a woman?''

''I doubt that has much to do with it. Being a man didn't protect Julia's first husband, did it? It's more a question of money and power and sheer clout. You have it, I don't.''

He released her chin and thrust his hands into the back pockets of his jeans. ''What do you know about Emery?''

''Nothing much. Julia just explained that you got rid of him a couple of years ago.'' Wishing fiercely that she'd never raised the subject, Kimberly chewed nervously on her lower lip. This was family business. Not her business.

''Tony Emery had been cheating on my sister for years. He couldn't have cared less about her or about Scott. Furthermore, he was swindling my father who had been soft enough to give him a job in the accounting department. He was garbage, and when he found out I controlled the financial side of things in the family, he left quite willingly. He knew I'd never support him the way my father had.''

"I understand," she said stiffly, refusing to meet his hard gaze.

"Do you? I doubt it. You think poor old Tony was in the same position as your mother was when she found herself confronting your grandparents. But it wasn't like that at all. I'd have made sure Emery had a job and a future if I'd thought for one minute that he cared about Julia and Scott. But he didn't.''

"So you got rid of him."

"As I said, it wasn't hard to convince him to go," Cavenaugh reiterated bluntly. "Kim, there's no similarity at all to your mother's position."

"Right," she agreed with unnatural briskness. "Well, it's getting late, Cavenaugh. I'm sure that even if your family thinks we're sleeping together occasionally, they won't be expecting us to do so under the family roof. Please don't feel obliged to stay any longer just for appearances' sake!"

"You're a sarcastic little witch at times, aren't you?" he growled.

"Only when I'm feeling pressured."

"And you're feeling pressured now, aren't you?" he asked with a gentleness she wasn't expecting.

"Yes."

"Kim, everything's going to be all right. You'll be safe here. I swear it."

She heard the underlying vow in his words and nodded mutely. She would be safe enough here from people carrying silver daggers but that didn't guarantee her any safety at all from Darius Cavenaugh. And both she and Cavenaugh knew it. Their eyes clashed in sudden, mutual understanding and in that moment Kimberly would have sworn that they really could read each other's minds.

Slowly Cavenaugh shook his head. ''No promises on the situation between us, Kim. Only that I'll protect you from others.''

He walked out the door, closing it softly behind him before Kimberly could think of anything to say.

TWO DAYS LATER Cavenaugh stood at the curving window of his office-study and watched Kimberly as she surreptitiously left the house and made her way through the huge garden. She glanced back over her shoulder two or three times, her amber hair gleaming in the wintry sunshine. He knew she was checking to see whether or not she was being followed.

At the far end of the garden she unlatched the gate and stepped outside. He knew exactly what was going through her head in that moment.

Freedom.

She was escaping, he realized. Two days of constant, even if well-meant, attention from everyone in the household had finally taken their toll. He had watched her deal politely with Julia's eager hospitality, Scott's excited efforts to entertain and the invitations to Aunt Milly's zany afternoon tea-leaf reading activities with Ariel. In addition, everyone on the estate from Mrs. Lawson to the gardener had displayed unabashed interest in her. They all knew the role Kimberly had played in retrieving Scott from his ordeal.

And they all thought they could guess the role she was destined to play in Cavenaugh's life.

Cavenaugh's mouth hardened a bit at the edges as he followed her escape route. She was on the other side of the garden now, striding briskly toward the low, electronically wired rock wall that was supposed to be the farthest she could wander from the house without an escort.

He had a grim feeling that she wasn't going to follow the rules today. She wanted some peace and quiet and privacy and she'd go beyond the rock wall to get it.

Glancing down at the manuscript pages he had picked up from the desk in Kimberly's room a few minutes before, Cavenaugh skimmed over the lines of fast-paced dialogue and equally swift action. *Vendetta* was undoubtedly going to be another highly successful novel in the Amy Solitaire series. Cavenaugh rather liked Amy. It was Josh Valerian he wanted to have dumped into one of the huge fermentation tanks over in the main production building.

It was damn tough competing with a fictional "other man." Especially when that other man was probably Kimberly's secret fantasy. He was pondering Valerian's excellent timing, both in the matter of coming to Amy's rescue and in bed when Starke entered the room.

"She's left the house, Dare."

"I know."

"Want me to go after her?"

"No, I'll go and get her. She's a little desperate at the moment." Cavenaugh turned away from the window and smiled bleakly at his friend. "I don't blame her. At times I know how she feels. Any leads on that business of the dagger?"

Starke shook his iron-gray head. "I wish we had a better description of it. This whole thing keeps getting screwier by the minute. I have a couple of possibilities to check out, though. There aren't that many sources for handmade silver daggers in this part of California. It's beginning to look as though we may be dealing with a pack of real crazies."

"Scott's witches?"

"Yeah. The authorities aren't interested in that line of

reasoning at all, however. Cranston prefers his own more straightforward theories. We'll have to keep following this one on our own.''

Cavenaugh nodded. He and Starke were accustomed to doing things in their own way. ''Have you got enough people working on it?''

''Three. But they're all good,'' Starke assured him.

''All right.'' Cavenaugh tossed down the manuscript pages he had been reading. ''I'd better go bring back our wandering houseguest.''

Starke eyed him thoughtfully. ''You didn't stay with her last night.''

Cavenaugh glanced up sharply. ''Your job is to keep an eye on this household, but that doesn't mean you have to turn into a voyeur!''

Starke lifted one brow with mocking politeness. ''Sorry.''

''About what?'' Cavenaugh growled.

''About overstepping the line between employer and employee,'' Starke said calmly.

Cavenaugh swore grittily and ran a hand through his hair. ''Don't give me that. You know very well you're hardly an employee.''

Starke relented. ''I know. Dare, you've been as tight as a compressed spring ever since you brought her here. The problem isn't that you're sleeping with her like everyone on the estate thinks—the problem is that you're *not* sleeping with her.''

''Stick to worrying about witches and daggers, Starke. I can do without the psychiatric advice.'' Back in front of the window Cavenaugh watched Kimberly disappear from sight. Behind him he sensed Starke shrugging.

''Whatever you say, *boss*.''

"Damn it to hell, Starke, what are you trying to do? Make me explode?"

"Not me. I've been with you on a couple of occasions when you've lost your temper. I'd rather you take it out on Kim. Something tells me she can handle it. Go release some of that tension with her. Since everyone on the place already assumes you've taken her to bed, you might as well go ahead and do it."

Cavenaugh slanted his friend a violent glance. "Your theories on handling a woman like Kim leave me gasping in amazement." He scooped up the manuscript pages of *Vendetta* and shoved them across the desk. "Want to find out what women really want in a man? Here, read this."

"What's this?" Curiously Starke picked up the pages and leafed through them.

"Part of the book Kim's working on at the moment. Pay particular attention to Josh Valerian."

Starke looked up. "Why?"

"Because he's Kimberly's ideal man."

Starke grinned, one of his rare, wolfish grins. "I take it you don't fit the role of Josh Valerian?"

"Valerian enjoys total communication with the heroine," Cavenaugh said dangerously. "He always seems to know what she's thinking, how she's feeling. What's more, he understands her thoughts and feelings perfectly."

"So? What's so tricky about that? You've always been good at reading other people. Don't you have a pretty fair idea of what Kim's thinking a lot of the time?"

"Yes. Unfortunately, it doesn't do me a lot of good." Cavenaugh moved around his desk to grab his suede jacket.

"Why not?"

"Because I don't always agree with or approve of what she thinks or the way she thinks."

Starke gave him a mildly astonished look. "Why should you? You're a man. She's a woman. How could you possibly react the same way to everything?"

Cavenaugh smiled wryly as he pulled on the jacket. "You know, Starke, you have a way of going straight to the heart of the matter. You're absolutely right. Why should I worry about not being Josh Valerian? Kim's an adult female. She doesn't need some mystical other half of herself. She needs a man."

"You."

"Damn right." Cavenaugh paused as something crinkled in his jacket pocket. He removed the folded, buff-colored envelope from the L.A. law firm. "Valerian isn't the only obstacle in my path right now." He handed the envelope to Starke. "See what you can find out about this situation, will you? I want to talk to one of those lawyers."

"You're going after Kim now?" Starke accepted the envelope.

"Thought I'd work off some of this excess tension you're complaining about," Cavenaugh muttered, striding for the door.

"By yelling at her or by taking her to bed?"

At the door Cavenaugh turned, green eyes narrowed in a way Starke had learned to respect over the years. "I'd thought I'd try a little of each. See which method works best."

"Probably the second one," Starke said quite seriously.

Cavenaugh slammed the door of the study and stalked down the hall to the door that opened onto the garden.

CHAPTER FIVE

THE BUILDING WAS NOTHING more than a storage shed tucked into the base of a hillside full of vineyards. But standing isolated and out of sight of the main house, it made an inviting refuge. When Kimberly spotted the shed after passing the forbidden rock wall she made straight for it. The day was deceptively moderate, considering the season. She'd only taken a light jacket with her when she left the house and after a few minutes of walking through the vineyards she had removed that.

Alone at last, she thought wryly, as she curiously plucked open the shed door and peered into the dark interior. She had realized this morning that if she didn't get away for a while she was liable to say or do something that would definitely border on the rude.

And heaven knew she didn't really want to risk that. Although the Cavenaugh household was overwhelming, she liked its various and assorted members, even the perennially visiting Ariel, who was constantly reading tea leaves, casting horoscopes or prescribing herb teas. She and Aunt Milly made quite a pair, Kimberly decided. Currently they had undertaken to plan a party. Julia was also involved, and when it looked as though they were all going to commandeer Kimberly, too, she had fled. She had finally reached a point where she needed to be alone for a while.

It was pleasantly warm inside the shed. Leaving the door swinging open on its hinges, Kimberly idly poked around amid the odd tools, stacked boxes and assorted equipment. Sunlight trickled through the cracks and chinks in the old wooden walls, providing a fuzzy sort of light here and there. Kimberly was examining an old leather harness, wondering what had happened to the horse who had worn it, when she became aware of a presence standing in the doorway behind her.

She swung around abruptly, Cavenaugh's warning about not going beyond the rock wall slamming into her head. For an instant as she stared at the figure silhouetted against the sun she couldn't see who it was. A shaft of fear sizzled through her. And then he moved.

"Cavenaugh! It's you." She smiled in relief. "You scared the daylights out of me."

He remained where he was, dark and rather intimidating as he filled the doorway. He had his familiar suede jacket hooked negligently over his shoulder. Dressed in jeans and a blue work shirt he could have passed for one of his own employees except for the air of grim command that emanated from him.

"Let's see how good our nonverbal communication is, Kim," he suggested sardonically. "Why don't you try reading my mind?"

Kimberly grimaced wryly. "Right now I can read you like an open book. You're angry because I disobeyed orders and went beyond the wall, aren't you? Going to yell at me?"

"I probably should. I didn't give those orders lightly, Kim. I gave them for your own protection."

"I know," she said, sighing. She slowly hung the old harness back on a rusty nail. "You'll have to make allowances for me. I've never been very good at taking orders from people who thought they knew what was best for me. Go ahead and yell."

He stepped through the door, his face moving out of the shadows and into a ray of light streaming through a crack. Green eyes met hers with a flash of genuine understanding. "I have a feeling chewing you out wouldn't do a whole lot of good. Besides, I know why you disobeyed orders in the first place. And I guess that if I'm perfectly honest I can't say I blame you. It can get to be a bit much."

She smiled weakly. "Your family and your employees are all very nice, Cavenaugh."

"But they drive you crazy at times."

She looked at him with gratitude. "I'm just not used to big families."

"You're not used to any kind of family, are you?"

"No, I suppose not. For a long time there was just mom and me and then there was just me."

"And you like it that way."

"It's been pleasant."

"Lots of freedom," he observed, taking a step closer so that he could look directly down into her face.

"Yes."

"Don't you think I know what that feels like? Not having to worry about anyone but yourself? Not having to solve everyone else's problems? Being free to come and go as you like? Not being on call for everyone from your sister to your aunt's nutty friends?"

And suddenly Kimberly realized that she wasn't the only one who craved some time alone. Her stay in the household was only temporary. Cavenaugh, however, was trapped by the responsibilities he had undertaken. And being the man he was he would never walk away from them.

"Ah, Cavenaugh," she whispered softly, lifting a hand to touch the side of his face. "I hadn't realized, hadn't understood how it was for you." Her amber eyes brimmed with comprehension and gentleness.

"Kim," he muttered, letting the suede jacket slide to the dusty floor. "Kimberly, I..." He bit off the words, reaching out to pull her into his arms with a rough hunger that seemed to explode out of nowhere.

His sudden passion swamped her. Kimberly felt his arms close around her, his hands sweeping with aching longing over her body as his mouth captured hers. She parted her lips willingly when he demanded the intimacy. And when he cupped her hips, drawing her jeaned thighs against his own, she moaned softly. His body hardened violently as it encountered her gentle curves. Beneath the snug fabric of his clothing she could feel the unmistakable evidence of his arousal.

The primitive knowledge thrilled Kimberly, filling her with a rush of heady desire. She had been telling herself for the past three days that she didn't know this man well enough to even think of becoming involved with him. What she did know about him seemed to indicate that he was all wrong for her, in any event.

Yet this afternoon she had finally understood that they weren't so very different, after all. Cavenaugh had been trapped in a situation she'd always avoided, but that didn't mean his longings weren't the same as her own. He could never be really free the way she was, but she empathized totally with what his self-denial must have cost him.

"Can you read my mind now, Kim?" he demanded huskily as he drew his mouth reluctantly away from her own. His palms slid up under her cotton knit shirt, finding the clasp of her bra. When it came free he groaned and let his fingers glide around her ribs until the fullness of her breasts rested on the edge of his hands. "You must know exactly what I'm thinking. I want you, Kim. I've been wanting you for two months. I *need* you."

"Yes," she managed breathlessly, answering all the

questions he had asked, both implied and explicit. "Oh, yes, Cavenaugh."

"Oh, God, Kim. Come to me, lady, and let me make love to you. I've been aching for you. You don't know what it's been like having you in my house but not in my bed."

The ardent plea unlocked the last of her reserve. Kimberly wrapped her arms around him and made no protest when he pushed the cotton shirt up over her head. Her loosened bra fell to the floor and Cavenaugh inhaled sharply as he drank in the sight of her breasts.

"Firm and ripe." He ran his thumbs over her budding nipples. "Just like my grapes at harvest. I want you so much, sweetheart."

Nestling her head against his chest, Kimberly closed her eyes and let the enthralling sensations sweep through her. Vaguely she was aware of Cavenaugh lowering her to the floor. She felt him spread the suede jacket under her before he urged her onto her back. And then he was lying beside her, undoing the fastening of her jeans.

"We're all alone," he rasped. "Just you and me. It's perfect. Absolutely perfect. *You're* perfect."

She smiled up at him, her eyes glowing with feminine mystery behind her half-lowered lashes. "I didn't think it could ever work between us...."

"Just let me do the thinking now, Kimberly. I'll take care of you. I'll make it good for you. I swear it." His palms tugged at the tight-fitting jeans until they were forced down over her hips. He dragged the bikini underpants along with them. A moment later she lay naked. Her body flushed under the heat of the desire she could read in him.

Tremulously she put her fingers on the buttons of his work shirt. He rested his palm possessively on the flat of her stomach as she fumbled with the task of undressing him.

"You're shaking like a leaf," he observed with passionate amusement.

"I know."

"Are you afraid of me?"

"Do I look afraid?"

He lowered his head to taste one of her throbbing nipples. "You look beautiful."

"Cavenaugh, I'm not the only one who's shaking. Are you afraid of me?"

"I probably should be," he growled, letting his fingers glide down to the juncture of her thighs. "Any sane man is afraid of witches." He seemed fascinated with the way her body moved instinctively under his hand.

She pushed his shirt off his shoulders and then began to struggle with his jeans. But he grew impatient with her fumbling and sat up to finish the job.

Kimberly took in the sight of his completely nude body, fascinated by his obvious need. Strong and hard and powerful, he gathered her close, letting her feel every tough plane and angle of him.

His fingers shaped her curves, exploring the softness of her as if discovering something totally unique. His unabashed delight in her was intoxicating, Kimberly discovered. She'd never experienced such excitement and anticipation. It was all swirled into a pervasive warmth that captured her senses.

"I want you," she finally choked.

"You sound astonished," he murmured as he forced her legs provocatively apart with his hand.

"I am. I've never wanted someone like this," she admitted in absolute honesty.

"Oh, Kim!"

As if her words were more than he could resist, Cavenaugh moved, sprawling along the length of her, finding a place for himself between her thighs. The heat of him burned into her skin and the heaviness of his smoothly muscled body was a glorious, crushing weight that seemed to excite every inch of her.

Kimberly caught her breath on a sob of expectation mixed with a strange trepidation as she felt his hardness poised on the brink of her feminine core. His hand moved between them briefly, teasing the exquisitely sensitive region until she cried out and sank her nails into his shoulders.

"You're so sweet, so ready for me," Cavenaugh muttered in tones of masculine wonder. "Do you really want me so much, witch?"

"Yes, ah, Cavenaugh, *yes!*"

And then he was thrusting deeply into her, the impact of him making itself felt throughout her body. Hot, demanding, deliciously overpowering, Cavenaugh took possession of her in a way that made him as much her captive as she was his.

Kimberly clung to the man above her, holding him close with legs that wrapped around him and arms that were silken bonds. Cavenaugh moved into her, claiming her body with elemental passion, giving her all of himself in return. The rhythm of his lovemaking claimed her and she was meshed in perfect harmony with his own pulsating desire.

When her body tightened in warning of the impending climax, Kimberly called Cavenaugh's name and he buried his mouth against her breast. She felt his teeth against her skin and the sensation sent her over some invisible edge.

"Oh, my God, Cavenaugh!"

"Now, Kim. Give me everything *now*. I'll keep you safe."

She shimmered beneath him and before the delicate convulsions had rippled completely through her body he was following her, huskily shouting his own release.

Kimberly sank down into a gentle oblivion, unaware of the hard floor beneath her, unaware of the unromantic surroundings provided by the old shed. She knew only that she had shared the most profound sense of intimacy that she had ever experienced. It might prove a fleeting thing, but while it lasted it was incredible.

And in that warm, vulnerable moment she was certain that Darius Cavenaugh had felt everything she had felt. The relationship between them was changed for all time.

Cavenaugh slowly released himself from her body, moving onto his side so that he could gather her against him. His cradling arm felt warm and comfortable and strong.

"Are you going to be furious with me later?" he asked evenly, green eyes poring over her love-softened face.

Mutely she shook her head. "For making love to me? No, Cavenaugh. It felt…right."

His mouth crooked gently. "I knew it was going to be like this."

"Did you?" She twisted lazily in his arms. "You should have told me."

"I think I tried to on a couple of occasions but you weren't listening."

"Ah, Cavenaugh. How was I to know?" she asked simply.

He leaned down and brushed his mouth against her lips. "In the future you'll just have to trust me to know what's best for you."

She smiled mischievously. "I wouldn't dream of putting

so much responsibility on your shoulders. You've already got more than enough to worry about.''

''More than enough?''

''Ummm.'' She ran her fingers through his silver-tinged hair. ''I've seen the way everyone in the household and on the estate turns to you for advice and help on even the most trivial matters. And you always stop and give it. It's a wonder you have time to get any of the winery's real business done.''

He exhaled slowly, as if enjoying the lingering moment of total relaxation. ''I suppose you're right in a sense. When I arrived two years ago everything was in such chaos that I had no option but to become totally involved both with what was left of the family and the business. People had been floundering. Julia's marriage was in a mess, Scott was having emotional problems because of his father's rejection of him, Aunt Milly was distraught over my father's death, the employees feared for their jobs and the wine wasn't doing well in the markets. On top of that, the estate was going into bankruptcy.''

''So you stepped in and took over responsibility for everything and everyone. You did your family duty, and now you're trapped by that duty.''

The brackets at the edges of his mouth tightened slightly. ''I don't see myself as trapped, Kim. I chose to do it.''

Instantly she was sorry she'd phrased her words the way she had. ''It doesn't matter whether duty chose you or you chose it. Your life has been completely changed by it. What was it like during the days you ran that import-export business?''

''I'm sure you'd describe my life-style back then as considerably freer than it is now,'' he said easily. Absently he stroked slow circles on her arm. ''A lot of traveling with basically only myself and Starke to think about. And Lord knows Starke can take care of himself.''

''Where on earth did you find him?''

''In the middle of a street riot in some miserable little country in the Middle East. I was in town making a deal for some rugs and Starke was there to make…well, another kind of deal. We were both in the wrong place at the wrong time. Things got nasty and by the time it was over we were partners. Two years ago when I decided to take over the winery after my father died, he opted to come with me.''

''You must be close friends.''

''Depends how you describe close friends, I guess. I probably know him as well as anyone, but there's a hell of a lot no one will ever know about Starke.''

''Why did you go into business for yourself? How did you escape being groomed to take over the winery?'' Kimberly asked.

''I had no interest in the winery when I was growing up. I wanted to do something more exciting with my life. I wanted adventure and action and the challenge of making my own fortune.''

''And you found all that?''

''Oh, yes,'' Cavenaugh agreed with a cryptic smile. ''I found it.''

''But when the chips were down, you came back to assume your responsibilities to your family.''

Some of the warm intimacy disappeared from Cavenaugh's green eyes. ''You have a way of making family responsibilities sound like a grim fate to be avoided at all costs.''

''Maybe it's just because I know how twisted they can become.''

Cavenaugh appeared to be sorting through his next words. ''Kim, if your father had really loved your mother he wouldn't have given her up to please his family. And he wouldn't have spent the rest of his life pretending you didn't exist. He would have fought to make his parents accept you and your mother.... Blame his own weakness for what he did to her, not his sense of family responsibility.''

Kimberly suddenly became very aware of a certain chill invading the old shed. "I think we're about to lose our sunny afternoon," she observed with a lightness she was far from feeling. "Clouds are starting to form."

Cavenaugh levered himself up beside her, slanting her a speculative glance. "Which, translated, means you don't want to talk about the situation regarding your grandparents, right?"

"Cavenaugh, I always said you do have some amazing powers of perception."

He finished pulling on his jeans and reached down to help her to her feet, his eyes lingering on her full breasts as she fastened her shirt. "You have some amazing powers, yourself, witch. I feel like a new man this afternoon."

His words halted her emotional withdrawal. Kimberly looked up at him and felt a return of the warmth she had been feeling earlier. But what she felt for him now, she thought fleetingly, went far beyond warmth or even passion for that matter. Deliberately she thrust the realization aside and smiled brilliantly.

"I hope I was a more interesting tonic than some of those concoctions Ariel is always serving up."

"You're much more than a tonic, Kim, and you know it." He took her hand. "Come on, honey, much as I hate to end this very satisfying idyll, I'm afraid we have to get back to the house. I've got a thousand and one things that have to be done this afternoon."

"Winery business?"

"Right. There's a new marketing plan that I've got to go over and a report from the accountant's office."

"It can't have been easy pulling the Cavenaugh Vineyards out of the red these past two years," Kimberly observed slowly as she allowed him to lead her back toward the house.

"It's been a challenge," he agreed dryly.

He didn't release her hand after they came within sight of the house. Instead he clasped her fingers tightly in his own all the way through the garden and up to the back door. Anyone watching from the house could not have missed the intimacy. And anyone watching would probably be able to guess how she and Cavenaugh had just spent the past hour, Kimberly realized uneasily. A part of her went on the defensive when she saw Julia hovering in the hall.

But Julia did not appear to be the slightest bit concerned that her brother might have just made love to their houseguest. She greeted them both cheerfully and glanced at Cavenaugh with obvious relief.

"Oh, there you are, Dare. I've been looking for you. Aunt Milly and Ariel want to invite half the world to this party we've been planning, and I said I'd check with you."

"No one gets invited who isn't personally known to either you or me, Julia, you know that. I don't want any strangers in the house until those kidnappers have been caught."

"That's what I told them you'd say. They're working up a guest list now for you to go over. Oh, and Scott has been scouring the place for you, too. He wants you to help him add a new section to his train track. And I was wondering if you'd talk to that car dealer for me. I'm not getting anywhere with him. He simply won't fix that problem in the transmission free of charge. Claims it's not under warranty. I know he'll back down if you deal with him.''

"Uncle Dare, Uncle Dare," Scott interrupted excitedly, tearing around the corner with a miniature train tunnel in one hand. "I've been looking for you. Come and help me set up my new tunnel."

Before Cavenaugh could respond, Aunt Milly appeared in the hall, the ever-present Ariel right behind her. "Here's the preliminary guest list, Dare. Julia said you'd want to go over it. We have to get the invitations out soon so we were hoping you'd get a chance to look at it this afternoon."

Cavenaugh reluctantly extended his hand to take the list. "All right, Aunt Milly. Scott, let's take a quick look at that train track. Julia, get me the dealer's phone number and I'll—''

It was too much. After two full days in the Cavenaugh household, Kimberly knew things were always like this. It was time to put a stop to it. She stepped forward and removed the guest list from Cavenaugh's hand. When he glanced at her in surprise she smiled serenely and turned to the others.

"I'm afraid Cavenaugh doesn't have time to worry about the guest list or the car dealer this afternoon. He has to go over a marketing report and some papers from the accountant." She glanced pointedly at her watch. "It's only three-thirty on a Wednesday afternoon. A time when every other executive in the country is concentrating on business. And that's exactly what Cavenaugh is going to do today. Scott, you just got home from school. Go find something else to play with for now. Your uncle will help you with the train track later. Julia, you can take a look at the guest list, can't you? You will know who's familiar and who isn't. The car dealer can wait until tomorrow.

Aunt Milly, I'm sure you and Ariel can begin filling out
the invitations. They can be addressed later after the guest
list is approved by Julia.'' She glanced around at the circle
of astonished faces. ''There, I think that does it. Go to
work, Cavenaugh. You have a winery to run. The rest of
the household can get along without you this afternoon.
No one will bother you until five o'clock. Personally,'' she
added firmly, ''I'm going to get some writing done.'' With
a challenging smile she invited objections. There were
none.

She shooed the others down the hall, leaving Cavenaugh
standing alone.

He stood there for a long moment after Kimberly's amber head had disappeared, savoring the memory of her in
his arms. And then he walked slowly toward his study,
letting himself inside and closing the door behind him with
a sense of satisfaction. He had an hour and a half of un-
interrupted time ahead of him. He could accomplish a hell
of a lot. Especially when he knew he wouldn't have to
worry about dealing with every small family crisis that
came along.

Picking up the copy of the marketing plan, Cavenaugh
sat down behind the desk that had been his father's and
went to work.

It was forty-five minutes later that he heard the knock
on the window behind him. Glancing around he saw Starke
staring back at him through the glass, hand poised to knock
again. Cavenaugh leaned across and opened the window.

''What on earth are you doing out there in the garden?''

Starke's somber face twisted in a wry grimace. ''Are
you kidding?'' He glanced furtively to the side, obviously
checking to make sure the coast was clear. ''This was the
only way I could get to you. If she catches me out here,
she'll probably skin me alive.''

"Kim?"

"Yeah. She's given strict orders you aren't to be disturbed until five o'clock. No one's allowed near the study unless they can claim a life-or-death emergency. What the heck's going on?"

"I'm working," Cavenaugh said with a grin.

Realization dawned on Starke's features. "And she's decided you need more privacy?"

"I'm an executive," Cavenaugh reminded him mockingly. "That means I get to set some rules about interruptions during working hours."

"Well, I'll be damned. The lady's going to get the household organized, isn't she? About time. I always did say you put yourself too much at the beck and call of everyone around here."

Cavenaugh glanced at his watch. "It's not five o'clock yet."

Starke arched one eyebrow. "So you want to know why I'm interrupting? Two reasons. The first is to tell you I set up a telephone call with one of those lawyers in L.A. for ten tomorrow morning."

"Thanks." Some of the quiet satisfaction left the emerald eyes as he contemplated the phone call. "What's the second reason you're standing outside my window?"

Starke grinned one of his rare grins. "I just wanted to see the results for myself."

"Results of what?"

"Your efforts to release a little tension this afternoon. Looks like it worked, Dare. You look real good. Nice and relaxed."

Cavenaugh gave him a sardonic expression and reached out to shut the window firmly in Starke's face. "Get lost, Starke, or I'll report you to Kim."

His grin wider than ever, Starke obediently disappeared into the garden.

UPSTAIRS IN HER ROOM Kimberly sat staring at the blank sheet of paper in her typewriter. She hadn't succeeded in typing a single word for the past forty-five minutes. All her thoughts were on the man with whom she had shared the passionate interlude in the shed.

There was no point deluding herself. The white-hot fires of his desire had crystallized her feelings. If she hadn't made love with him perhaps she would have been able to go on pretending that what she felt was only a physical attraction.

Now she knew different. The incredibly, shatteringly intimate experience in the old shed had forced her to acknowledge the truth. She was falling in love with Darius Cavenaugh. No, even that statement didn't disclose the full truth. She was in love with him. Full stop.

Dazedly Kimberly stared at nothing, trying to sort through the ramifications of what had happened. She had been telling herself all along that he was the wrong kind of man for her. Yet at every turn the intimacy between them was growing deeper and more pervasive. There were times when she really did wonder if they were reading each other's minds. And the bonds that existed between them now after that scene in the shed were deeper than anything else she had ever known. She didn't understand how it could have happened so completely or so quickly. But she couldn't deny that it had happened. Love was not a matter of logic or rationality, Kimberly discovered.

With a heart full of trepidation she tried to picture her future. Cavenaugh was inseparable from this house and the wine business. If she became involved with him, she became involved with everything that went with him.

After all her years of avoiding anything that even hinted of competing loyalties and inescapable family obligations—two things that had the potential for destroying love—Kimberly wondered if she could learn to adjust to such a situation. There was no doubt that the Cavenaugh household was a cheerful one. Cavenaugh himself might make the major decisions yet there was no denying he was also trapped by his role. Just look at the way the rest of the family felt free to impose on his time, Kimberly thought grimly. If she moved in here permanently, she'd certainly do some major reorganizing.

And then she realized just how far her thoughts had taken her. Moving in here permanently was an absolutely idiotic notion. No one, least of all Cavenaugh, had invited her to do so!

Just what had he felt after making love to her, she wondered. Some of the warm certainty that she had felt herself returned. Kimberly knew that for Cavenaugh the experience had been more than just a casual interlude. Surely she couldn't be deluding herself about something as crucial as that.

No, this growing sensation of sureness, of understanding and empathy between herself and Cavenaugh was very much for real. It was, Kimberly decided, almost like the invisible bonds she was building between Amy Solitaire and Josh Valerian.

And with that euphoric knowledge blazing in her mind, Kimberly finally managed to go back to work on *Vendetta*.

NO ONE SEEMED UPSET that evening at dinner. It was as though the entire household, including Starke, had accepted her right to rewrite the rules under which they all functioned. As promised, Cavenaugh disappeared after the meal to assist Scott with his railroad construction. Julia told

Aunt Milly that she had gone over the guest list and recognized everyone on it.

"Wonderful," Aunt Milly enthused. "Ariel and I can address the envelopes in the morning. We wrote out all the invitations this afternoon," she added as an aside to Kimberly who was quietly sipping tea near the fireplace.

"Will it be a large party?" Kimberly asked.

"Fairly large. We used to have parties all the time when Dare's father was alive, but since Dare has taken over we don't entertain nearly as often."

"No one felt much like having a party for quite some time after mom and dad died," Julia put in quietly. "And then I was going through that awful divorce." She smiled at Kimberly. "It's taken a while to put the family back on its feet emotionally as well as financially. You were right to step in this afternoon, you know. It made me realize how much we've all come to lean on Dare. He's been fulfilling a number of different roles for all of us during the past two years. I don't know how he does it at times."

"I think he finds it all worthwhile," Kimberly assured her gently.

"Of course he does," Aunt Milly put in with serene confidence. "After all, he's the head of the family. It's his duty to hold things together."

Kimberly said nothing but for some reason she happened to catch Starke's eye as he looked up from the newspaper he was reading across the room. She wasn't certain she could read the message in his quiet eyes but she thought she saw approval there.

"A man trying to hold things together for everyone else," Starke murmured softly, "needs a woman who can understand him and occasionally protect him from all that responsibility."

There was an embarrassed silence among the three

women in front of the fire. Starke appeared oblivious to it as he went back to reading his newspaper.

"By the way," Aunt Milly announced forcefully, as if to distract everyone from Starke's comment, "Ariel said to tell you that she's ready to tell your fortune, Kim. She'll give you a reading tomorrow."

"I'll look forward to it," Kimberly replied ruefully, knowing there was no polite way to escape the promised session.

"She's very good at card reading, you know," Aunt Milly went on chattily. "She even predicted you'd be returning with Dare."

Julia laughed. "The whole household predicted that. We all know where he'd gone and why. I was the one who answered the phone that day you hung up, Kim. When I told Dare, he seemed to know immediately it was you. Why didn't you stay on the line?"

"I had a few second thoughts."

"Well, I'm certainly glad you're here now," Aunt Milly intoned. "You're going to be very good for Dare."

At ten o'clock Kimberly excused herself and climbed the stairs to her room. Cavenaugh, who had long since returned to the living room to read the paper, said a polite good-night. She felt his eyes on her as she made her way up the staircase. And in that moment she was very certain she knew exactly what was going through his head. He was remembering the passion they had shared that afternoon. Well, Kimberly, thought, so was she.

An hour later she heard the door to her room open. It was a small sound in the darkness, a sound fraught with inevitability.

Turning sleepily in bed she stared at the shadowy outline of the man who stood on the threshold. Her voice was a soft, husky whisper as she greeted him.

''Hello, Cavenaugh.''

Without a word he closed the door behind him and walked across the room to stand looking down at her in darkness. Although she could not make out their emerald color in the shadows, Kimberly could see the way his eyes gleamed. She sensed the hunger in him because it was much the same as her own.

Kimberly held out her arms and he went to her with a heavy groan of need and desire.

CHAPTER SIX

CAVENAUGH LAY watching the dawn stream through an uncertain cloud cover and lazily contemplated the sense of satisfaction that permeated his body. He felt good. More than that, he felt great. He couldn't remember feeling quite like this ever in his life.

It was as though something vital had been missing in his world and now he had it in his grasp. He would be a fool to let it go. But he was also, he discovered, a very greedy and possessive man. He didn't just want to warm himself beside the fire that was Kim. He wanted that fire to engulf him.

Beside him Kimberly shifted as she began drifting awake. Her bare foot brushed against his leg and the curve of her hip was pressing his thigh with unconscious invitation. Cavenaugh told himself it was probably adolescent or, at the very least, ungentlemanly to wake up in a state of semiarousal but here he was, doing exactly that. And all because of the woman beside him.

With the practical approach of his sex, Cavenaugh had decided to stop trying to figure out why this particular woman exercised such power over him. He wanted her; he needed her. Having possessed her, it was now impossible to even think about the possibility of giving her up.

And he could make her want him. That thought brought a savage satisfaction. She was like hot, flowing amber in his arms, clinging to him as she surrendered to the intimate

demands of his body and her own. Yet he lost himself in
her even at the moment when he claimed her most completely. It was a paradox which, being male, he decided
not to waste time analyzing. It was the way things were
and he was content to accept the situation. He was old
enough and intelligent enough to realize that a relationship
such as this came along once in a lifetime if a man was
very, very lucky. Only a fool would question it or analyze
it to death.

It was far more crucial to spend his time assessing the
threats to the relationship. And when it came to dealing
with threats, Cavenaugh was more than willing to spend
time analyzing, evaluating and ultimately neutralizing
them. He had already taken steps to protect Kimberly from
the strange hints of physical menace that had cropped up
around her. Certainly that battle was the most urgent one.

But there were other threats of a more subtle nature and
therefore more difficult for a man to analyze and defeat.
Number one on the list was the wariness she had of families and the responsibilities and pressures that went with
them. He had to find a way to show her that the past could
not be allowed to dictate how she lived and loved in the
present. Once he had shown her that her grandparents were
not the personification of callous, selfish arrogance she had
always thought them to be, he could remove a large measure of her distrust of men who had family loyalties.

And then there was that damned Josh Valerian to deal
with.

Cavenaugh felt his body harden into full arousal as Kimberly stirred in his arms. He watched her face as her lashes
fluttered open and he smiled slightly. The momentary confusion in her gaze amused him. It also pleased him.

"You're not accustomed to waking up beside a man, are
you?" he murmured. He turned on his side, hooking a hair-

roughened thigh over her legs. "Better get used to it. There are going to be a lot more mornings like this one." He bent his head to drop a small, possessive kiss on her warm shoulder.

"Are there?" she asked, looking up at him with unreadable mysteries in her eyes.

"Definitely." He let his palm glide luxuriously upward until it covered her breast, and the morning hunger in him escalated. "Most definitely," he repeated, aware that his voice had roughened. "What's more, I don't intend to share them with that other man."

She blinked in sleepy astonishment. "What other man?"

"Valerian."

"*Josh Valerian?*"

"Umm." He pushed his knee between her silky thighs and tasted the dark grape that tipped her breast. "I've been thinking about him."

"Come to any earthshaking conclusions?" she asked uncertainly.

"Only the obvious. I think the fastest, most effective way of getting one man out of your head is to keep reminding you that another, namely me, now possesses your body." He pushed himself forward until his manhood was at the soft gate of her femininity.

"Cavenaugh, are you joking?"

He smiled a little grimly as he met her questioning gaze. "What do you think?"

The tip of her tongue touched the corner of her mouth as she tried to assess just how serious he was. Cavenaugh didn't mind this evidence of female wariness. It meant she was focusing on him, not some illusion of a perfect man.

"I...I don't think you are joking."

Slowly he thrust into her, taking his time so that he could experience every centimeter of her clinging, velvety core.

She grew hot and damp around him and the soft little gasp at the back of her throat sent ripples of satisfaction through him.

"You're right," he growled as she instinctively lifted herself against his loins. "I'm not joking. You see how well we're communicating these days?"

"Cavenaugh, you can be an arrogant beast at times," she managed as her body warmed and tightened beneath him. Her fingers were splayed on his shoulders and her legs twisted around his in growing demand.

"But I'm real. And you need a real man, not some fictional wimp who will never be able to hold you like this or make you come alive in his arms."

"Josh is not a wimp!"

"He's no good to you right now, is he? Right now you need *me*. Admit it," Cavenaugh rasped as the delicious tension built between them. "Tell me you need me!"

"I need you, Cavenaugh. Please. Now. All of you. *Ah, Cavenaugh!*"

A long time later Kimberly lay in bed and watched Cavenaugh pull on his jeans and thrust his arms into his shirt. He didn't bother to do up the buttons. As he had explained, he was only going to duck back across the hall to his bedroom.

"Not that there's any hope the entire household won't know where I spent the night," he growled humorously as he came to stand beside the bed. "But it might be easier for you to go down to breakfast if you can pretend that we observed the proprieties."

"That's very, uh, considerate of you," she said demurely, thankful for his understanding of just how awkward this sort of situation could be for a woman.

His emerald eyes gleamed with buried fire. "Lady, if I was only considering myself, I'd move you into my room today and say the hell with the proprieties. But I'm not totally insensitive. I also realize that I'm supposed to be protecting you, not taking advantage of you." He bent over the bed, planting a hand on either side of her body. "So I'm going to try very hard to behave myself until we get things sorted out between us. If that's the way you want me to behave, I suggest you don't tempt me too far."

"If you come to my room again in the middle of the night I'll have no one but myself to blame?" she taunted wryly.

"Right." He kissed her forehead and then straightened. "See you at breakfast." With a proprietary slap on her hip, Cavenaugh turned and strode out the door.

Kimberly watched him go, half amused, half enthralled by the self-assured, unabashedly male arrogance in him. He was feeling very good this morning, she decided. Men were probably at their most dangerous when they felt that good. On the other hand, it gave her an undeniable pleasure to know she was the cause of his wholly masculine satisfaction.

ARIEL'S CARD READING that morning was far from being a private affair. She arrived complete with a new burgundy turban for the occasion and a wonderfully clashing flowered dress in pea green. By the time she was ready to deal the deck of ordinary playing cards into a series of numbered squares, Julia, Mrs. Lawson and Aunt Milly were gathered around. Good-naturedly Kimberly sat in front of the inlaid table Ariel was using and waited to have her fortune told.

"She's really quite good," Julia confided cheerfully. "A few months ago she predicted Mark and I would become engaged and that's exactly what happened."

Aunt Milly nodded enthusiastically. "And she predicted

I'd get sick at the little restaurant in Mexico last summer. She was right."

"Lots of people get ill eating unfamiliar food in foreign countries," Kimberly felt obliged to point out. "And after seeing Mark and Julia together, I think I could have predicted an engagement, too."

Julia laughed. "Don't ruin it all by being too analytical."

"Julia's absolutely right," Ariel declared roundly as she shuffled the cards. "You'll spoil all the fun if you start analyzing the whole thing."

"Okay, okay, I promise not to intellectualize about it."

"Have you ever had your fortune told?" Ariel asked.

"Nope."

"Well, once the cards are dealt they all have a relationship to one another in addition to their own independent meanings. It can get very complex. Each of these squares stands for a certain aspect of life. This square concerns prosperity. That one deals with projects you might be thinking of undertaking and that one is your love life."

"I can't wait to see what card turns up on that square," Julia said with a chuckle.

"As if we don't know," Mrs. Lawson put in with bland emphasis.

"Ready?" Ariel asked lightly as she began to deal the cards into the squares.

"Ready," Kimberly agreed in resignation.

Ariel became unexpectedly serious as she dealt the cards. When she began to turn them over and study them she seemed to become completely involved with the task.

"Excellent," Ariel murmured as she turned over a heart on the square representing prosperity. "You will enjoy success in your work. Money is no problem for you. This next square represents changes in your life. Here you have a spade. Hmmm. That's not so good. A spade indicates a change for the worse. Perhaps actual danger. However, it appears to be mitigated by the King of Hearts next to it in the square for happiness.''

The card reading continued, largely a vague and ambivalent process as far as Kimberly could determine. Whenever a card representing misfortune turned up, Ariel seemed to find one next to it that lessened or canceled out the first. There were good cards for such things as health, ambition, money and travel.

"A recent trip may lead to major changes in your life," Ariel noted as she turned over the card on the travel square.

Kimberly resisted the impulse to say "no kidding." But she caught Julia's eye and found the other woman grinning at her.

"And now we come to your love life," Ariel finally declared grandly. Her listeners leaned forward expectantly. Kimberly felt a wave of embarrassment and wondered if all the others were aware of how she had spent the night. She watched as Ariel turned over a King of Clubs.

"Hmm," the older woman said, eyeing the card. "He'll be faithful, at least."

"Well?" Kimberly pressured. "Is that all it indicates?"

"Not quite. It implies that although you can trust him implicitly, he will not be without faults."

"What man is?" Julia asked rhetorically.

"In fact," Ariel went on as she turned up another club, "he might prove quite infuriating at times."

"As Julia said," Mrs. Lawson interrupted, "what man isn't?"

Ariel bent over the cards, turning up others in the vicinity of the "lover" square. "There is more than that here," she said slowly. "There is danger again. You will know fear, Kim."

"Fear? Of what?"

Ariel ignored the question and turned up a diamond. "There is much pain from fraud and deceit."

"Probably refers to some of the royalty statements I've had from various and assorted publishers. Forget that one. Tell me what I'm supposed to be afraid of."

Ariel shook her head slowly. "It is difficult to say, Kim. I see darkness. Darkness and silver."

Kimberly froze as an image of the dark, cowled figure holding the silver dagger leaped into her head. "A man?" Her mouth suddenly felt quite dry.

"Perhaps, perhaps not." Ariel frowned and then turned over the next card. She gave a few more vague analyses and then sat back, collecting all the cards into a neat pile.

"Is that the end of it?" Aunt Milly asked cheerfully.

"That's it," Ariel said.

"Well, Kim, it sounds as though you'd better be wary of a dark, dangerous lover with silver in his hair," Julia commented, laughing.

"But who can be trusted," Aunt Milly put in firmly.

"Sounds to me like someone we all know very well," Mrs. Lawson declared happily.

"Yes, well, it's been fun, Ariel," Kimberly said, getting decisively to her feet. "Now, if you'll all excuse me, I really must get back to work. That dark, dangerous man sounds like the villain in my latest novel. I'd better go see how he's getting along."

The card reading party broke up as Julia and Mrs. Lawson went back to their own projects. Kimberly was halfway out the door of the sitting room they had all been using when Ariel stopped her with a small, fluttery hand on her arm. Kimberly was astonished by the intent look in the older woman's eyes.

"The cards should not be dismissed lightly, Kim. They are not always simply a parlor trick."

Kimberly smiled gently. "I'll remember that, Ariel. Thanks. Oh, by the way, how is the party planning going?"

"Wonderfully," Aunt Milly enthused. "The invitations go out today. The party is scheduled for this coming Saturday night."

"Rather short notice for everyone, isn't it?"

"Oh, we phoned everyone this morning to tell them about it. The invitations are just a formality," Ariel explained complacently, removing her hand from Kimberly's arm. "As it turns out, Saturday is an especially propitious time for the affair. Run along dear. Milly and I are going to work on the menu today."

Aunt Milly nodded in agreement. "We want everything just right for this particular event."

"What's so special about this party?" Kimberly asked unwisely.

Aunt Milly looked at her in amused astonishment. "Why, because you'll be there, of course. Now do as Ariel says and run along, dear."

Kimberly didn't need any urging. She was far enough behind in *Vendetta* as it was.

SHORTLY AFTER TEN O'CLOCK on Saturday evening Cavenaugh glanced across the crowded living room and managed to catch a glimpse of Kimberly. He considered himself lucky. It had been difficult keeping track of her tonight. From the moment the guests had begun arriving she had been the focal point of one after the other.

The fact that some of the people in the crowd had read her books certainly accounted for some of the attention she was receiving, but Cavenaugh was aware there was a lot more involved. The details of the kidnapping had been in the local papers, and Julia had seen to it that everyone knew Kimberly was the woman who had rescued Scott. In addition, everyone in the Cavenaugh household was treating Kim virtually as a member of the family.

That last undeniable fact was being interpreted by the vast majority of the guests to mean that Kim was due shortly to become a member of the family. In the past half hour Cavenaugh had overheard at least three clusters of people discussing when the marriage would be announced.

He had done nothing to squelch the speculation. Just as he had done nothing to stem the gossip that had arisen among his employees after he'd taken Kim on a tour of the wine-making facilities earlier this week.

By now Cavenaugh was fairly certain that Kimberly herself had realized just how everyone was viewing her presence. She looked up as he glanced across the room and the wariness was back in her eyes. For an instant their gazes clashed, and then she took a long sip from the glass of Cavenaugh wine she was drinking and went back to her discussion with a group of local wine makers. They seemed enthralled with whatever she was saying.

Cavenaugh retreated to the edge of the crowd and helped himself to another glass of wine. Then he stood quietly and watched Kimberly for a while longer. Other than the familiar wariness in her eyes, she looked good tonight, he thought, wryly aware of a fierce sense of possessiveness.

Kimberly and Julia had gone shopping yesterday under Starke's supervision. They had returned with the turquoise and yellow silk gown Kimberly wore tonight. Tiny, strappy turquoise sandals and a small strand of gold at her throat constituted the remainder of the outfit. Cavenaugh had wanted to pick up the tab for the obviously expensive dress but had prudently refrained from making the offer. Something told him that Kim would be furious. She had a fierce pride that he respected, even if it did annoy him at times.

He studied her amber hair, which was caught high on her head in a deceptively careless cascade of curls. The thought of tearing the concoction apart with his fingers later on elicited a now-familiar, heavy ache in his body. Deliberately he put the image out of his mind. There were matters that had to be cleared up before he took Kim back to bed. Or so he kept telling himself.

He swallowed some more of his excellent Merlot wine and let himself fantasize about what it would be like to be able to take Kimberly up to bed after everyone left tonight. He had been savagely strict with himself following the one night he had spent with her. There was still too much that lay unsettled between them. The talk with the lawyer in L.A. had made that clear.

Cavenaugh suspected that Kimberly merely assumed he was staying away from her bed out of a sense of gentlemanly behavior. He had allowed her to believe that, because he hadn't yet figured out how to tell her there was much more involved. It was becoming increasingly difficult to keep his hands off her. Soon, he promised himself, he would have it all sorted out and Kimberly would be free of her past. He was letting himself speculate on the future when Starke moved quietly up beside him.

"She's doing all right," Starke observed, his gaze on Kimberly.

"Especially for someone who's accustomed to being a loner," Cavenaugh agreed.

Starke shrugged. "Everyone's alone in some ways."

"Why is it you always get philosophical after a couple of whiskies, Starke?"

"Brings out the intellectual side of my nature."

"I see."

"She's good for you, Dare. I like her."

Cavenaugh's mouth twisted faintly. "Knowing how selective you are about people, that's saying something. As it happens, I agree with you."

Starke's eyes were on Kimberly. "So when are you going to get this other thing out of the way so you'll be free to stop playing games?"

"I've arranged the meeting for the day after tomorrow."

"On neutral grounds?"

Cavenaugh nodded. "The lobby of a San Francisco hotel."

"You're sure this is the right way to go about it?"

"You got a better idea?" Cavenaugh challenged grimly.

Starke sighed. "No."

"I want her free of the past, Starke. The only way to do that is to confront it. Besides, they'll hound her until they get to her. They're desperate. Better to arrange the meeting on our terms rather than theirs."

"You're just going to spring the whole thing on Kim?"

"She'll never agree to a meeting with her grandparents."

"I don't know, Dare. Women don't like surprises."

"Kim will understand why I did it. When it's all over she'll see it was the only way."

Across the room Kim managed to excuse herself from the cluster of people around her and drifted out onto the patio. It was nippy out there, but after the crowded, overheated environment of the party it was a relief to her.

She was experiencing that trapped sensation again. There was no doubt about what people were thinking when they looked at her. They were seeing her as the new Cavenaugh bride, and none of the Cavenaughs was doing anything to discourage the assumption. Not even Darius Cavenaugh.

What was going on in his head tonight, Kimberly wondered as she walked to the edge of the patio. There were times when she thought she could tell exactly what he was thinking. But there were other occasions when he remained unfathomable.

He hadn't been back to her room since that one night they had spent together. For the hundredth time Kimberly considered that fact. Was he truly playing the gentleman or was there more to it? Perhaps he hadn't found her as physically satisfying as she had found him.

Kimberly's fingers closed tightly around an awning pole and she stood looking out in the darkness. Before her was a section of shadowy garden, and beyond that the rock wall she had been forbidden to pass. In the distance the building that held the fermentation tanks loomed in the darkness. The acres of grapes stretched out on all sides, gliding over gentle hills beneath a pale moon. It was a lovely, prosperous, peaceful setting. Kimberly wondered how it differed from the kind of life-style Cavenaugh had lived before he had returned home.

"Isn't it a little cold out here, Kim?"

She whirled at the sound of Starke's familiar, gravelly voice and smiled at him. She had decided she liked this strange, aloof man, even though she couldn't quite figure him out.

"I needed some fresh air. I'll come back inside in a few minutes," she told him. "Having a good time, Starke?"

"I'm not much for cocktail parties," he murmured blandly.

"Neither am I. Is Cavenaugh?"

"There's a lot you don't know about him yet, isn't there?"

Surprised by the question, Kimberly shook her head.

"Sometimes I think I know him. Other times..." She let the sentence drift off into the darkness.

"He feels the same way about you, I think. Human nature."

Kimberly slid him an amused glance. "You're a student of human nature?"

Starke held up the glass in his hand. "It's the whiskey. Brings out my intellectual qualities, as I was just explaining to Cavenaugh."

"Fascinating. What other observations have you got on the subject?"

"Of you and Cavenaugh? Just the obvious, I guess."

"Which is?"

"That you're right for each other," Starke explained. "He needs you, Kim."

"I don't know, Starke," she replied gently. "He has so many other things and people in his life—the winery, his duty to his family. So much. Why would he need me?"

"Because you can keep those things from taking over his whole life. You can give him a separate world where he can relax and be alone with someone who puts him first."

She stirred uneasily. "Maybe that's what I want, too, Starke. Someone who can put me first in his life."

"You don't think Cavenaugh can do that?"

"How can any man in his position do that?" she asked helplessly.

"You still don't know him very well. Give him a chance, Kim. And—" Starke hesitated and then finished bluntly "—try not to be too hard on him on the occasions when you don't understand him completely. He's only a man."

Kim's lips lifted in a teasing smile. "So are you. Are you sure you're qualified to explain the species to me?"

Starke took a long swallow of whiskey. "Probably not, but I guess I felt obliged to try."

Instantly Kim softened. "You're very loyal to Cavenaugh, aren't you?"

"He saved my life a long time ago. Later on I was able to return the favor. That sort of thing builds a certain bond between two people."

"How did he save your life?" Kim demanded with a slight frown.

"It's not important now," Starke said, shifting with an uneasiness that told Kim it was a subject he wished he hadn't brought up for discussion. "I had gotten myself into a messy situation in the Middle East. I was trying to make contact with someone and got caught in the middle of a riot. Cavenaugh had also gotten trapped on the street. All hell broke out and, being the nearest Americans in the vicinity, we got mistaken for devils by the local crowd. I found myself up against a wall, literally. And then Dare arrived. He knew someone in the neighborhood with whom he'd done business. That association gave him enough clout to get me free from the mob. By the time everyone figured out that his connections shouldn't be allowed to stand in the way of a little mob vengeance, we were clear. Dare used his contacts to pull some strings and got us both out of the country about two steps ahead of the full-scale war that broke out a day later."

Kimberly drew a deep breath. "I had no idea the import-export business could be so, uh, volatile."

"It had its moments," Starke reflected, lifting his glass again. He stared into the whiskey for a few seconds, as if seeing something Kimberly couldn't. "Especially the way Dare ran things."

Kimberly couldn't be sure she'd heard those last few words. Her voice sharpened. "When did you save his life,

Starke?'' It occurred to her that there was more to this man than met the eye. His laconic speech and quiet mannerisms belied the harshness of his appearance.

He looked at her and blinked owlishly. ''There was a knife fight in some alley in Hong Kong. Dare was trying to deal with three punks who had waylaid him outside his hotel. I was on my way to see him and found it all going down in the alley a block from the hotel. I'm pretty good with a knife,'' Starke explained blandly.

Kimberly shivered. ''Oh.''

Starke's brows bunched together in a heavy line. ''Promise me you won't tell Dare I told you all this, okay? He'd have my head if he thought I was out here scaring you to death with those kind of stories.''

''Why are you scaring me to death with those tales, Starke?'' Kimberly asked perceptively.

''I guess I just want you to understand that there's a lot more to Dare than may seem obvious by looking at Cavenaugh Vineyards.''

''I know that, Starke,'' Kimberly said gently.

Starke looked suddenly relieved. ''Sure you do. If you didn't, you wouldn't love him, would you?''

Kimberly recoiled, a protest rising automatically to her lips. Her love was still a private, personal matter at this point. She had not dreamed that others knew of it. But before she could find the words to make Starke understand that it was much too soon to make such statements, he was slipping out of his jacket and handing it to her.

''Here,'' he said gruffly. ''If you're going to stay out here awhile, you'd better put this on.'' Then he turned and strode back into the house.

With a sigh, Kimberly walked off the patio and into the garden. She really didn't want to go back into the house just yet. The thought of all those people looking at her, speculating on her relationship with Cavenaugh, perhaps coming to the same conclusion Starke had, was suddenly overwhelming. She needed some time alone.

Not that she would be able to stay out here very long. Julia, Aunt Milly, Ariel, Mrs. Lawson or even Cavenaugh or Starke was likely to miss her and start looking for her. So many people who would concern themselves over her. She wasn't accustomed to it. Kimberly glanced up as she wandered into the garden. The light in Scott's room was finally turned off. He had been sent to bed a couple of hours ago, but only under protest. It had been his future father, Mark, who had taken on the task of putting Scott to bed. Kimberly had seen the warmth in Julia's eyes as she watched her fiancé handle the boy.

At the edge of the garden Kimberly came to a halt again and stood staring at the dark winery facility several yards beyond the rock wall. A few outside lights illuminated the beautiful grounds in front of the building where tourists gathered during the days. The rear of the large structure was shrouded in darkness.

This was as far as she ought to go. In another few feet she would be crossing the low, rambling rock wall. Doing that would set off the alarms, which in turn would certainly put a damper on the Cavenaugh party tonight, she thought humorously. Aunt Milly and Ariel would never forgive her.

That was assuming, of course, that Starke hadn't had a little too much whiskey tonight and was able to realize an alarm had been triggered.

As for Cavenaugh's reaction, he was more likely to turn her over his knee than make love to her if she pulled that stunt again. Once was forgivable. Disobeying orders a second time probably wouldn't go down well with the lord and master of Cavenaugh Vineyards.

With a wry smile at the thought, Kimberly reluctantly

turned to walk back up through the garden to the patio and into the noisy, well-lit house.

The statue-still figure in a cowled robe was waiting for her, blocking the path through the garden.

Kimberly was so stunned by the dark apparition that for a timeless moment she couldn't even scream. Frozen in the moonlight the two stared at each other and then the robed figure raised both hands, revealing the ornate silver dagger he held.

Kimberly did scream then but it was the kind of scream one had in a nightmare, a choked soundless cry that reached no one. Fear stifled the first attempt and before she could make another, the cowled creature took a menacing step forward.

Kimberly got the scream past her lips this time but even as it echoed through the night she told herself that no one would hear it over the noise of the party. She was at the rear of the garden, much too far from the safety of the house.

The dagger flashed in the watery moonlight and the movement freed her. She picked up the skirts of her silk gown and began to run, attempting to dodge around the hooded threat that stood so obscenely in the beautiful garden.

The creature in the robe shifted position, easily blocking her path. He held the advantage. There was no way she could get past him and back to the house. When he moved toward her again, Kimberly did the only thing she could do; she fled out of the garden toward the low rock wall.

Risking a glance over her shoulder she saw the cowled figure pursuing. He seemed to be having some trouble managing the bulky skirts of his robe. Silver from the wicked blade of the dagger flashed in the darkness and memories of Ariel's card reading chilled Kimberly even more than she already was. As she ran Starke's jacket slipped from her shoulders. It landed on the rambling rock wall as Kimberly scrambled over the top.

Her only hope was that the discreet alarms in the house had been triggered and that Starke would not be too deep into his whiskey to know it.

Panicked, Kimberly fled for her life toward the only possible protection she could imagine, the winery building. If she could reach it far enough ahead of her pursuer perhaps she would be able to get inside and lock a door behind her.

The turquoise sandals proved treacherous on the sandy path that led through the vineyards. Several times she stumbled and nearly fell, but sheer blind fear drove her on toward the looming building.

The cowled figure seemed to be having more trouble running than she was in the heavy robes he wore, and that gave Kimberly hope. Perhaps the flowing garment would hinder his movements enough so that she could get inside the building before he did. Once inside there were phones she could use to call the main house. She had seen them several days earlier when Cavenaugh had taken her on a tour of the production facilities.

Her breath was like fire in her lungs as she fled toward the rear entrance of the building. Behind her she could hear the crunch of pursuing footsteps. For some insane reason the menacing sound came almost as a relief. Surely only a real human being would make such a sound as he ran. At least she was not being pursued by a specter. Out here alone in the darkness it would've been easy to believe she was dealing with a supernatural threat.

Gasping for breath, her heart thudding from fear and exertion, Kimberly slammed to a halt in front of the door at the rear of the building. She didn't even hesitate. She'd decided what she would do while she was still several yards away.

Whipping off one of the turquoise sandals, Kimberly shattered the door's window. She had her hand inside, reaching to unlock it before the glass had even struck the floor.

A lacerating pain sliced into her arm but she ignored it. The door opened and she was inside, slamming it shut behind her.

In the hall all was in darkness. Kimberly was forced to slow to a walk. Behind her she heard the door open and close again. Then there was silence. The utter darkness must be as much a burden to her pursuer as it was to her.

But Kimberly had one advantage. She knew where she was in the building. With any luck the man with the knife would be forced to wander aimlessly, trying to follow her by sound alone.

Taking off her other sandal so that she could move as silently as possible, Kimberly groped her way carefully down the hall toward the huge, high-ceilinged room that held the fermentation tanks and the rows of casks used to age the wine.

CHAPTER SEVEN

THE GENTLE HUM of machinery and the unique, sharp smell of wine in the making greeted Kimberly as she pushed open the door of the huge room. Towering stainless-steel tanks and several rows of wooden vats loomed around her. They made her think of dinosaurs dozing in the muted darkness. At the far end of the room near a short staircase a dull light gleamed. Otherwise all was in shadow.

For an instant Kimberly hesitated. The room that she thought might promise some shelter seemed suddenly to be filled with giant, alien machines that were half alive. No, she thought hysterically, it wasn't the tanks that were alive, it was the wine inside them. Hadn't Cavenaugh explained that to her on the tour? The process of fermentation and aging was a living process, a process of constant evolution and change. The vats and tanks around her were the wombs that nurtured the wine while it developed and matured.

She listened for sounds behind her and heard nothing. Then, slipping into the shadowy room, Kimberly darted to the left. She would weave a path through the tanks, using them for cover while she made her way toward the dimly lit stairs at the far end.

Cavenaugh, help me. Hurry. For God's sake, hurry.

Halfway toward her goal, unable to hear sounds of pursuit above the hum of the tanks, Kimberly's bare foot came down in a puddle of cold liquid. She gasped aloud and then immediately bit down on her lip, cursing silently. With any luck her pursuer hadn't heard her faint, startled exclamation.

She felt her way along the darkest side of the room, staying behind the last row of tanks. While the sound of working machinery was a cover for her own progress, it also covered the approach of the creature in the robes. The room at the top of the stairs seemed miles away instead of only a few feet. She had to reach it. It was the tasting room, the last stop on a tour. In it lay a telephone. There was also a fire alarm, Kimberly recalled vaguely. She would break the glass cover on it. That should summon help in a hurry.

But first she had to get through the jungle of tanks.

Every soft sound behind her was a new source of terror. Kimberly kept glancing back over her shoulder, expecting to see the silver dagger plunging toward her at any second.

Arriving at the last tank in the row, Kimberly eyed the stairs with trepidation. To reach them she would have to make a dash out into the open and the small light on the wall would illuminate her quite clearly. She had no reason to think that the door at the top would be locked, but if it were she would be trapped at the top of the stairs.

Cavenaugh, where are you? I need you.

There was no point delaying the inevitable. Her only chance was to reach the tasting room and barricade herself inside while she phoned for help. Collecting her skirts in one hand, Kimberly darted out from behind the shelter of the last tank and ran for the door at the top of the stairs.

With the primitive instinct of the hunted, she knew it was too late. There wasn't going to be enough time. The creature was behind her. He must have guessed her goal.

Kimberly's hands were on the doorknob, twisting frantically when she glanced over her shoulder and saw him.

The dagger was in his fist as the man in the robes raced toward her down the center aisle between the tanks. He was only a few paces behind. No time, she thought wildly as the door obediently opened inward. There was no time.

Kimberly slammed the door behind her but her pursuer struck it with such force that it crashed back against the wall. She whirled and fled behind the ornate bar of the tasting room. The pale glow from the light at the top of the stairs filtered into the dark room, illuminating the rows of glasses and the neatly stored bottles of Cavenaugh wine.

Without even thinking clearly about what she intended to do, Kimberly grabbed the nearest bottle. It didn't seem like much against a silver dagger but it was all that was available. Grasping the neck of the bottle as though it were a club she swung the end against the highly polished edge of the bar. Then she wondered half-hysterically if this sort of thing only worked in vintage westerns.

Glass shattered. Wine gushed to the floor, spilling over her bare feet. Kimberly was left holding a jagged, crystal blade.

At the open end of the bar the hooded figure halted, silver dagger raised. He was only steps away and for the first time Kimberly could see the dark gleam of human eyes beneath the shrouding cowl. The dim light glinted off the broken wine bottle in her hand as she held it in front of her.

"Cavenaugh will kill you if you so much as touch me," she bit out.

"Your friend Cavenaugh can go to hell."

The voice was low and harsh and it had the sound of city streets in it. It didn't sound at all supernatural or sepulchral. She was facing a street punk, not a warlock, Kimberly thought wildly.

"He'll see you there first. I can promise you that much."

"I'll worry about him later. You're my job for tonight."

He rushed her then, holding the dagger now like a fighting blade, not a sacrificial one. Coming in low and fast, the man in the robe covered the few steps separating him from his victim with a frightening ferocity.

"Cavenaugh!"

Kimberly screamed the name as she tried to sidestep the attacker's rush. There was so little room to maneuver here behind the bar. But the punk must have had some respect for the jagged bottle in her hand because when she instinctively lashed out at him with it, he faded to the side.

Kimberly swept past him, toward the open end of the bar. He whirled, slashing the dagger through the air in a violent arc.

Kimberly picked up another bottle, still holding on to her first weapon. She hurled the full wine bottle toward the man who, in turn, ducked. The glass cracked on the counter behind him and liquid poured onto the floor.

"You bitch!"

Kimberly was throwing every bottle she could get her hands on now and more than one of them found its target. The bulky robes seemed to provide protection, however, and none of the blows proved devastating.

With a roar of rage, her attacker sprang forward, intending to throw himself into one final rush that would plunge the dagger deeply into her body.

Kimberly turned to run and then heard the scream of fury behind her as the robed figure slipped on the wine-slick floor. She heard the thud as he fell to the tile, and without stopping to think, Kimberly picked up one more bottle of wine.

She brought it down on the back of the cowled head with every ounce of force she possessed.

"Kim!"

Cavenaugh came through the door, a dark lethal shadow in his evening clothes. The glint of metal caught Kimberly's eye as she stood over her victim. Cavenaugh held a gun in his hand. Starke was right behind him, grabbing for the light switch on the wall.

Cavenaugh reached her as the lights came on, yanking her away from her prone attacker. She felt the taut violence in him as his hand closed over her shoulder. Then he was bending down beside her victim, turning him over to feel for a pulse beneath the heavy hood. Starke stood tensely, waiting for the verdict. He, too, was armed. Both men, she thought dazedly, looked very comfortable with a gun in their hands.

Cavenaugh straightened slowly, shoving his weapon out of sight beneath his elegant evening jacket.

"He's out," Cavenaugh growled. His hard, emerald eyes raked Kim from her head to her bare feet. "She knocked him unconscious."

"Smells like it took half a case of wine to do it," Starke commented as he examined the situation. "Looks like it took half a case, too. We've got a regular swimming pool in here."

"I didn't know neatness counted," Kimberly managed, her stunned eyes never leaving Cavenaugh's.

"Lady," Cavenaugh grated harshly, "the only thing that counts in a situation like this is who's still standing when it's all over. My God, woman, you've taken ten years off my life tonight! Are you all right?"

She nodded mutely, unable to move. Still clutching the jagged blade she had created from the first bottle, Kimberly faced him. Then, with a groan of savage relief, Cavenaugh reached for her. She dropped the bottle and fell into his arms.

"You're bleeding! If that bastard…"

"It's all right. I just cut myself a little on the glass in the door. Oh, Cavenaugh, I thought you and Starke would never get here," she whispered from the safety of his hold.

"Doesn't look like you needed us too badly," Starke said. "You seem to have handled things pretty well on your own. The next time we find ourselves in a barroom brawl, Dare, we'll have to make sure she's along to back us up."

"She'll be there if that's where I happen to be. I'm never going to let her out of my sight—"

"How did you find me?" she interrupted hastily. There was still a fierce tension flowing in him. She could feel it as he held her close.

"Starke's beeper went off when you crossed the wall. We excused ourselves to go check the control panel, thinking the alarm must have been set off by an animal. Somewhere along the line we noticed that you were nowhere to be found," Cavenaugh explained. Very gently he disengaged himself from her tight hold and turned the water on in the small sink. Then he thrust her bleeding arm under the flowing tap.

"I told Dare I'd last seen you on the patio," Starke put in calmly, bending down to yank back the hood of the attacker. Beneath the mysterious cowl was the face of a dark-haired young man in his early twenties.

"Neither of us could believe you'd be stupid enough to actually take a midnight stroll over the wall, of course," Cavenaugh went on.

"I didn't exactly go strolling over that damned wall, you know. I was in the garden, about to start back to the house when this turkey got in the way. I knew I couldn't run past him. So I tried to run away from him, hoping that when we went over the wall, the alarm would go off. Ouch. Cavenaugh, that hurts."

He ignored her and slapped a bar napkin over the small wound. "We found Starke's jacket and knew it was you and not some deer who had triggered things. But we couldn't figure out where you'd gone at that point. When you broke into the winery you tripped another alarm, though, which pinpointed your location. We were right behind you. And then we started hearing all those bottles you were throwing around with such cheerful abandon." Cavenaugh's mouth twisted wryly. "Some of my best Cabernet Sauvignon, by the way. I may send you a bill."

"Of all the nerve!"

"On second thought," Cavenaugh said consideringly, "I think I'll just take it out of your sweet hide." He released her to bend over the young man in the robes. Fumbling beneath the flowing garment he retrieved the silver dagger. "Call the cops, Starke. And see if you can get hold of that Detective Cranston we've been working with."

"Right." Starke picked up the phone and dialed.

IT WAS SEVERAL hours later, nearly two in the morning, before Kimberly finally got to bed. Julia and Aunt Milly and Ariel had fussed over her while Mrs. Lawson fixed a soothing herbal tea according to Ariel's directions. Aroused by the hubbub, Scott had wandered sleepily downstairs to see what was going on. Cavenaugh and Starke dealt with the police, while concerned neighbors and guests asked countless questions of one another and of Kimberly.

"Maybe you'll be able to work this into one of your plots," Mark Taylor said lightly at one point.

"Mark!" Julia scolded. "Don't joke like that."

But ultimately the guests and the authorities took their leave. The man in the monk's robes was thrust into the back of a patrol car and taken away, too. He had revived by then but to the best of anyone's knowledge he hadn't said a single word.

Alone at last, aware of her own exhaustion but feeling too restless and wound up to sleep, Kimberly slipped into her T-shirt and crawled into bed. She lay in the darkness and reran the entire episode over and over in her mind. It seemed to her that it would be a long time before she could get the image of that raised dagger out of her head. Every time she closed her eyes it was there, poised and ready to strike. Her body seemed periodically racked by fine shivers. It was just reaction, she knew, but she couldn't seem to control it.

She was lying on her side, staring out the window when her bedroom door opened softly and then closed again. Kimberly knew who had entered the room without having to see his face.

"Cavenaugh?"

"I told you I wasn't going to let you out of my sight again."

She heard him undressing in the darkness and she turned slowly to meet his shadowed gaze. Her amber hair was spilled around her on the pillow, and the sheet was pulled taut across her breasts. Cavenaugh's possessive eyes moved over her as he slipped off his ruffled evening shirt.

"What about the proprieties? What about the, uh, awkwardness of my position as a guest in your household? What about your concern for my potential embarrassment?" She tried to make the words light and teasing, but the truth was she was incredibly glad to have him here and she knew it must have shown in her voice.

"What about moving over?" he countered as he stepped out of the last of his clothes. "I may not have mentioned it the last time I slept here, but I happen to prefer the left side of the bed."

"I'll keep that in mind." Obediently she moved to the opposite side. But the forced lightness in her words ended as he got into bed beside her. With a small cry she went to him, clinging to his reassuring warmth and strength. "Ah, Cavenaugh, I was so scared tonight."

"I know how it feels, sweetheart," he rasped thickly. "Believe me, I know how it feels. God, you were brave." He stroked her hair, twining his legs with hers. "You looked like a warrior queen when I came through the door. I wanted to kill that punk on the floor. If you hadn't already knocked him out, I probably would have. It was too close, Kim. Much too close for my peace of mind. That's why I couldn't let you stay alone tonight."

"I would have had nightmares," she confessed.

"You think I wouldn't have had them, too? That little scene in the tasting room is going to haunt me for a long time." He continued to stroke her, not with passion but with long, soothing motions.

"I can't seem to calm down," Kimberly whispered tightly. "All my nerves feel as though they've been plugged into an electric outlet."

"It's reaction, honey, just reaction. Takes a while for your system to settle down after something that traumatic."

"You seem to understand."

"I do."

She thought about the way he had come through the door with the gun in his hand. "You've been through this kind of scene before," she said softly.

"No, never quite like this," Cavenaugh denied flatly. "I've never walked into a room and found my woman facing an armed punk."

"You didn't exactly 'walk' into the tasting room. You and Starke came through that door like the U.S. Marines."

His arms tightened around her and Kimberly snuggled

gratefully into his embrace. Inside she savored the words "my woman."

"Don't ever do that to me again, Kim," Cavenaugh ordered harshly.

"Believe me, I didn't set out to do it to you tonight! Or to myself."

"You shouldn't have gone out into the garden alone."

Kimberly lifted her head. "Cavenaugh," she protested. "No one ever said anything about not going out onto the patio or into the garden. That electronically rigged rock wall was the only barrier!"

He groaned, pushing her head back down on his shoulder. "Technically, you're right. What I'm really trying to say is, don't wander out of my sight again. Understand?"

She smiled faintly in the darkness, inhaling the earthy, masculine scent of his skin. "I understand. I'm not sure how practical that will be, but I understand."

"Damn it, Kim, I wasn't going to yell at you tonight."

"No? You were going to wait until morning?"

"Yes, as a matter of fact I was. I still intend to wait until morning. This isn't the time."

"Why not?"

"Because you're in shock. I told you, I know what the reaction feels like."

"How is it you know so much about it?" she asked softly. "Just what sort of import-export company did you run before you returned to Cavenaugh Vineyards?"

"A perfectly legitimate and profitable one."

She sensed him smiling against her hair. "Rugs and trinkets and doodads from all over the world?"

"Something like that," he agreed absently.

"Do you still own the business?"

"No, I sold it two years ago when I came back here."

"Do you miss it?" she pressed. "All the travel and free-dom and everything?"

She felt him hesitate. "No. That part of my life is over. I'm content making my wine. It's a very satisfying kind of work, Kim."

"I know what it's like to have a satisfying career. I'm very lucky to have my writing."

Again she sensed a hesitation in him and then Caven-augh said quietly, "It won't always be enough for you, Kim. I realize that you think it will because right now your life seems to hold everything you need. But you're a warm, sensitive woman. You weren't cut out to spend your whole life alone."

"I don't intend to spend it completely alone."

His hand moved impatiently on her thigh. "I know. You're looking for your real-life Josh Valerian. The perfect man, unencumbered by family and responsibility. But he's not out there, Kim. He doesn't exist except in your books. And you're far too passionate and real to be content with a fictional lover."

Surprised by the vehemence in his voice, Kimberly didn't argue. "I agree with you," she said simply.

"What?" Green eyes narrowing, Cavenaugh rolled her over onto her back and trapped her beneath him.

"I said, I agree with you." Smiling up at him, she wrapped her arms around his neck. "Make love to me, Cavenaugh. I need you."

"Not half as much as I need you," he groaned huskily, lowering his head to taste the sweet skin of her shoulder. "Oh, God. Not half as much as I need you. But I won't stop trying until you realize you want me more than any-thing else on this earth!"

He slid his hands up along her sides, pushing the T-shirt out of the way. When her bare breasts were revealed in the shadows he tantalized the tips gently with the palm of his hand until they became firm.

Kimberly felt the hardness of his arousal as he pressed himself strongly against her thigh. When he drew one of her hands away from his neck and guided it down to his manhood, she moaned in soft wonder.

"Such gentle hands," Cavenaugh muttered achingly. "You drive me out of my mind, sweetheart."

He let his fingers glide teasingly along the inside of her thighs until she was arching against his hand. Then he touched the dampening heart of her and Kimberly gasped aloud.

Cavenaugh lifted his head from her breast to drink in the sight of her parted lips and luminous eyes. She caught at his shoulders, pulling him to her.

"Love me, Cavenaugh. I love you so much!"

"Kim!"

She hard the ravishing hunger in his voice and then he was forging into her, taking her completely. The elemental power of his lovemaking captured her, binding her to him in the most primitive of ways. Kimberly clung, her nails leaving small marks of passion in his shoulders, her legs wrapped tightly around his driving thighs.

And then came the moment when her head tipped back over his arm and her body shuddered delicately beneath him. Kimberly was vaguely aware of Cavenaugh calling out her name and heard his fierce demand.

"Tell me again, Kim. Say you love me."

"I love you, Cavenaugh. I love you—" Then the words were cut off as he poured the essence of himself deeply into her body. The long moment of violent, male release drained both of them.

It was a long while before Cavenaugh stirred and slowly

uncoupled himself from her warmth. Kimberly turned into him, seeking shelter and comfort and empathy.

"Did you mean it, Kim?" he asked finally, his hands moving through the tangled mass of her hair.

"I love you, Cavenaugh."

He muttered something she couldn't understand and folded her more tightly against him. "Remember that, sweetheart."

"How could I forget?"

"Kim, I have to be certain you know what you're saying," he said after a moment. "Do you understand? I want to be sure you know exactly how you feel. I want you to be completely free to love me."

"Don't worry. I'll give up Josh Valerian. It will be hard on the poor man but I expect he'll survive."

"Honey, I'm not joking." Cavenaugh tilted her chin up so that he could study her face. His own was harsh and unreadable. "I don't want there to be any barriers between us."

Kimberly's mouth curved with love. "Stop worrying, Cavenaugh. I know what I'm doing. You're so good at reading my mind occasionally, can't you read it tonight?"

"I'm not sure." His eyes were hooded and brooding in the darkness. "Kim, the day after tomorrow I want to take you into San Francisco with me. We'll spend the night there."

Kimberly glowed. "A little time to ourselves?"

"There's some business we have to handle but then, yes, we'll have the night to ourselves." He hesitated and then asked carefully, "Would you like that?"

"Very much."

A sigh escaped him. "Go to sleep, Kim. You've had a hell of a night."

She nestled closer and allowed herself to drift comfortably off into oblivion. The last thought on her mind before she fell into a surprisingly dreamless sleep was that Cavenaugh hadn't told her he loved her. He was saving that for San Francisco, she decided.

At dawn Kimberly awoke to find herself deeply enmeshed in Cavenaugh's embrace. She lay quietly for a time, thinking about the night.

"Are you awake, sweetheart?" he murmured into her hair.

"Umm. Cavenaugh, I've been thinking about something."

"Not always a good sign in a woman."

She pinched his hip and he growled, nipping her shoulder in sensuous retaliation. "I'm serious. There's something we didn't talk about last night."

It seemed to Kimberly that he stiffened slightly at her words. "What didn't we discuss?"

"Well, the whole point of your alarm system along the rock wall is to keep intruders out."

"True."

"The only alarm you got last night was the one I set off when I ran toward the winery building."

"Uh-huh."

"But the character in the robes who was chasing me was already inside the grounds. In fact, he was inside the garden, near the patio. How did he get there without tripping the alarm when he arrived?"

"That," Cavenaugh muttered, "is a little matter I've been lying awake thinking about for the past hour."

"Did he slip in when the invited guests arrived?"

"I don't see how. Starke was monitoring everyone's arrival through the gates and Julia greeted everyone at the door. After the last guest arrived the gates were locked. Starke is very thorough about these things."

Starke. The strange man who shared Cavenaugh's past. Kimberly shivered. But she was afraid to bring up any possible suspicions. Cavenaugh and Starke apparently went back a long way together. Cavenaugh would not thank her for voicing any doubts about his friend.

Besides, Kimberly thought, dismissing her momentary questions, she had no reason to doubt Starke in the first place. His loyalty to Cavenaugh had been proven in the past.

"What are you thinking about, Kim?"

"Loyalty," she answered truthfully.

"A difficult concept to deal with at five o'clock in the morning."

"Yes."

"Are you sleepy?"

"No."

"Want to get up?"

"No."

He smiled. "Want to tell me you love me again?"

"How about if I show you?"

"I'm at your mercy."

"I've always had this thing for passive, submissive men."

"Witch," he rasped huskily, pulling her down on top of him.

BY NOON THAT DAY Starke had a preliminary report on the man who had attacked Kimberly the previous night. He sat with Kimberly and Cavenaugh and told them what little he knew.

"This is all unofficial at this point. Cranston gave me the information off the record. The guy's name is Nick Garwood. He's got a record that goes back to his kindergarten days. Questioned twice last year during an investigation of a stabbing death in L.A. The police down there think it was a contract killing. Right now Garwood is busy demanding his rights and a lawyer but Cranston thinks they can get him to talk.''

"Any word on the source of that dagger?" Cavenaugh asked calmly, as if discussing a business matter. Kimberly was amazed at the matter-of-fact way he and Starke were handling this whole thing. As if they had dealt with such things often in the past.

"Not yet. But Cranston let me take a look at it. It's not a cheap, stamped-out knife, Dare. The handle is genuine silver and it's heavily embossed. Looks like some kind of ceremonial thing. A collector's item. Not the kind of knife a punk would use to carry out a neat, tidy contract killing. It's—'' he slid an apologetic glance at Kimberly ''—it's not exactly an efficient sort of weapon.''

"Lucky for me," Kimberly tossed back smoothly.

"Lucky for all of us," Cavenaugh grated. "Any theories on how he got inside the gate without triggering the alarms?''

Starke shifted his gaze to the garden outside the study window. "Dare, the only thing I can think of is that he somehow snuck in with the other guests. I don't see how, but it must have happened that way. I've been so damned careful…!''

Kimberly saw how harsh Starke was being on himself and felt compelled to interject. "Is it possible someone inside, one of the guests, let him in?''

Cavenaugh and Starke both turned to look at her.

"Do you realize what you're saying, Kim?" Cavenaugh finally asked gently.

"That someone you know is behind this? Yes, I realize it. It's just a passing thought." She smiled bleakly. "I guess I've written one too many crime novels.''

Cavenaugh shook his head. "Don't apologize. It's something that has to be considered. Starke and I went over that ground this morning. We couldn't come up with anything useful, though. Everyone here last night is a good, solid, substantial citizen of the community."

True, Kimberly reflected. In fact, realistically speaking, the newest people on the scene locally were Cavenaugh and Starke.

It was getting very involved, she decided. "With any luck the authorities will get that Nick Garwood to talk," she offered firmly. "Perhaps he's the only villain."

"Don't forget the woman. The one who held Scott captive."

"True. But if she's a girlfriend of Garwood's, it should be easy to trace her." Starke fell into a musing silence.

"What doesn't fit in all this is the weird part," Cavenaugh put in bluntly. "The rose with the needle in it, the silver dagger, the robe Garwood was wearing. None of that fits a straight kidnap or murder attempt."

"I know," Starke muttered in dark frustration.

Cavenaugh leaned forward in sudden intensity. "Starke, see if you can get Cranston to give you a photograph of that dagger."

"Sure, but why?"

"You and I imported a lot of odd things during our time, pal. We had to get them appraised occasionally. We've got a lot of contacts who know a lot about weird items. I want to show some of them a photo of that dagger."

Starke was on his feet, heading for the door. "I'll get on it right away, Dare." The man was obviously grateful to have something useful to do. At the door he paused for a moment to glance back at Cavenaugh.

"Are you still going to take Kim into San Francisco tomorrow?"

Kimberly wondered at the disapproval in his voice but Cavenaugh ignored it. "We'll be leaving in the afternooon. As soon as I finish that meeting with the marketing people. Any objections?"

"Would they do any good?"

"No," Cavenaugh said harshly. "I know what I'm doing."

"I'll see you later," Starke said and walked out the door.

Startled at the unexpected discord between the two men, Kimberly frowned at Cavenaugh. "What was all that about?"

He switched his emerald-hard gaze to her. "Forget it, Kim. Like I told Starke, I know what I'm doing."

"I never said you didn't, but—" A sudden, bleak thought struck her and she went on in a tight whisper, "Doesn't Starke approve of...of us? Is he trying to warn you not to get too involved with me?"

Cavenaugh's mouth tilted wryly at the corner. "In case you haven't noticed, I already am involved with you. And if it makes you feel any more comfortable about it, yes, Starke does approve of you. Most emphatically. So does everyone else around here."

"Oh." A sense of relief went through her. "It's just that I know how demanding families can be in a situation such as this," she began gently. "If they don't approve—"

"No," Cavenaugh cut in with cool deliberation. "You do not know how families are in a situation such as this. You only know how one family was and that was twenty-eight years ago. Before you were even born!"

Kimberly got to her feet, astonished and annoyed at his biting attitude. She had gotten very accustomed lately to being cosseted by Darius Cavenaugh. "Occasionally I forget how overbearing you can be when you choose," she told him as she walked to the door. "I'll see you at dinner."

"Kim, wait!" He was on his feet behind his desk, green eyes urgent and compelling.

"What is it, Cavenaugh?" she asked warily, her hand on the doorknob.

"Kim, you do know that whatever I do, it's because I want everything right between us? I know there are times when I seem like a tyrant to you, but you do understand that I only want what's best for you? And for myself," he added dryly. "I can't pretend to be totally altruistic about all this."

She tilted her head to one side. "About all what?"

"Never mind. Just remember what I said. Oh, and Kim, why don't you have Mrs. Lawson set out a bottle of that new Riesling for dinner."

"Of course," she said politely and closed the door behind her. *And while I'm at it,* she decided grimly, *I might as well tell her I'd like to see a bottle of hot sauce on the table. I may not be sure of my status around here, but I must have some rights!*

He came to her room again that night and while he didn't exactly flaunt the relationship to the rest of the household, it was obvious Cavenaugh had no intention of trying to pretend that he wasn't sleeping with her. No one seemed to mind the obvious intimacy. In fact, everyone seemed quite pleased about it as far as Kimberly could tell.

But it seemed to her that he made love to her with a kind of fierce energy that night, as if he was trying to imprint himself on her senses. He should realize by now, Kimberly thought fleetingly, that he had succeeded completely in wiping out her image of a fictional lover. She would be satisfied now only with the very real love of Darius Cavenaugh.

CHAPTER EIGHT

SOME DEEP INSTINCT warned Kimberly of impending disaster as Cavenaugh escorted her into the ornate lounge of the elegant Union Square hotel. If she were honest with herself she would have known that the promised trip to San Francisco was not really destined to be the romantic idyll she had anticipated.

There had been a tension about Cavenaugh since the day before, when he had made a point of telling her that whatever he did would be for her own good. When people, especially men, started telling you that what they did was for your own good, a smart woman ran. As fast and as far as she could.

But she hadn't been a smart woman lately, Kimberly reflected. She had been a woman in love. Quite a difference.

Cavenaugh's tension had communicated itself to Kimberly until she herself bristled with it. He had been almost silent during the drive into the city that afternoon. There had been an implacable, forbidding aura about him that had squelched her attempts at conversation.

When they had checked into the hotel he had taken her upstairs to the room and brusquely suggested she change for the evening. Out of a fleeting wish that the atmosphere between them might be explained and mitigated before the night was over, Kimberly had dressed with hope.

The sophisticated little black knit dress with its piping

of gold at the collar and cuffs had been discovered by Julia yesterday during a shopping trip. Together with black, high-heeled evening sandals and hair brushed into a chic twist at the back of her head, Kimberly felt as ready as she ever would to face what promised to be an uncertain evening. It had seemed to her that Cavenaugh had dressed as though he were going to war. He looked formidable and aloof, essentially masculine in the dark evening jacket and dazzling white shirt. She felt the distance between them grow more frighteningly intense with every passing second. Her dreams of an evening of love and promises faded.

By the time they were facing the smiling hostess in the lounge, Kimberly knew that something devastating was about to occur. Beside her Cavenaugh spoke with quiet authority.

"We're expected by the Marlands."

Kimberly went absolutely still even as the hostess nodded politely and turned to lead the way.

"Cavenaugh, what have you done?" Kimberly whispered with a bleakness that reached all the way to her heart. She turned vulnerable, stricken eyes up to his unyielding gaze. "What have you done to us?"

His mouth tightened as he looked down at her, and for an instant she thought she read desperation in the depths of his emerald eyes. But it was masked almost immediately by fierce determination.

"It had to be this way, Kim. You would never have agreed to meet them otherwise."

She shook her head, trying to clear it. "I knew from the beginning that you were arrogant, but I never thought you would do this to me."

His hand closed around her wrist. "Let's get it over with, Kim. It's not going to be as bad as you think it will be. Trust me."

She looked up at him uncomprehendingly. "Trust you? But Cavenaugh, after tonight I'll never be able to trust you again, will I?"

Fury hardened his features even more than they already were. "You don't know what you're saying. Don't fight it, Kim. And don't be afraid. I'm with you, remember? I won't let anything happen to you."

"What more could happen?" she asked. "Do you know that I thought you were bringing me to San Francisco so we could spend some time alone? And I thought tonight was going to be a very special one for us. I always thought I kept my fantasy world confined to the pages of my books but apparently I allowed it to slip over into real life."

"I'm no fantasy, damn it!"

"No. But the man I fell in love with is."

"We'll deal with this later, after you've faced the Marlands and found out that there's no need to deny your heritage."

"Cavenaugh…" she whispered distantly as he led her through the crowded lounge.

But it was too late. They were confronting a refined-looking couple seated at a round table in the corner. Her grandparents must have been in their seventies, Kimberly realized vaguely as Wesley Marland got to his feet and politely extended his hand to Cavenaugh. But even as the older man went through the formalities, neither he nor his expensively dressed, silver-haired wife could take their eyes off their granddaughter.

When she looked into Wesley Marland's face, Kimberly found herself meeting eyes the same amber color as her own. Marland must have been a handsome man in his youth, she reflected as she acknowledged the quiet introductions with the barest inclination of her head. Without a word she took the chair Cavenaugh held for her, refusing to look at him as she did so. He sat beside her, close and protective.

No, not protective. Possessive perhaps, but not protective. A man who cared enough to protect her would never have thrown her into deep water as Cavenaugh had done tonight.

"Oh, my dear Kim," Anne Marland murmured as though she could no longer restrain herself. "You have your father's eyes."

"With any luck," Kimberly said coolly, "that's all I inherited from him."

Mrs. Marland flinched and withdrew the hand she had been extending tentatively toward her granddaughter.

"Kim," Cavenaugh began, softly warning, but Wesley Marland interrupted him.

"No, Mr. Cavenaugh, she has a right to be bitter."

Kimberly lifted her chin. "Let's get one thing straight. I will not be patronized. I'm sure Cavenaugh has explained to you that this whole thing has been sprung on me without any advance notice. I would appreciate it if we could keep everything short and businesslike. Let's get this momentous occasion over with as quickly as possible."

Before anyone could respond the waitress appeared at the table, politely requesting drink orders. When the other three hesitated, as though their minds had been anywhere but on drinks, Kimberly smoothly gave her order.

"I'll have a glass of your house wine as long as it's not from the Cavenaugh Vineyards."

"Uh, no, ma'am, it's not," the waitress said, surprised. "Cavenaugh wines are much too expensive to serve as house wines."

"I'm beginning to realize that."

The Marlands quickly ordered and Cavenaugh asked for

a Scotch on the rocks. When the young woman took her leave, Kimberly faced her grandparents.

"Now suppose we get down to business so that we can all be on our way. What do you want from me?"

It was Cavenaugh who responded, green eyes gleaming with faint threat. "Kim, the Marlands only wanted to meet you. There's no reason to be aggressive. Just relax."

Mrs. Marland said hastily, "Your fiancé is right, dear. We only wanted to meet you."

Kimberly's eyes widened in mocking astonishment. "My *fiancé?* Who on earth are you talking about?"

Wesley Marland frowned. "Mr. Cavenaugh here has given us to understand that he intends to marry you."

"Really? First I've heard of it." Kimberly smiled in a brittle fashion as the cocktail waitress returned with the order.

"Marriage is a matter I intend to sort out with Kim after this meeting takes place," Cavenaugh said calmly.

"Another little surprise you were going to spring on me, Cavenaugh?" Kimberly took a deep swallow of her wine. It wasn't nearly as good as a Cavenaugh vintage but it certainly tasted better to her tonight than any of the noble bottles Cavenaugh produced. "Hmm, not bad," she offered dryly, holding it up to the light. "It has a clean, *honest* taste."

"Stop it, Kim," Cavenaugh ordered gently. "You're acting like a child."

"What?" she asked sardonically. "Aren't things going the way you had planned? Did you expect me to throw myself into my grandparents' arms after all these years? How terribly disappointing for you."

It was Wesley Marland who interceded as his wife looked on unhappily. "Kim, we understand this is difficult for you and that it's been something of a surprise. But we honestly didn't think we could get you to agree to meet with us in any other way. The lawyers told me that you categorically refused any overtures.''

"Categorically,'' Kimberly agreed.

"We had to see you, Kim,'' Anne Marland whispered. "You're all we have left now. It's taken us so long to find you, dear. Years, in fact. We started looking a long time ago but all we found out was that your mother had died. It took the lawyers forever to trace you. It wasn't until your books started appearing in print that they finally got a lead. They contacted your publisher and your agent, neither of whom would give out your address until we convinced them that we really were your only surviving relations.''

Kimberly looked into the aging, once-beautiful face and thought of what this woman had done to her mother. "You're twenty-eight years too late, Mrs. Marland.''

"Don't you think we know that?'' Wesley Marland asked bitterly. "But we can't undo the past, Kim. We can only work with the present and the future.'' He drew a deep breath and then announced grandly, "We want you to know that, as our only surviving descendant, you will be inheriting everything we own.''

Kimberly stared at them, utterly astounded. "My God,'' she gritted. "Do you really think I'd touch a penny of your money?''

The Marlands stared back at her, obviously not prepared for the vehemence in her words. Cavenaugh quietly sipped his drink and watched Kimberly over the rim of his glass.

Wesley cleared his throat. "Forgive me, my dear. It's just that, well, we understand it takes quite a while to become, uh, financially successful as a mystery writer and we thought that...Kim, our money can be a legacy to your children. Perhaps you should think of them before you allow pride to dictate your answers.''

"What children?" she asked politely.

Anne glanced uneasily at Cavenaugh. "Surely when you and Mr. Cavenaugh are married you'll want children?"

"Not only has Cavenaugh failed to discuss marriage with me, he has certainly not brought up the subject of children." Kim flashed a brilliant smile at the man beside her. "Another little example of our failure to communicate, I suppose."

"Kim," he said roughly, "you're making this hard on everyone, including yourself. Why don't you deal with the situation like the warm, sensitive woman you really are?"

"What did everyone expect to accomplish with this dramatic encounter?" she demanded tightly.

"A chance to get to know our only grandchild," Mrs. Marland said softly. "After your father was killed and we realized there was no hope of...of..."

"No hope of ever having a properly bred Marland heir?" Kim offered helpfully.

"You don't understand how it was twenty-eight years ago," her grandfather said quietly. "Your father was so young. We were convinced that what he felt for your mother was only infatuation that would wear off quickly. Frankly, we believe that's exactly what did happen. John didn't put up all that much of a battle in the end. He seemed, well, almost relieved when we arranged the divorce for him. I know that's not what you want to hear, but that's the truth."

"Did it ever occur to either one of you that you had no right to arrange his life for him?" Kimberly demanded.

"John had certain responsibilities," Anne Marland began firmly. "Or so we convinced ourselves at the time."

Kimberly nodded. "I understand completely."

"You do?" Marland looked at her in surprise.

"Certainly. Cavenaugh, here, is a perfect example of

how family responsibilities can dictate a man's entire life. I really do understand the kind of pressure my father must have been under.'' She met Cavenaugh's eyes and the angry aggression in her began to disintegrate. "All of you have been the victims of that inbred sense of responsibility and loyalty. When I was very young I used to feel I had been denied something important because I had been disowned by my grandparents and by my father. Now I realize that I was very, very lucky. I grew up without the kind of pressure all of you must have endured. I grew up to be independent and self-contained. And I don't need my grandparents now. I don't need anyone." What a joke that was. If only she had never met Cavenaugh. The words might actually have been true before she'd fallen in love with Darius Cavenaugh.

Anne Marland leaned forward urgently. "Kim, my dear, you are on the verge of a very good marriage. The Cavenaughs are a solid, respectable, old California family. By acknowledging your grandfather and myself you can bring something important to that family. You can bring a solid, respectable background of your own."

Kimberly set down her glass with fingers that trembled. "Is that what this is all about?" She looked at Cavenaugh. "Were you hoping to establish a proper background for me before bringing me into the family?"

Grim fury flared in the emerald ice of his eyes. "You know very well that's not why I did this."

And quite suddenly Kim knew she believed him. She believed all of them. Closing her eyes briefly she summoned a small sad smile. "I know," she whispered. "I know. You were only doing what you thought was best for me."

"For all of us, Kim," Wesley Marland said quietly. "Please believe me. Anne and I don't want to hurt you any more than we already have. We want to make up for what happened twenty-eight years ago. You were the one innocent victim in the whole mess.''

''There was my mother,'' Kimberly pointed out wearily.

Anne flicked a quick glance at her husband and then looked directly at Kimberly. ''Darling, your mother was very young and very desperate to hold on to John.''

''What's that supposed to mean?''

Wesley sighed. ''Kim, your mother deliberately got pregnant when the divorce proceedings started. She admitted as much to John. She hoped that a baby would hold the marriage together. We never heard from her after that. In fact, we all assumed...well, we assumed she'd probably had an abortion when she realized she wasn't going to receive a large settlement.''

Kimberly shook her head. ''I'm not going to argue with you. You may be right for all I know. Women have done less intelligent things when they're in love.'' She was aware of Cavenaugh slanting a cool glance at her but she ignored it. ''There's really no point in rehashing the past, is there? No good can come of it now. What's done is done.'' She smiled wryly at the Marlands. ''But I'm afraid you really will have to find something else to do with your money. Give it to a worthy charity. How about starting a fund for impoverished, unpublished writers?''

Wesley looked directly at Cavenaugh. ''Don't let her throw away her inheritance, Mr. Cavenaugh.''

Cavenaugh shrugged. ''I don't care what she does with the inheritance. I only brought her here today to reestablish contact with you. I wanted her to see that her grandparents weren't monsters and that she doesn't have to be afraid of families that are bound by loyalty and responsibility.''

''Are we such monsters?'' Anne Marland asked sadly.

"We did what we thought was best at the time. We were wrong."

Kimberly shook her head. Her grandmother had paid a heavy price for interfering in her son's life so many years ago. "Who am I to punish you now? You've lost everything that really counted, haven't you? Your son and heir, a granddaughter to spoil, the hope of future generations who will acknowledge you on the family tree. No, Mrs. Marland, you're not a monster. I wish you and Mr. Marland all the best. I truly mean that. I'm not holding a grudge against you any longer. But neither can I give you back everything you threw away twenty-eight years ago."

"You can give us great-grandchildren," Wesley Marland stated gruffly.

"You wouldn't deny us our great-grandchildren, would you, Kim?" Anne asked desperately.

"I don't have any to offer you," Kimberly pointed out simply.

"Yet," Cavenaugh interjected coolly.

She wasn't going to argue with him now. Kimberly was feeling emotionally drained. There wasn't enough energy left over for an argument with Cavenaugh. Besides, there was nothing left to argue about.

An awkward silence descended on the table as the four people sitting around it confronted one another and themselves. Then Wesley asked cautiously, "Would it be too much to hope you and Darius will join us for dinner, Kim?"

Too much to hope? These proud, wealthy, influential, eminently respectable people had reached the far end of their lives and found themselves reduced to begging for some time with their granddaughter. Twenty-eight years ago they could not possibly have dreamed that it would all turn out this way. Twenty-eight years ago they had probably assumed money could buy them anything. They had learned the hard way that it had its limits. It could not buy a meal shared with a granddaughter. They could only hope that the granddaughter would grant it to them.

Cavenaugh waited for her answer along with the Marlands. He made no effort to force her into the next step of the fragile relationship.

"Cavenaugh and I will have dinner with you," Kimberly said quietly.

The relief and gratitude in the proud eyes of her grandparents were eloquent thanks. But it was the satisfaction in Cavenaugh's gaze that roused some of Kimberly's anger and despair.

Who did he think he was to play God with her life like this?

Sitting next to her, Cavenaugh felt the immense effort of will Kimberly was exercising to maintain a cool, polite facade, and his own sense of foreboding increased.

He had been so certain that the way he had chosen to handle the situation was the best, so convinced of the rightness of his instincts in the matter. Now he was not so sure. Starke had warned him that women didn't like surprises.

Cavenaugh watched Kimberly as she carefully chatted with her grandparents. She was behaving very civilly now, although there was not yet any sign of her relaxing. There was even an occasional smile. It was almost painful to see how eagerly the Marlands greeted the faint hints of Kimberly's softened mood.

They couldn't be any more grateful than he was, Cavenaugh thought as he finished his drink. For a while there he thought he'd set a match to a powder keg. Now, although the threat of immediate explosion seemed to have passed, he knew he was still dealing with a woman on a very short fuse.

She wasn't used to having someone else in her life, he assured himself as they all rose to go into dinner in the hotel dining room. Kim was so damned independent, so accustomed to making her own decisions without any input from people who cared, that it was probably difficult for her to adjust to what he had done tonight. But she was an intelligent, sensitive woman and she would understand that he'd handled this the only way he could.

Ultimately, Cavenaugh decided as he ate his trout mousse, Kim would relax and accept the situation. After all, just look how much progress had already been made. Here she was communicating quite politely, if a little stiffly, with people she had once sworn to never even contact.

But even as he tried to cheer himself with that thought, Cavenaugh couldn't shake his own sense of apprehension. He was both thankful and wary as the evening drew to a close.

"I want both of you to feel free to visit us at the winery soon," Cavenaugh said as he shook Wesley Marland's hand in farewell.

"Thank you," his wife answered gratefully. "We'd like that very much." She looked uncertainly at Kim, obviously not sure how to say good-bye to her newfound granddaughter.

Cavenaugh realized he was holding his breath but he needn't have worried. Kimberly hesitated and then leaned forward to quickly kiss her grandmother's pale cheek. Mrs. Marland patted her awkwardly on the shoulder and then turned away with tears in her eyes.

"You've made her very happy, Kim," Wesley Marland said quietly. "We shall always be grateful for your generosity tonight."

"Don't thank me," Kimberly said. "Thank Cavenaugh. It was all his doing."

Marland shook his head. "He set things up but you're the one who made it work. Good night, Kim." He turned away to take his wife's arm.

Cavenaugh watched them walk through the lobby to a waiting taxi. Two intensely proud people. What it must have cost them to acknowledge the mistake they had made twenty-eight years ago, he thought.

"Well, Cavenaugh, you pulled it off. Congratulations. I never even suspected that you had this little scene up your sleeve when you said we were going to spend an evening in San Francisco." Kimberly collected her small, black evening bag and smiled at him with the same brittle expression he'd already seen on her at various times during the confrontation.

"It's over, Kim," he murmured as he took her arm. "You handled it very well."

"Golly, thanks. You can't imagine how terrific that makes me feel."

Warning signals hummed along his nerve endings. Cavenaugh kept a very tight grip on Kimberly's arm as they made their way out of the dining room. He had the oddest impression that if he didn't physically hang on to her he might lose her tonight.

"You're through the hard part, honey. You've made the contact and found out that, while they may be far from perfect, your grandparents aren't inhuman despots, either. No one is going to make you accept them completely but you needed to face them and understand them."

He didn't like the innocently blank look she gave him. "Why?"

Cavenaugh felt his tension increase. This was going to be more difficult than he had anticipated. "Because I wanted you to get over your fear of a certain kind of…of family relationship. I didn't want you holding the actions of your father's family against me for the rest of your life. I wanted you free of the past. Can't you understand that, Kim?"

"I was free of my past. I had absolutely no contact with it. How much freer can a woman be?" she asked with an unnatural calm.

"The hell you were. It was between us constantly. You were wary of me from the beginning because of it. You constructed your Amy Solitaire character to be as unfettered and emotionally free as *you* wanted to be and then you gave her the perfect mate, Josh Valerian. A man who has no other responsibilities in the world except the ones he has to Amy. Damn it, Kim, I felt I had all these ghosts from your past to deal with before I could have you."

She came to a halt in the middle of the lobby, amber eyes cool and fathomless under her lashes. "You've already had me, remember? The ghosts didn't seem to get in your way."

Cavenaugh gritted his teeth. "How long are you going to punish me for the way I handled this whole thing tonight?"

She turned away. "I'm not going to punish you, Cavenaugh. I don't have that kind of power."

He caught her arm but when she shot him a defiant glance he released her. The last thing he wanted was a major scene here in the lobby. Kimberly was walking swiftly toward the bank of elevators. Lights from the heavy crystal chandeliers dappled the amber of her hair. Her head was high and she carried herself with a pride he had just witnessed in two other people. Cavenaugh strode forward, catching up to her as she paused to punch the elevator call button.

"It wasn't just your grandfather's eyes you inherited, Kim. You've got the Marland pride. Just imagine how they felt tonight."

To his surprise she inclined her head, not looking at him. "I know it must have been difficult for them. Twenty-eight years ago I'll bet they couldn't have managed it. Time changes everyone, I suppose."

"Everyone, Kim," he emphasized meaningfully as one of the bronzed elevator doors slid silently open. "Including you."

She shrugged elegantly in the sleek black dress. "Look me up in twenty-eight years and I'll let you know."

"I'm not going to wait around that long for you to forgive me," Cavenaugh snapped, beginning to feel goaded. "When you've had a chance to think about it you'll realize I handled this the only way I could."

"Will I?" She stepped inside the elevator and he followed quickly.

Cavenaugh drew a deep breath, seeking patience. "I know you're upset, honey, but by morning you'll have calmed down. You're too intelligent not to realize this has all been for the best."

She didn't answer him, her gaze fixed steadfastly on the closed elevator doors. Kimberly maintained her silence all the way up to the room and by the time he unlocked the door Cavenaugh knew he was more than tense. He was getting damned scared. She wasn't coming out of it as fast as he had anticipated. When she slipped past him into the room he shut the door and leaned back against it, watching her through narrowed, brooding eyes. Kimberly went immediately over to the closet and began pulling out her small suitcase.

"What do you think you're doing?" Cavenaugh asked harshly.

"What does it look like I'm doing?"

He came away from the door, moving toward her with such obvious intent that she stepped back a pace. Instantly Cavenaugh halted. "Damn it, Kim, don't look at me like that."

"If you don't want me looking at you like that then I suggest you don't threaten me."

"I am not threatening you. But neither am I going to let you pack up and leave this room," he growled.

"Why would you want me to stay?" she asked too calmly.

"Because you belong here!" His patience was fraying to a dangerous degree, mostly because of his growing fear that he'd done something incredibly stupid tonight. "You belong with me, Kim. Hell, you belong *to* me. You love me, remember?"

"Ah, Cavenaugh," she whispered hopelessly. "I remember. But the problem is that you don't love me. You proved that tonight. I had fooled myself into believing that you did, you see. That was sheer idiocy on my part, of course. You never gave me any reason to think that you did. When I told you that I loved you, there was no answering response from you, was there? Do you know I had decided that tonight was the night you would tell me how much you loved me? I thought that this trip to San Francisco was planned by you to give us a chance to be alone so that you could tell me your true feelings."

"Kim, now that we've gotten through that confrontation with your grandparents we're both free to talk about the future."

"I don't see much future for myself with a man who doesn't love me," she flung back in a tight voice.

"Give me a chance, Kim. This wasn't the way I wanted everything to go, damn it!" He ran a hand restlessly through his hair. His whole body was seething with frustration and anger. Standing with his feet braced slightly apart, adrenaline pouring through his system, he knew he was poised to reach out and grab her. He wanted to pull her down onto the bed and shut off the flow of her resentment with the kind of lovemaking that would remind her of just whose woman she was.

"A man who really cared for me would never have done what you did tonight. He would never have set me up like that. He would have understood that I had a right to handle my past in any way I saw fit. He would have respected the fact I'm an adult and entitled to make my own decisions. He would have empathized with my feelings about my grandparents, even if he thought I should confront them. He might, conceivably, have tried to talk me into a meeting with them but he would never have arranged one behind my back the way you did."

"Kim, I wanted it over and done, can't you understand? I had to know you were really free to love me. It's because I want you so much that I had to make certain what you felt was real. I didn't want any barriers between us, and I thought your wariness of families that wielded their power the way your grandparents once did was standing in the way of our relationship."

"So you decided to wield a little power of your own, is that it? Was tonight's act of sheer, unadulterated arrogance supposed to reassure me? My God, do you realize I had actually begun to think that you could almost read my mind? That we were becoming emotionally and intellectually intimate? That you understood me?"

"Kim, I'm a man!" Cavenaugh gritted, his fists clenching in impotent fury. "Men see some things differently than women see them. Sometimes we make mistakes dealing with women because we can't think like them. Maybe

I made a mistake tonight. But I didn't intend to set you up. I only wanted you to face your past and deal with it. That's the way I do things, Kim. I face them. I don't pretend they aren't in my life. I don't build a fantasy world for myself as a way of dealing with real life.''

"A fantasy world!'' she snapped. "You think I live between the pages of my books?''

"Well, haven't you done exactly that?''

She stared at him as though seeing him finally for the first time. "Cavenaugh, you don't know me at all, do you?''

"Kim, wait…!''

She turned her back on him and disappeared into the bathroom. A moment later she was back with her toothbrush and a handful of other items, stuffing them into her small case. Yanking the blouse in the closet off the hanger, she dumped it in on top of the rest and closed the lid.

"Just where do you think you're going tonight?'' Cavenaugh was almost afraid to touch her, fearing that once he did he would do something drastic. But he had to stop her. He knew his fingers closed much too tightly around her fragile wrist but she disdained any protest.

"I'm going to find a place to spend the night,'' Kimberly told him simply. "Alone.''

"You're spending the night here. With me.''

"No.''

He grappled with that single word. It would have been easier if she'd yelled something along the lines of "not if you were the last man on earth.'' He could have dealt with that kind of outrage. But Cavenaugh freely admitted to himself that he wasn't at all sure how to handle Kim in her present mood. He released her wrist as he realized that his hand was beginning to shake with the force of his barely restrained emotions.

As soon as he freed her she turned and started toward the door.

"That's far enough, Kim. You've not leaving this hotel. For both our sakes, don't push me." He heard the lethal threat in his own voice and knew she understood it, because at the door she stopped and turned around to face him. Her head was still held with dignity but he could see the uncertainty in her eyes. *Nice going, Cavenaugh. Now you've managed to frighten her. You're really handling this whole thing with finesse.*

"If you're going to threaten me, Cavenaugh, be up front about it. What exactly are you going to do if I exercise my right to leave this room?"

He closed his eyes in exasperation and then glared at her thorugh narrowed lids. *Back off, Cavenaugh, or you're going to blow this completely. Give her time. She needs a little time.* He forced himself to speak calmly.

"If you're absolutely determined to run instead of staying with me tonight, I'll call the front desk and get you another room in this hotel." Without waiting for her response he picked up the phone on the nearby end table.

Kimberly watched him in utter silence. In fact, Cavenaugh reflected a few minutes later as he escorted her down the hall to another room on the same floor, he got the distinct impression she didn't quite know what to make of his actions. Obviously getting her a room of her own without further protest was not what she had expected him to do. As he opened the door of her new room, he looked down at her.

"This isn't how I wanted it to be between us tonight, Kim. You know that, don't you?"

"It isn't how I wanted it to be, either, Cavenaugh. As you've already taken pains to point out, I live in something of a fantasy world. But the fantasy I was living in was taking place in real life, not in one of my books.''

"Damn you," he gritted and reached for her.

He pulled her into his arms, deliberately giving her no opportunity to resist. Frustrated hunger and a large dose of his seething fury combined in the kiss. His mouth closed over hers with a possessiveness he made no attempt to hide. She might choose to sleep alone tonight but she would go to bed with the taste of him on her lips.

Kimberly didn't fight him but that was probably because he didn't allow her to do so. Cavenaugh wasn't interested in a response tonight. He only wanted to imprint himself on her in a way that would last until morning. He wanted her to lie awake thinking of him all night, he realized. The same way he was going to lie awake thinking of her. When he finally released her she stumbled back a step, her fingers lifting to touch her sensually bruised mouth. It seemed to Cavenaugh that he had never seen her golden eyes so wide or so unreadable. For a long moment they looked at each other and then Cavenaugh shook off the spell.

"Good night, witch. Go to sleep. If you can."

Two hours later the uneasiness became so intense that Cavenaugh knew he had to act. He hadn't slept at all but this restless feeling wasn't from lack of sleep. Something was very, very wrong.

Unable to stand it any longer he climbed out of bed, pulled on his slacks and his shoes and went out into the hall.

He was too late. Kimberly had left the hotel.

CHAPTER NINE

SHE HAD BEEN A FOOL, Kimberly told herself. A fool to think that she had achieved some kind of rare, magical intimacy with Darius Cavenaugh. A fool to let him trick her into that confrontation in San Francisco. A fool to let herself believe that Cavenaugh was somehow different from other men in his position.

Most of all, she decided ruefully as she gripped the wheel of the rental car, she was a fool for making the long drive up the coast at one o'clock in the morning. But when you were running from your own foolishness, home was where you instinctively wanted to hide. And if home lay a hundred and fifty miles away, you just kept going until you got there.

In spite of the lousy weather.

Kimberly struggled with the tension of fighting the steady rain as well as her own inner anxiety. Refusing to spend the night with Cavenaugh hadn't been enough for her high-strung nerves. She'd needed to be alone, really alone. Kimberly didn't have any misconceptions about what would have happened if she'd stayed in the hotel.

Cavenaugh would have been at her door when she opened it in the morning, waiting to see if she had gotten over her snit. And he would have continued to haunt her, arguing his case, condemning her own behavior until she finally admitted that he had been right. It infuriated her to think that she had been so blissfully unsuspecting about that trip to San Francisco. She should have paid more attention to her instincts. After all, there had been plenty of evidence that the trip wasn't starting out as a romantic jaunt for two! But she had chosen to ignore Cavenaugh's increasing silence and tension.

When you were in love, Kimberly reflected sadly, you saw things the way you wanted to see them, not as they really were.

Cavenaugh had been right about one thing. He was a man and he didn't think like a woman. More importantly, he didn't think the way she, Kimberly Sawyer, did. That was the bottom line. He didn't think the way she did. He might at times be able to almost read her mind, to know what she was thinking, but that didn't mean he shared the same emotions or analyzed those thoughts the same way she did.

He wasn't Josh Valerian. How many times had he told her that, Kimberly asked herself wryly. She supposed it had been his way of trying to warn her that the warm, shared intimacy that she imagined was beginning to take shape between them had its limitations.

The truth was she had never confused him for a moment with her fictional male character. It would have been impossible to mistake Cavenaugh for anyone but himself. He was too real, too dynamic, too solid and far too virile to be a stand-in for Josh Valerian or anyone else.

Everything about him was unique, Kimberly realized as she slowed the car to compensate for the increasing rain. The taste of his mouth, the earthy scent of his body, the feel of him as he crushed her deeply into the bedclothes. She would never forget the physical side of him.

But what she would miss the most were the more intangible aspects of their short-lived affair. Damn it, she thought, there *had* been moments of shared understanding.

She hadn't imagined them all. The night he had held her in his arms and told her he knew what it was like to be wired with tension after a frightening confrontation with violence, for instance. He had comforted and soothed her and she knew he understood exactly what she was going through.

There had been other times, too, Kimberly remembered. He had understood her need to be alone in a busy household. He had been quietly, deeply appreciative of the way she had interceded to establish some rules for his working hours.

How could a man who seemed so in tune with her in so many instances do to her what Cavenaugh had done tonight?

The answer was simple enough, Kimberly thought grimly. He'd given it to her himself. He was a man. More than that, he was *Cavenaugh*. The basic masculine arrogance in him was an intrinsic part of his nature as was his sense of responsibility. It was instinctive of him to take charge of a situation and do what he thought had to be done. That part of him would never change.

Accepting Cavenaugh as her lover meant accepting the total man.

Tonight had been one of the most difficult in her life. It had been traumatic facing the grandparents she had sworn never to meet. But on the whole, the confrontation had not gone the way she would have expected. It was impossible to hate the Marlands.

Kimberly wasn't sure, yet, exactly what she felt toward the elderly couple who had been forced to beg her to acknowledge them. They seemed like strangers to her—people whom she had heard about from her mother and from the lawyers who had written to her explaining the history of the situation. But they were people whom she'd never actually met and on some levels they had remained unreal until now.

Tonight she had learned that they were two very human people who were trying to salvage something they had once foolishly thrown aside. It was impossible to hate them.

Kimberly bit her lip as she reflected on her own pride. Cavenaugh had been right about that aspect of her personality. Just as he'd been right about the fact that she had nothing to fear in meeting her grandparents. Cavenaugh was no doubt right about a lot of things.

But that didn't mean he was the right man for her to love, she told herself. Unfortunately, telling herself that and learning to unlove him were two entirely different matters. In spite of the turmoil of her emotions tonight, she knew that she loved the man.

The anger and resentment that had driven her from the hotel in search of solitude had faded into a dull, sad ache by the time Kimberly pulled into the drive of her darkened beach house. The storm was really raging at this point on the coast, and she was exhausted from fighting it for the past hundred and fifty miles.

Lightning crackled as she stood on the porch, fumbling in her purse for the key. She had changed into a pair of jeans and the full-sleeved white blouse she had intended to wear on the drive back to the Napa Valley, but she hadn't brought along an umbrella. The rain had almost drenched her just during the short dash from the car.

Her fingers trembled slightly as she finally located the correct key and thrust it into the lock. It seemed that every nerve in her body was being delicately probed with a razor. It was no wonder that she was suddenly so shaky. It was nearly four o'clock in the morning. She had been through a great deal tonight and the drive through the worsening storm had not helped. What she needed was a glass of wine and bed. Taking a grip on herself, she turned the key in the lock and pushed open the door.

And saw at once that the last things she was fated to get tonight were a glass of wine and the privacy of her own bed. Panic smashed through her, scattering her senses for a timeless instant.

It was the candle burning in the middle of the pentagram that caught her eye first. The ancient, magical symbol had been drawn on her living room floor and the candle glowed evilly in a low, squat metal holder that sat at the center of the design.

The candlelight was the only light in the room but it was enough to illuminate the hooded figure who sat cross-legged on the far side of the pentagram.

"Come in, Kimberly Sawyer. You are expected."

Kimberly flinched at the familiar voice but before she could react two other figures stepped out of the darkness and into the faint light of the candle. They were both hooded and robed but one had his hand extended and in it was a gun.

"Close the door," a man's voice commanded from the depths of the flowing cowl.

Kimberly desperately tried to weigh her chances. He could kill her easily before she could dash back through the door, she realized. She might have been able to outrun a knife but no one could outrun a bullet. Slowly, she closed the door behind her. She felt a distant kind of surprise that her chilled muscles responded to the silent effort. The door seemed very heavy.

"The power is strong tonight, my lady," murmured the second standing figure. "It has brought her here, right into our grasp." There was awed wonder in the tones and also a touch of familiarity. Kimberly knew she had heard that voice sometime in the past, too.

"The power," intoned the woman who remained seated in front of the pentagram, "grows stronger every day. Have I not told you that?" She lifted her head so that her features were illuminated beneath the shadowy hood. "Good evening, Kimberly."

Kimberly stared back at her, calling on a kind of pride that only tonight she had learned was inherited from her grandparents. That pride was all she had to get her through this terrifying encounter. With an effort of will she forced a measure of cool mockery into her response.

"Hello, Ariel. Graduated from tea leaves to the big time, I see." The sardonic comment startled her because it didn't reflect the panic that seemed to have invaded every corner of her mind. She discovered that managing the cool remark gave her a measure of courage, however. Kimberly seized on that spark of strength.

Ariel Llewellyn smiled back at her, but the cheerful, scatterbrained expression of the woman who had been virtually a member of the Cavenaugh household for almost a year was gone. A hint of madness gleamed in her eyes and there was an unnaturally serene smile on Ariel's mouth, as if she could see into the future and found it satisfying.

"You have been incredibly foolish, Kim. And now you will pay."

Kimberly concealed the tremor of fear that went through her. Ariel meant it. "Well, I know a one-hundred-fifty-mile drive through a storm probably isn't the brightest thing someone can do at three in the morning, but what can I say? I was bored."

Ariel shook her head once as if unable to believe such stupidity. "Foolish woman. You had no option but to make that drive tonight. You were summoned. That was not a matter of choice for you. No, you made your mistake two months ago when you chose to interfere in matters that did not pertain to you.''

''The little matter of the kidnapping?'' Kimberly swallowed the sickening taste of fear and swung her gaze to the standing woman. ''You're the one who was holding Scott in that beach house, aren't you? The one I took him away from so easily that night.'' She turned her attention back to Ariel. ''It seems to me you've got some problems in the personnel section of your organization, Ariel. I know good help is hard to get but you've really picked some blunderers. This idiot didn't even hear me the night I came by to fetch Scott. And then there was that turkey with the knife who kept tripping over his Halloween costume. This guy with the gun probably forgot the ammunition.''

There was an ominous growl from the armed man and the nose of the gun lifted menacingly.

''I assure you it is loaded,'' Ariel said calmly. ''But I do hope you won't force him to use it. We have much more interesting plans for you, Kim.''

''Wonderful. Are we going to sit around and read cards?''

''I told you the day of the card reading that you should take the omens seriously. Of course, I knew you wouldn't. But you learned a lesson that night, didn't you, Kim?''

''Why did you do things the hard way the other night, Ariel? Why make your hit man use an antique silver dagger, which, I have on the best authority, isn't a particularly efficient weapon? Stylish, yes. Efficient, no.''

Ariel's mouth hardened and in the glow of the candle flame her eyes seemed to glitter. ''It was important that you die properly. It has been a hundred years since the Dagger has been blooded. You were chosen as its victim.''

''Because I interfered in the kidnapping.'' Kimberly

nodded, as though it all made perfect sense. "Why did you take Scott two months ago? Was he the original choice for the sacrifice?"

"Oh, no. Kidnapping Scott was purely a financial move," Ariel assured her. "We needed the money. It was decreed that Cavenaugh should be the source."

"You mean this magical power of yours can't conjure up something as simple as a credit card?"

That seemed to crack Ariel's unnatural serenity. "It was the power that decided the money should come from the Cavenaughs!"

"But you never got it, did you?"

"We will in time," Ariel declared, calming again. "All will happen as the power said it would happen. In time."

Kimberly glanced at the shadowed faces of the other two people in the room. "Are you guys as crazy as she is? Do you actually believe in all this inane nonsense? Sooner or later, you know, the whole mess is going to cave in on you and you're going to get caught. That turkey who tried to kill me the other night is probably singing his heart out to the cops now!"

"That punk knows nothing," the figure with the gun assured her. "No names, no faces. It was all arranged very carefully. He knew only that he had to do it in the pre-scribed manner, using the Dagger, because he would not be paid otherwise."

"You're out of your mind if you think he won't be able to provide the authorities with some clues. The knife alone is a very big one."

"No one but the Select know the meaning and purpose of the Dagger," Ariel put in evenly. "There are only a few of us in each generation. The secrets are always guarded most carefully. The authorities will learn nothing from the Dagger."

"Where did you get it, Ariel?" Kimberly couldn't think of anything else to do except keep the conversation going. Ariel seemed willing enough to chat about her "power" and the other two seemed totally under her control.

But before Ariel could answer, the phone rang.

Kimberly wasn't the only one who flinched at the unexpected, shrill command of the instrument. The guy with the gun must have jumped an inch, she decided. And the young woman looked momentarily panicked.

Without even having to think about it, Kimberly knew who was on the other end of the line.

"That will be Cavenaugh," she said quite clearly. "He'll be checking to see that I got home safely."

"No!" The sharp denial was from Ariel.

"Of course it is," Kimberly assured her. "Who else would be calling at four in the morning? Why don't you get out your fortune-telling cards and see if I'm right?" The phone rang again, harshly demanding. "The only problem," Kimberly continued, "is that by the time you've dealt the cards to determine who's calling, Cavenaugh will have given up and decided something must be wrong. Knowing him, I expect his next move will be to call the Highway Patrol. With his name and clout he'll probably get them to come check on me."

The phone rang again and the man with the gun was definitely nervous now. He looked at Ariel for guidance.

"We'd better let her answer it, my lady."

Ariel lifted an admonishing hand. "I will decide, Emlyn." Her once-cheerful eyes were full of threat as she nodded brusquely at Kimberly. "Answer it. And be very, very careful what you say, Kim, or I will have Emlyn kill you where you stand. Tell Cavenaugh you're fine. Then get rid of him."

Aware of the other three watching her with violent intensity, Kimberly moved to answer the phone. She was so certain it would be Cavenaugh that she wasn't at all surprised at the sound of his voice. What did surprise her was the urgent concern in his words.

"Kim? Are you all right?"

"I'm fine, Cavenaugh. It was a long drive, but I'm home. I told you there wouldn't be any problem, didn't I?"

"You didn't have the courtesy to tell me a thing," he exploded softly. "You just did a midnight flit without bothering to mention the little fact that you were leaving town."

"You know how writers are, darling. They get the oddest compulsions at the oddest hours. I just had to come back here to finish what I started."

Across the room Ariel glowered at her, motioning her to get off the phone.

"You don't work like that. You work regular hours. What the hell are we discussing your writing for, anyway? You know that's not what's wrong between us. Kim, listen to me. We've got to talk about what happened tonight."

Kimberly steadied herself, deliberately dropping her voice to what she hoped would sound like a sensuous purr to the three people watching her so malevolently. "You know I'll look forward to that. I always enjoy our pillow talk. Remember the last chat we had in bed?"

"Kimberly, you're not making a whole lot of sense. But, yes, I do remember the conversation," Cavenaugh said roughly. "You told me you loved me. Are you trying to tell me that you've realized you still do?"

"Actually, I was referring to the other topic we discussed," she murmured lovingly. Emlyn raised the snout of the gun in a gesture of warning. "I remember how you assured me that you understood. Your understanding would mean a great deal to me right now, Cavenaugh.''

There was a taut silence on the other end of the phone. Kimberly could almost feel Cavenaugh sorting through her words. When he spoke again there was a new edge in his voice, one she had never heard before.

"You were scared that night."

"Yes, darling," she whispered lightly.

"And tonight?"

"Oh, I still feel the same way, Cavenaugh. Even more so."

He swore with soft violence. "How much time have I got?"

Kimberly swallowed. "I don't know how I'll make it through the rest of the night without you," she said, some of the purring quality draining from her voice.

"How many of them?" The question was as hard and cold as a knife blade.

Kimberly swallowed. "I've got three chapters to get done for that deadline. A lot of work so I really must get to bed. It's been a very long, tiring drive. Take care, darling. I'll look forward to seeing you when I've finished *Vendetta*." She hung up the phone before an obviously nervous Emlyn could get any more restless.

The younger woman looked relieved and glanced at Ariel for direction. Ariel nodded. "Tie her up, Zorah, and put her in the bedroom for now. We have preparations to make." She flung a coldly amused look at Kimberly. "It's a good thing you had the sense to keep Darius out of this. Loving him as much as you do, I'm sure you wouldn't want him hurt. Take her away, Zorah. Emlyn, give her a hand and then come back here. There is much to be done before tonight."

Loving him as much as you do. The words played about

in Kimberly's brain as she submitted to having her wrists bound behind her back and her ankles tied. Emlyn supervised the process, his gun never wavering.

Loving him as much as you do. The old witch was right, Kimberly realized as Zorah and Emlyn left the room. Maybe Ariel really did have some power. Kimberly tested her bonds carefully. Her captors had left her trussed up in the middle of her bed.

Loving him as much as you do. There was no point in denying it, Kimberly told herself bleakly as she lay staring at the far wall. Self-honesty seemed appropriate when you found yourself in such dangerous circumstances. She loved Cavenaugh. Perhaps when she had run from the hotel tonight she had only been running from the truth.

She knew she had made him understand that something was wrong but what would he do next, Kimberly wondered. He was probably still back in San Francisco. The only thing he could do was call the local authorities and ask them to check out the situation.

Her fate was in his hands, Kimberly reflected. On the whole, she couldn't imagine trusting anyone other than Cavenaugh with her life.

SEVERAL MILES DOWN THE ROAD Cavenaugh hung up the pay phone in the all-night convenience store and went outside to the waiting Jaguar. So the compelling sense of urgency, which had been governing his actions since the moment he knew he had to go to Kim's room, had been based on something more than the uneasiness left by a lovers' quarrel. He had left the hotel a little more than an hour behind her, but he'd made better time than she had. He was only a half hour from her home.

Cavenaugh yanked open the car door, his mind spinning as he considered the possibilities that lay ahead. Kim had implied there were three people in the house with her. There wasn't much time, but then, there never was in situations like this. He would go into this as prepared as possible. Before starting the engine he leaned down and removed a couple of items from underneath the front seat. The knife he slipped inside his low boot, strapping it to his ankle. He shoved the small, flat, metal box inside the waistband of his jeans so that it lay snug against his spine. Then he turned the key in the ignition and pulled out onto the rain-slicked road.

Given the driving conditions, it should have been a thirty minute trip to Kimberly's beach house. Cavenaugh decided that with a little effort he could make it in twenty. That was a good deal less time than it would take to try and rouse the local authorities into efficient action.

KIMBERLY WAS INCHING HER WAY across the bed, trying to get close to the glass-based bedside lamp when the door to her room opened. The woman called Zorah stood in the doorway. She was holding a small brazier in her hands.

"I didn't phone for room service," Kimberly managed. She was very scared now.

"You are foolish to mock what you do not understand," Zorah informed her softly. She set the brazier down on the floor and knelt in front of it. "But soon you will pay the price. Your life will be forfeited to the Darkness, Kimberly Sawyer."

Kimberly watched uneasily as the woman applied a match to the small pile of coals in the bottom of the pan.

"Look, Zorah, don't you think this has gone far enough? Why don't you get out of it before you're trapped? You know it's only a matter of time before Ariel is discovered. She's not clever enough to cover her tracks or yours for much longer. And after I disappear you can bet Cavenaugh won't stop until he's uncovered the truth."

"Darius Cavenaugh cannot deal with my lady's power," Zorah said serenely.

"What power? Everything Ariel's arranged so far has been screwed up. The kidnapping went wrong. The attempt to kill me fizzled. What makes you think she'll pull off her next trick successfully?"

Zorah glared at her, some of the assured serenity faltering. "She brought you here tonight with her power, didn't she?"

"Not exactly. I think we can write tonight off as one very large coincidence. A coincidence she was shrewd enough to capitalize on. Did she really tell you that she would make me appear this evening?"

"She said we had to come here to your house in order to discover the best method of dealing with you. The emanations of your essence are strongest here where you live, and the power can be wielded most effectively in such an environment."

"But did she actually promise to produce me?" Kimberly prodded. "Or did she just say you'd do a bit of hocus pocus and decide on your next course of action?"

Zorah sprinkled powder from a small leather packet onto the glowing coals and got to her feet. "You are wasting your time trying to put doubts in my head. I believe in my lady's power. Someday she has promised it will be mine!"

Zorah turned and walked out of the room, closing the door firmly behind her. Kimberly lay eyeing the heated coals in the brazier. A strange scent was beginning to permeate the room.

Kimberly inhaled cautiously, wondering what was happening. The fragrance was curiously tantalizing. An herbal smell that was both acrid and sweet. Perhaps it was some sort of ritual, she decided. Turning back on her side she continued her interrupted worm crawl across the bed.

Kimberly had reached the far edge of the quilted surface and was studying the lamp, looking for a way to break the glass base without making too much noise when she began to question her actions. She inhaled deeply, absently enjoying the strange fragrance from the brazier and wondered if this project was worth all the effort she was exerting.

It would be so much easier to close her eyes and rest for a few minutes. Perhaps after she'd had a small nap she would be able to think more clearly about the task of breaking the glass lamp base.

In fact, Kimberly thought critically, why should she even want to break such a lovely piece of glass? It had something to do with a vague notion of using the sharp edges to cut her bonds but that seemed highly unrealistic now.

The herbal scent was filling the room, drifting into the corners, hanging lightly over the bed. Kimberly took another, deeper breath and realized she hadn't felt so relaxed in ages.

It had been a hard night, she decided. She needed to unwind. There had been that confrontation with her grandparents, the quarrel with Cavenaugh and then the long drive through the storm.

The storm.

Outside her bedroom window thunder rolled and lightning crackled over the ocean. The momentary brilliance jarred her. There was something she was supposed to be doing, some task that demanded attention. Glass. It had to do with glass.

Once before she had used broken glass, Kimberly remembered dazedly. She had been defending herself. There had been a silver dagger and a man in robes. Glass. She needed a piece of broken glass.

Ridiculous. Who had any use for broken glass? Gazing over the edge of the bed, Kimberly stared at the coals in the brazier. Such beautiful coals. And they gave off such a lovely fragrance. Too bad Cavenaugh wasn't here so that he could enjoy the aroma with her.

But Cavenaugh was safely in San Francisco. Or was he safe? Her mind drifted around that thought. It wasn't like Cavenaugh to keep himself safe while she was in danger. He was a man who understood responsibility. And he had definite responsibilities toward her.

He was her lover, Kimberly told herself, and he felt it was his job to protect her. So how could he be sitting safely in a hotel room right now? No, he must be coming after her. It was the only logical conclusion.

Danger. Where was the danger? It was so difficult to keep her mind focused on it. Yet when a person was in peril surely her attention should be riveted on it? Somehow it all seemed like such an effort.

Ever since she had begun enjoying the scent of the brazier smoke she had been having a hard time remembering that crazy Ariel Llewellyn was out there in the living room going through who-knew-what nutty rituals. It was even harder to remember that she, Kimberly, was going to play a starring role in the upcoming drama.

Ariel. Ariel and smoke. Ariel knew a lot about herbs. There were those herbal tea concoctions she was always fixing for people. Certain herbs released their power when heated. Kimberly frowned, remembering the packet of powder Zorah had sprinkled on the brazier.

Lightning sparked angrily outside the window, as though demanding Kimberly's attention. For a moment she obeyed, turning her head to gaze out into the darkness. Soon it would be dawn but the storm was raging so wildly it would be a long time before the sky grew light.

Herbs sprinkled on the brazier coals. Cavenaugh making his way through the storm to get to her. Witches and daggers. A ripple of fear pulsed under Kimberly's unnatural relaxation. That smoke was doing this to her, she thought, twisting on the bed. Smoke was dangerous.

Desperately she sought for a new focus of attention. Images of Cavenaugh flashed into her head. Cavenaugh making love to her, holding her, telling her he understood. Cavenaugh forcing her to meet her grandparents. Cavenaugh on the phone tonight, comprehending immediately that she was in real trouble. Cavenaugh, who could almost read her mind at times and who, at other times, infuriated her with his male arrogance. Cavenaugh whom she loved.

He was the reason she had to keep trying to break that glass lamp base, Kimberly realized with sudden clarity. Cavenaugh would expect her to at least try. But that damned smoke was so overpowering. Desperately Kimberly twisted, knocking her shoulder against the end table.

The crash of the lamp as it fell to the floor coincided with the opening of her bedroom door. The destruction of the bulb left only the glow of the brazier coals for light. In the sudden darkness Kimberly heard people moving around.

"What the hell have you done to her?"

It was Cavenaugh's voice, Kimberly realized dreamily. "Ah, Cavenaugh. I knew you'd get here. What took you so long?"

The light from the hall shafted through the haze in the room, providing just enough illumination for Kimberly to see that Cavenaugh was not alone. Emlyn was behind him.

"Oh, dear. They got you, too," she whispered sadly. "I'm so sorry, Cavenaugh. I think I made a mistake tonight."

"You've drugged her with this goddamned smoke," Cavenaugh said somewhere in the haze.

"She'll live until tonight. Just thought we'd give her a little something to keep her quiet. She's the kind who would have made trouble. Wonder why she pushed that lamp over? Oh, well, if she wants to lie here in the darkness, that's her problem. Get on the bed. Zorah, tie his ankles. And be careful."

"Do you think it's safe to leave both of them here together?" Zorah asked.

"The smoke will keep them under control. Besides, where else can we put him? Ariel won't want him watching her preparation rituals."

Kimberly felt the bed give beside her as Cavenaugh obediently allowed Zorah to finish binding him. A moment later the two had left the room, leaving Kimberly and her companion in smoky darkness.

"Kim, are you all right?"

"The smoke," she tried to explain sleepily.

"Yeah, I know." He was moving, sitting up beside her and shifting around. "Wake up, honey. This will go a lot faster if you help. That smoke will get to me soon."

"Help? How?"

"There's a knife inside my boot. Turn around so you can reach down and pull it out."

Kimberly struggled to concentrate as he urged her onto her side. She felt his leg and then the leather of one boot. Behind her back her fingers fumbled awkwardly.

"Why did you let them get you?" she whispered unhappily. "I didn't want them to get you, Cavenaugh."

"I had to let them take me. I had no way of knowing where you were or what they might have already done to you. So I just walked up to the front door and pretended total ignorance."

"Quite a surprise seeing Ariel, wasn't it?" For some reason that seemed inordinately funny. Kimberly giggled and her fingers slid off the boot.

Cavenaugh swore. "When I think of harboring her under my roof for the past twelve months…Kim, stop it," he ordered harshly.

"I'm sorry," she mumbled guiltily. "Didn't mean to laugh. Just seemed funny."

"Get the knife!"

The command in his voice cut through her foggy senses. Another moment of clarity returned and Kimberly managed to get her fingers inside his boot. She felt the handle of the knife and tugged.

"That's it, honey," he said approvingly. Then he coughed. "Now hold it as firmly as you can. And be careful, it's very, very sharp."

"I'm not a little kid. I know about sharp knives," she informed him loftily. But obediently Kimberly held the knife firmly. She was vaguely aware of him turning around so that he could rub his bonds against the sharp blade but her mind was on another matter.

"About the mistake I made this evening, Cavenaugh."

"We both made a few. We'll talk about it later," he gritted. "Damn it, Kim, hold the knife still!"

"You're always telling me what to do," she said with a sigh, but instinctively she responded to his orders and tightened her grip on the knife handle.

"You'll get used to it."

A moment later something gave and Cavenaugh moved away from her. She heard him cough again and through the shadows saw him rip the pillowcase off one pillow. Holding the material over his mouth, he quickly freed his ankles. Seconds later he was kneeling on the bed, opening the window behind it.

The cold, wet air rushed into the room and into Kimberly's brain, clearing it a little. The strange sense of amusement she had been feeling faded rapidly as the effects of the smoke subsided. Panic returned. Then Cavenaugh was working on her bonds, slicing through them with efficient ease.

"Now what?" she whispered, gulping in the fresh air. Her brain still felt very foggy.

"Now we get out of here."

But even as Cavenaugh pushed her toward the window, the hall door opened. Light poured into the room.

"They're getting away!" Zorah screamed.

CHAPTER TEN

"LET'S GO, KIM," Cavenaugh ordered. "She's not armed. Hurry!"

Kimberly tried frantically to obey him, scrabbling for the windowsill. But the smoke seemed to have played tricks not only with her brain but with her body. She felt oddly lethargic still, and her muscles refused to coordinate with her mind.

"My lady!" Zorah screamed, "They're escaping!"

"Come on, Kim, *move*." Cavenaugh reached for Kimberly's arm, trying to push her through the open window, but she was unable to cooperate in her own escape. Every movement seemed to require incredible effort.

"Cavenaugh, I can't...!"

"Goddamn it, Kim!" Cavenaugh grabbed her, trying to forcibly stuff her through the window. He was interrupted by another voice from the doorway.

"You shall not escape the power this time!" Ariel's shrill screech of fury was backed up a second later by Emlyn's uneasy command.

"Stop where you are, Cavenaugh, or I'll shoot the woman."

"Which woman?" Cavenaugh asked, sounding vastly annoyed. "Right now all three of them are giving me a headache."

But he reluctantly stopped trying to push Kimberly

through the window and stepped down off the bed to face Emlyn's gun.

The smoke from the brazier continued to waft through the room. It was diluted now by the effects of the open window and door but it had not completely dissipated.

Kimberly remained on the bed, her legs feeling shaky as she stared at the three people in the doorway. "Aren't these about the poorest excuses for witches you've ever seen, Cavenaugh?" she muttered.

"Yeah," Cavenaugh agreed, his eyes narrowed on Emlyn's gun. "Pretty poor. Kim, stay right where you are."

"You have mocked the power one too many times," Ariel shrieked at Kim. She lifted her hands high above her head. The full sleeves of her robe fell back revealing a variety of odd bracelets on her wrists.

"Uh, my lady," Emlyn began with what Cavenaugh thought was superb diplomacy under the circumstances. "Perhaps we should wait until later?"

"Let her teach the bitch a lesson," Zorah interrupted fiercely. "Call up the power, my lady! Let the darkness rain on her. Let her see what it is she mocks!"

Oh hell, thought Cavenaugh. Looking straight at Emlyn he said coolly, "This whole scene is getting a little out of hand, isn't it? Maybe it's time for you to split. I think you can write off any money you might have been hoping to see."

Emlyn glowered first at Cavenaugh and then at Ariel who was still standing with her hands raised above her head. The older woman had shut her eyes, her face twisted intensely. She was beginning to chant.

"Let the power that dwells in the depths of darkness come forth to answer the challenge of this foolish creature of light," Ariel intoned while Zorah watched in anticipation. "Let that which lives on the fringes of the universe and in the center of the Earth rise to smash the impudent being.''

"Cavenaugh…" Kim began uneasily and then closed her mouth. This was nothing but a crazy woman's act. It was probably just the remnants of the smoke lingering in her head that made Ariel seem so menacing.

Cavenaugh ignored the new fear he heard in Kim's voice. Right now the only one who held any real power was the guy with the gun, and Emlyn was looking distinctly unhappy. That didn't make him any less dangerous.

"My lady," the male witch tried again, "I think it would be better if we saved this bit for another time."

"Shut up!" Zorah hissed.

Ariel's voice was rising in intensity now, filling the room as she chanted.

"All that answers to me; all that I have chained and bound according to the ancient laws, hear me now!" Ariel called.

"Hear her," Zorah echoed fervently, her eyes glittering with excitement. "As her handmaiden I, too, call on that which is raw power!"

Kimberly shuddered and didn't know if the shiver was caused by the cold night air pouring into the room or Ariel's chanting. But she obeyed Cavenaugh and stayed very still on the bed.

Emlyn moved uneasily. "Zorah, stop her, we've got to get these two under control. She can use her witchcraft later!"

Zorah turned on him violently, her eyes wild. "Hush! You are only a man. You will never understand the depths of the power you serve. Leave my lady alone!"

Ariel droned on, oblivious to the conversation. "Out of the bottom of the pit of darkness, gathering the forces of the ancient magic as it rises, lifting up into the surface

world, flooding in from the farthest reaches of emptiness..."

Cavenaugh slanted a glance at Kimberly who was still
sitting on the bed. At least she was staying put although
she appeared half-mesmerized by Ariel's chant. When he
made his move he didn't want her getting in the way.

"The time has come," Ariel shrieked. "Fill this space,
oh spirits of the great void, fill it with fire and darkness
and destruction..."

"Zorah," Emlyn snapped, "this has gone far enough.
She's nuttier than a fruitcake. Stop her!"

"You, too, shall suffer for mockery and disobedience!"
Zorah promised him. "Only my lady and I will be left
alive in this room!"

"*Now!*" Ariel yelled. "Let it be now!"

"*Now!*" Zorah screamed, lifting her own arms high
above her head.

Emlyn lost patience and reached out to grab one of Ariel's raised arms. "Stop it, you dumb broad!"

"Don't touch her, you fool!" Zorah shouted. "The
power is flowing now!"

It might as well flow now, Cavenaugh decided, agreeing
silently with the woman. Emlyn's full attention was on
dealing with Ariel and Zorah. There wasn't going to be a
better opportunity.

With a quick movement Cavenaugh reached behind his
back and withdrew the flat metal case that he had concealed there.

"The moment of power is here!" Ariel cried out.

"Let it be now!" Zorah yelped, trying to fend off Emlyn.

"You've got it, ladies," Cavenaugh muttered and hurled
the flat case at the feet of the trio in the doorway.

An instant later brilliant, blinding light flashed through

the room. Screams from everyone except Cavenaugh
echoed from one end of the house to the other as each
sought to cover his or her eyes. Cavenaugh had already
prudently covered his own eyes with his hand. He counted
to five and then opened them.

The fiery white light produced by the exploding chemical compound in the case was still blazing but the initial
brilliance had faded. Cavenaugh was careful to keep from
looking directly at the case as he leaped across the room.

Seconds later he reached Emlyn who was shouting idi-
otically. The gun lay on the floor where it had been
dropped during the first shock of the explosion. Zorah was
screaming.

"My eyes! My eyes!" Emlyn yelled. "I can't see."

Ariel seemed stunned. She fell back, reeling, holding her
hands protectively out in front of her. Temporarily blinded,
she stared sightlessly at what she must have been convinced she had just unleashed.

Kimberly was still on the bed, her palms over her eyes.
"Cavenaugh!"

"Right here, Kim. It's okay. You'll be able to see in a
couple of minutes."

"Oh, my God, Cavenaugh, what happened?" She lowered her hands to her sides, her head turned in the direction
of his voice.

Cavenaugh looked at his brave, temporarily blinded
witch. "Everything's under control, honey. I've got the
gun."

She blinked rapidly a few times. "I can't see!"

"It's just the light. You'll be all right soon," he soothed
as he grabbed Emlyn and began tying the man's hands
behind his back with the rope belt that Emlyn had worn.
Soon the still-stunned Ariel was secured. He was working

on Zorah when Kimberly got shakily up off the bed. She was still blinking rapidly.

"That's a hell of an act, Cavenaugh. You should take it on the road," she murmured, still sounding shocked. "You never told me you were into witchcraft, yourself."

He smiled grimly as he finished tying Zorah's wrists. "You learn a lot in the import-export business."

"So I see. I think I've asked this before, but what exactly did you import?"

"I'll tell you later. How are your eyes?"

She shook her head as if to clear it. But when she looked at him Kimberly was focusing almost normally. "Okay, I think. Geez, Cavenaugh, what was that stuff?"

"A chemical powder that reacts with oxygen. When the case is broken the chemical explodes in a bright flash."

"Like a small bomb," she said in awe. "I could use that in a book."

"Be my guest. How are you feeling?"

"Odd."

"Yeah, you look a little odd. Get some water from the bathroom and put out the coals in that brazier."

Kimberly looked at the still-glowing brazier and then nodded obediently. She walked into the bath and returned a moment later with a drinking glass full of water. Very carefully she poured the contents over the coals. There was a hissing sound and a small cloud of steam.

"Now go call the cops," Cavenaugh ordered distinctly.

Kimberly started out of the room and then stopped for a moment in front of Ariel. The older woman's eyes were wet with tears.

"She's crying, Cavenaugh."

"Yes, so she is," Cavenaugh said gently. "Go make the phone call, Kim."

"IT'S ALL SO SAD," Kimberly said several hours later as she reached into her cupboard and pulled out a bottle of Cavenaugh Riesling. "Aunt Milly is going to be crushed when she hears how Ariel was deceiving her."

Cavenaugh took the bottle from her and inserted a corkscrew. With a smooth, thoroughly expert movement, he removed the cork and started pouring the wine. "I don't feel so good about it myself. When I think of how none of us suspected what a fruitcake Ariel really was, I get cold chills." He swore softly and took a large swallow of wine from one of the two glasses he's just filled. "What a fool I was."

Kimberly watched him from under her lashes. This was the first time they had been alone since the authorities had come to collect Ariel and her pals. There had been endless questions and statements and explanations. But finally everyone had left.

"I know how you must feel," Kimberly said softly as she picked up her own glass of wine. "But no one realized what she was really like."

He looked at her broodingly. "It was my responsibility to protect my family and you. I blew it."

Kimberly picked up a platter of cheese and French bread she had prepared. "Nonsense. You saved us all. And I for one am extremely grateful." She led the way over to the two chairs in front of the fireplace. "You do realize what was on the agenda for me this evening? Ariel was going to make me the star attraction in her first sacrifice ceremony. Nothing like being a guinea pig in some witch's act." She shuddered and flopped back in one of the chairs.

Cavenaugh followed slowly, pausing to stoke up the fire he had started an hour earlier. For a moment he stood staring down into the flames. "Are you sure you feel okay?"

"What? Oh, you mean am I suffering any aftereffects

of that herb Ariel used on me. No, I'm fine, really I am. As brilliantly clear-headed as I've ever been."

His mouth crooked faintly in spite of his mood. "I'm not certain that's very reassuring."

Kimberly grinned briefly. "Poor Cavenaugh. You've had a rough time of it lately, haven't you? And all because of me."

"I wasn't the only male who was having trouble with females this morning. I almost felt a twinge of sympathy for poor Emlyn."

"Emlyn!"

"Well, he was only playing at being a witch because he really thought Ariel's plan for kidnapping Scott would work. After it fell apart, I guess she convinced him she had another scheme up her sleeve. It must have been a shock when he realized what a real nut she was."

"I wonder how he and Zorah met Ariel."

"The cops are wondering, too. They promised to let me know the whole story when they've finished dredging it out of those three. The first thing they'll have to do is find out Emlyn and Zorah's real names!"

"I thought they sounded a bit on the theatrical side," Kimberly noted. "How did Ariel become such friends with Aunt Milly?"

Cavenaugh's face hardened. "They met in a garden club." He winced. "I can still remember Milly telling me what a 'magical' touch Ariel had with herbs."

"She does know a lot about them. Probably from studying all sorts of arcane books. Ariel really feels she's this generation's keeper of some sort of witchcraft mysteries. I'll have to work her into a book...."

"Just as long as you don't feel you have to do any hands-on research," Cavenaugh growled forbiddingly.

Kimberly's response was a yawn that she barely managed to cover. "My God, I'm exhausted. You must be, too."

"I am. In spite of what you may be thinking, this really has been a slightly abnormal day, even for members of the Cavenaugh household," Cavenaugh said with real feeling.

Kimberly smiled briefly and then fixed him with a very earnest expression. "But it's all over now. You've more than kept your promise. You've fulfilled the responsibility you felt you had toward me. I want you to know that, Cavenaugh. You don't owe me anything else." It was important to her that he understood he was free in that sense, Kimberly realized. "You've kept your promise."

"My promise to take care of you? Kim, I want to talk to you about that." He walked over to the other overstuffed chair and lowered himself into it.

Kimberly watched him obliquely. She liked watching him, she reflected. There was an easy, masculine grace in his movements, even when he was simply taking a seat.

"What's to talk about?" she tried to ask lightly. "It's over. You've done what you said you'd do. And without a lot of help from me, either," she added wryly.

"You did your part," he interjected.

Kimberly took another sip of wine. "Thank you for coming after me, Cavenaugh. You saved my life." She didn't meet his eyes, her gaze on the fire instead.

"I owed you any protection I could give you," he returned bluntly.

"Why?"

"Why?" He frowned. "For a lot of reasons. Because of what you did for Scott, naturally, and because you're my—"

"No, I mean, why did you follow me from San Francisco?"

"Oh, that." Cavenaugh hesitated. "Well, there are a

number of reasons for that, too. I didn't get much sleep last night. None at all, in fact. And somewhere around two in the morning I had the feeling something was really wrong.''

"More of your telepathy?" she mused.

"It wasn't telepathy. Just the restless brain of a man who knows he's handled something very badly."

She flicked him a wary glance. "You're referring to the way you set up that meeting with my grandparents?"

"I didn't handle it well, Kim. I admit it. My only excuse is that I honestly thought I was dealing with a difficult situation in the most efficient manner. I thought…I thought that after you got over the shock and had a chance to put it all in perspective you'd realize I'd done the right thing. I see now that I had no business springing it on you like that."

"Was it so very important that I be made to confront my grandparents, Cavenaugh?" she asked quietly.

"Yes," he said flatly. "I saw your relationship with them as the last barrier between us."

"You were really that worried about the fact your current bed partner had a mental block when it came to dealing with powerful families?"

He looked at her until she was compelled to switch her gaze from the fire to his face. The emerald eyes gleamed with a relentlessness that astonished Kimberly.

"I was not concerned about my current bed partner's feelings toward families. I was concerned with how my future *wife* dealt with the issue."

"Your wife!"

"I'm asking you to marry me, Kim. I was only waiting until we'd gotten the meeting with your grandparents out of the way."

She swallowed uncomfortably as her fingers tightened

around the stem of her wineglass. Eyes wide, she stared at him. "Cavenaugh, you don't have to go that far out of some misguided sense of responsibility."

"I know you're not much interested in marriage, Kim," he returned softly. "You've gotten along fine for years without anything that really resembles a family. After pushing you into that meeting with your grandparents, you probably haven't changed your mind much. Especially when it comes to overbearing, arrogant males who happen to be heads of families. But I know that if you'll give us a chance we'll be good together in a lot of ways, not just in bed. I also know that I am not in a position to install a live-in lover in my household. Having you for a guest will work for a while, but quite soon everyone's going to want to know when I intend to marry you. Your grandfather will probably be at the head of the line demanding explanations."

Kimberly sat very still, totally unable to read his mind at all now. "I don't particularly care what my grandparents think."

Cavenaugh sighed. "No, I don't suppose you do." There was a long period of silence. "You said once that you loved me. I realize you've had some, uh, second thoughts thanks to the way I forced you into that scene with your grandparents."

"I have done some thinking," Kimberly admitted cautiously. She remembered that under the influence of the herbal smoke she had been trying to tell Cavenaugh that she had made a mistake. He hadn't had time to listen then and so she had not told him that she still loved him, in spite of the scene in San Francisco. Perhaps it was just as well. After all, she had no real idea of how deep his feelings went for her.

Except for the fact that he's asking you to marry him,

she reminded herself. That didn't mean he was in love with her, of course. He was attracted to her and he felt a strong sense of responsibility toward her. Cavenaugh might also have found her useful in organizing his household. What was it Starke had said? Something about Cavenaugh needing a woman who could occasionally protect him from his own sense of duty.

"Sitting here now reminds me of that evening I came to get you, after you'd phoned the house a couple of times," Cavenaugh mused. "You were just as wary and cautious then as you are at the moment."

He was right, Kimberly thought. She was wary. But for different reasons. Falling in love with Darius Cavenaugh had been a dangerous thing to do. It left her vulnerable in a way she had never been before. She wished desperately that she really could see into his head. What was he thinking, she wondered. How did he feel? How long would it take him to fall in love with her? Or would his feelings always be limited to a combination of duty, responsibility and attraction?

"I think," she began hesitantly, choosing her words carefully, "that we need more time."

To her surprise, he nodded and lifted his glass to his mouth. "I agree with you. We need time for you to get to know me well enough to trust me again. Unfortunately, time is not something I have a great deal of to spend as I choose. You've lived in my house for several days. You know what it's like. Someone or something is always needing attention. It would be hard just trying to get away to see you on occasional weekends. And I don't want to limit our time together to just weekends."

"A life full of responsibilities," she said thoughtfully, more to herself than to him.

"It's the life I've chosen, Kim. Or perhaps it chose me.

I don't know and it doesn't matter. That's the way it is. That's the way I am.'' His voice had roughened and it seemed to her that the emerald in his eyes was lit with implacableness.

''And you want me to be a part of that life?''

''I think you can be happy in it if you'll give yourself a chance. I know it will be a change for you and I know there will be adjustments. But you've already proven you can handle the day-to-day hassle. You've taken control of it rather than let it control you. Things are so much more organized at home now and they'll be even calmer when Julia and Scott move out. You can have all the privacy you need for your work. I'll make certain the staff understands that. I'm asking you to make changes, I know, but I think that a woman who is brave enough to taunt a witch and face an attacker with only a broken wine bottle in her hand is brave enough to risk a new life-style.''

''Cavenaugh, I think…''

He lifted a hand to silence her. ''Let me finish, Kim. I said I understand your need for time, and I'm proposing to give it to you.''

''How? You've just said you would find it uncomfortable to install me as your live-in lover,'' she gritted, thoroughly irritated with the description.

''I'm asking that you marry me. In return I'll give you the time you want.''

She looked at him blankly for a second, not comprehending. And then it hit her. ''Oh, I see.'' She was suddenly, inexplicably embarrassed. ''We'll, uh, have separate bedrooms after we're married?''

Cavenaugh took a very long swallow of wine. Kimberly had the feeling he was nerving himself up for something. ''I thought it would take some of the pressure off you,'' he explained evenly. "I realize that for you the sex is more than just, well, pleasant."

"Pleasant?" she repeated faintly, wondering how going to bed with Darius Cavenaugh could ever be described by such a mundane word as *pleasant*. "Is that all it is for you?"

"No!" The glass in his hand suddenly appeared very fragile as his knuckles whitened around it. "You know damn well it's not just pleasant. Now let me finish!"

Kimberly arched an eyebrow but kept her peace. It was becoming clear that Cavenaugh was straying near the bounds of his normally excellent self-control. She wondered why. Perhaps it had something to do with the fact that he hadn't had any sleep in the past twenty-four hours.

"As I was trying to say," he went on, "I am aware of the fact that you give a great deal of yourself when you go to bed with me. To be blunt you give yourself completely." His eyes locked with hers as if daring her to deny it. Kimberly again kept her mouth shut and covered the uncomfortable moment with another sip of wine. Cavenaugh continued cautiously. "I feel that asking you to share my bed would be putting an added strain on you while you settle down in my household as my wife. It might make you feel too vulnerable, too committed to something you weren't yet really sure you wanted."

"And you don't think just the existence of the wedding license would put a similar sort of strain on me?" Kimberly inquired far too politely. "Are you trying to tell me that if I decided I don't like being married to you I will be free to walk out the door? That I will feel free to do so because we're not sleeping together?"

Cavenaugh set down his wineglass with an audible snap. "Don't twist my words, Kim!"

"I'm not twisting them. I'm only trying to figure out what they mean!"

He surged to his feet, striding over to stand in front of the hearth. With one hand resting on the mantel he turned to glower at her. "I don't see how I can make the matter much clearer. I'm asking you to marry me. I'm sorry if I'm botching up the job but this is the first time I've tried it."

"You're nearly forty years old and you've never asked a woman to marry you?" she asked disbelievingly.

"Up until two years ago I wasn't particularly interested in marriage. There was no room in my life for a permanent woman. Since then I've been too busy trying to put the winery back on its feet financially," he explained harshly.

"And now you've come to realize that it's time you married," she concluded with a nod of comprehension. "You have, after all, a responsibility to continue the family line, right? People will expect you to marry. You'll need a wife to lend the proper background to your role as an established, prosperous vintner. And, of course, I now have a thoroughly respectable background myself, thanks to your tracking down my grandparents."

He watched her through narrowed eyes, his lean body dangerously poised. "I warned you not to twist my words, Kim."

"I'm just trying to get all the details straight," she flung back, feeling increasingly incensed. "So far I can see what's in it for you, but I'm not sure what's in it for me."

"You need a husband!" he blazed. "You need me!"

"I do?"

He moved toward her with unnerving intent, reaching down to pull her up out of the chair. Cavenaugh's emerald eyes reminded Kim of a bird of prey, and quite suddenly she knew she had goaded him too far.

"Cavenaugh, wait...!"

His hands closed around her waist, holding her securely. "Little witch," he muttered, "you don't know when to stop, do you? Did you think you could just sit there and provoke me indefinitely?"

Before she could respond, his mouth was crushing hers. Kimberly stood trapped in his arms and let the storm of his emotion break over her. The frustration and implacable determination she sensed in him told her more than words could have just how close he was to the end of his tether.

The strange thing was that her instincts were to yield and soothe rather than resist. Kimberly parted her lips obediently when he demanded entrance to the warmth of her mouth and she let her body sway against his. Cavenaugh moved his hands up to cradle her head. His low groan of need and hunger reverberated through his chest, touching her at a deep level of awareness. He wanted her. She knew that with a certainty that went beyond words.

His tongue probed deeply, simulating the primitive rhythm of lovemaking until Kimberly moaned softly in response. Then she felt his teeth nip at her lower lip with passionate care. Keeping one palm wrapped around the nape of her neck, Cavenaugh ran his other hand down her back to her buttocks, pulling her up and into the heat of his lower body.

"You have a talent for driving me crazy," he rasped against the curve of her throat.

"Cavenaugh, listen to me," Kimberly pleaded with the last remnants of her intelligence. "This is dangerous. Neither of us is in any condition to handle a major discussion about our future right now. I'm sorry if I've provoked you. But the truth is both of us need sleep and...and some time to think. We're exhausted and we've been through some very traumatic scenes in the past twenty-four hours."

"I've tried to reason with you," he growled, his fingers on the buttons of her blouse. "And I've tried to set up an unthreatening situation. But you're determined to resist every inch of the way."

"That's not true!"

"Yes, it is. But I know one way you won't fight me. Like I said earlier, when you're in my arms, you give yourself completely. I'm going to make love to you until you can't say anything but 'yes, Cavenaugh,' until you're shivering and hot and completely mine." His hands were moving inside the parted edges of her shirt.

"Is this what I could expect if I agree to your proposal? If I marry you will you immediately forget your promise to give me some time before demanding your conjugal rights?"

There was a moment of lethal stillness. Kimberly realized belatedly that she was holding her breath. And then Cavenaugh slowly raised his head to look down at her with eyes that were dark and dangerously enigmatic.

"Lady, you sure know how to walk a risky line." His hands fell away from her, and he moved slowly back to stand in front of the fire. "You'd better go to bed, Kim," he went on in an unnaturally level voice. "I'll sleep out here on the couch. I know where the blankets are."

Kimberly trembled with love and emotion. She could feel the leashed emotion in him even though she couldn't be certain just what those emotions were. The intensity of his manner ate at her heart and she longed to comfort him. But there was a self-protective wariness in her, too. Cavenaugh had the power to hurt her as no one else could. And she was still uncertain of his underlying feelings for her.

He was asking her to take all the risks, Kimberly told herself as she watched the rigid line of his back. No, that wasn't strictly true. Whatever he felt for her, it was not superficial. She knew that with her deepest instincts. While she couldn't actually read his mind, she did know that the intensity and power of his commitment was genuine. He would be a strong, dependable, honorable husband. And she loved him.

"Cavenaugh," Kimberly whispered, "I'll marry you."

He swung around, his gaze piercing in the soft light. But he made no move toward her. A curious tension hovered between them.

"You're sure? Be sure, Kim, because I won't let you change your mind in the morning."

She shook her head. "I won't change my mind."

He took a deep breath and inclined his head almost formally. "I will do my best to make you happy, Kim."

In spite of her tension, Kimberly found herself smiling. "Yes, I think you will. And I'll try to make you a good wife, Cavenaugh."

They stood quietly for a long moment, absorbing the impact of their simple promises to each other. And then Kimberly turned to walk down the hall to her bedroom.

"Good night," she said, not quite knowing what else to say. It was obvious he didn't intend to follow her.

"Good night, Kim."

She was almost at the door of her bedroom when his voice stopped her once more.

"Kim?"

Her head came up quickly. Had he changed his mind about sleeping with her? She would welcome him, she thought. She would welcome him with all her heart.

"I think you should invite your grandparents to the wedding, Kim."

Kimberly's mouth curved wryly and she lifted silently beseeching eyes heavenward.

"You don't know when to quit, do you, Cavenaugh?" She slammed the door of her bedroom behind her.

CHAPTER ELEVEN

STARKE HAD IGNORED the wedding champagne and concentrated on whiskey most of the evening. Kimberly decided he'd had enough to put him in one of his philosophical moods, and when she found herself momentarily alone she decided to talk to him.

Holding her champagne glass in one hand she lifted the skirts of her wedding gown with the other and moved quickly across the crowded room.

"Enjoying yourself, Starke?" She smiled.

His craggy face cracked into a genuine grin. "Would you believe this is only the second wedding I've been to in my entire life?"

"When was the first?"

"My own."

"Oh." Kimberly tilted her head, uncertain about whether or not to pry further. "Somehow, I don't see you married," she ventured.

"Neither did I. But I was only nineteen and the girl claimed she was pregnant." He shrugged his massive shoulders. "I thought I ought to do the right thing."

"But she wasn't pregnant?" Kimberly hazarded.

"No. And my wife quickly decided that marriage wasn't all it was made out to be. Not when you're nineteen and stone broke. We split by mutual agreement within six months."

"I see."

He gave her a sharp glance. "Hey, you're not drawing any parallels here, are you? Believe me, if you're pregnant, Dare's going to be thrilled!"

Kimberly felt the blush stain her cheeks and concentrated determinedly on the cluster of men across the room. Cavenaugh, austerely formal in his conservative wedding jacket and ruffled shirt, was the focus of the laughing, jesting group.

She was married to him now, Kimberly had to remind herself. Tied to him with vows and a band of gold. But she felt more nervously uncertain about his true feelings and thoughts tonight than she had at any point during the entire time she had known him.

It was no wonder she was so apprehensive. For the past six weeks they had seen relatively little of each other. Kimberly had stayed in her beach house working on *Vendetta*, and Cavenaugh had only come to see her on the weekends. When he was there he had slept on the sofa. On the one or two occasions when she had spent a weekend at his home, he had kissed her good night at her bedroom door.

She did not fully understand his restraint or the rather cautious, distant way he treated her. Kimberly knew it probably had something to do with Cavenaugh's determination not to "pressure" her. But she couldn't help wondering if he intended to spend his wedding night in his own bedroom. There was no telling how far Cavenaugh would let his sense of responsibility and duty take him.

"Kim?" Starke's voice held a note of concern. "Don't look so uneasy. Dare won't mind at all."

"Mind what?" She pulled her attention away from her husband's hard-edged profile.

"If you're pregnant."

"That's very reassuring," she said with commendable lightness, "but as it happens, I'm not."

"Oh. Too bad. Dare should have a couple of kids."

"To, uh, carry on the Cavenaugh name?" Kimberly asked dryly.

"No, just because he'd make a good father."

Kimberly peered at her oblivious husband. "Do you think so?"

"Yeah. Your grandparents would love some, too. They're having a good time tonight, aren't they?" Starke glanced with satisfaction to the far edge of the crowd where Wesley Marland and his wife were chatting enthusiastically with Aunt Milly and several of her friends. Starke was right. They were delighted with the wedding, embarrassingly grateful to have been invited. And they would adore a couple of grandchildren.

"Cavenaugh made me invite them, you know," Kimberly confided after another sip of champagne. "Or perhaps I should say he strongly advised it."

"Dare wanted to tie up all the loose ends," Starke said bluntly. "He's like that. How are you getting along with the Marlands?"

"With cautious politeness," Kimberly admitted honestly.

"Well, look at it this way," Starke advised, "some people don't even have a cautiously polite relationship with their relatives!"

"I suppose you're right."

"Do you really hate them?"

Kimberly thought about that for a split second and then shook her head. "No." It was the truth. She still wasn't certain how she felt about her grandparents but she knew she didn't hate them. Perhaps she was simply too much in love with Cavenaugh to have any emotion left over for something as useless as hate.

"I told Dare he was an idiot to force you into meeting

them," Starke informed her, sipping his whiskey. "But maybe he was right. Maybe it was the most efficient way of handling the situation. Dare's instincts are usually pretty solid."

"Uh-huh, well, if he ever springs a surprise like that on me again, I'll probably break his neck."

"I don't think you'll have to worry about Dare doing anything so risky for a long while," Starke said consideringly. "He's been handling you with kid gloves for the past six weeks."

Kimberly bit her lip, knowing Starke was right and knowing, too, that she didn't really want that kind of cautious treatment from Cavenaugh. Determinedly she changed the subject.

"Aunt Milly finally seems recovered from the shock of finding out Ariel was the villain of the piece. I was afraid she was going to go on blaming herself indefinitely for what happened."

"Dare wouldn't let her do that," Starke said with a wryly crooked mouth. "He insisted on taking all the blame himself."

"He's big on assuming responsibility." Kimberly sighed.

"It's in his blood," Starke opined. "Comes naturally to him. Some men are like that."

Kimberly slanted him a sardonic glance. "Is that so?"

"Yeah. But there's a price tag attached."

"What do you mean?"

Starke hesitated, as if trying to find the best way of saying what he had to say. "Men who have the guts to handle a lot of responsibility usually have the, well, uh, the *assertiveness* it takes to make sure things get done right."

"Assertiveness?" Kimberly tasted the word. "You mean the arrogance, the overbearing, domineering, stub-

born machismo that it takes to railroad everyone into doing
things the way said male wants them done?''

Starke looked pleased at her understanding. ''Something
like that.''

''Forget assertiveness. Tell me about the dagger. What
did you ever find out about it?''

Starke shrugged. ''Dare was right. Some of our old contacts in the import business finally recognized it. The design dates back a few centuries to a style that was used in
Europe at one time by people who called themselves
witches.''

''How did Ariel get hold of it?'' Kimberly asked.

''This particular dagger wasn't really old. It's a copy.
Ariel apparently found a drawing in one of her occult
books and took it to a knifemaker who made it up for her.
We would have eventually found the guy who did it. There
aren't that many good custom knifemakers around. But we
wouldn't have found him in time.''

''Did the authorities ever find out how Zorah and Emlyn
came to be involved with Ariel?''

''Zorah's real name is Charlotte Martin. Emlyn's name
is Joseph Williams.''

Kimberly grimaced. ''So much for the exotic names.
Ariel's doing, no doubt.''

''She ran into them when she was exploring sources for
some of the herbs she was always experimenting with.
Charlotte ran an herb shop and Joe was her boyfriend. Poor
Charlotte really wanted to believe in Ariel's power and the
possibility of having it passed on to her. Joe was far more
practical about the situation. He's the kind of guy who will
always be looking for a fast buck. He thought Ariel's kidnapping plans might work. When they didn't he stuck
around because he still thought there was a possibility of
getting money out of Dare. When Ariel said they had to

kill you he went along with it because you were the only one who could identify Charlotte. You'd seen her face to face at the house the day you rescued Scott.''

Kimberly shuddered. "So they hired some street punk to do the job. Ariel was the one who let him onto the grounds that night, I suppose.''

Starke nodded. "Luckily Ariel insisted it had to be done in a ceremonial fashion. She's the one who said he wouldn't get paid unless he wore the right outfit and used the proper weapon. The punk is still complaining about the limitations she put on him, according to Cranston.''

"All of which probably saved my life that night." Kimberly shook her head ruefully. "What a situation.''

"Going to get a book out of it?''

"You bet!''

"I like your books," Starke told her seriously. "That Josh Valerian guy's a little strange, but I like the stories.''

"What's wrong with Josh?'' Kimberly demanded.

"Well, he's not exactly realistic," Starke said carefully. "I mean, all that business about being able to understand the heroine isn't so weird. But having him always feel the same way about things, see them in the same way she does. That's weird.''

"You think so?'' Kimberly asked wistfully.

"Yup. Valerian's supposed to be a man. Men don't see things quite the same way women do. Nearly drove Dare crazy trying to figure out how he could compete with a fantasy.''

"He managed," Kimberly shot back dryly.

"Does Dare know that?''

Kimberly glanced up at him quizzically. "I think so,'' she said very seriously.

"Then why's he acting so carefully around you?''

"You noticed?''

"Who hasn't?"

"Your guess is as good as mine," Kimberly said evenly. Then she told herself that now was as good a time as any to ask a question that had been on her mind. She gauged the amount of whiskey Starke had had to drink and decided to take the plunge. "I've been wondering about something, Starke," she began with deceptive lightness.

"Hmm?"

"What is it exactly that you and Cavenaugh imported and exported?"

Starke blinked owlishly. "Stuff."

"What kind of stuff?"

"Junk. Trinkets, jewelry, odd things from different corners of the world. Cavenaugh bought whatever took his fancy and whatever he thought he could sell."

"Starke, why do I have the feeling you are not being one hundred percent straightforward with me?"

"Uh, I think Cavenaugh is trying to get your attention."

"Starke…" She gave up. "I think I'd like more champagne."

"What a coincidence," Starke said brightly. "Here comes Dare and he's carrying two glasses."

Cavenaugh's emerald eyes seemed to glitter with a curious intensity as he took in the sight of his wife, but his voice was lacking in expression. Instead he was as coolly polite as he had been for the past six weeks.

"More champagne, Kim?"

She smiled equally coolly, setting down her empty glass to accept the full one he handed to her. "You must have read my mind."

"I do my best. Starke, I just saw Ginny Adams. She's looking for you."

To Kimberly's astonishment the normally unflappable Starke suddenly looked slightly nervous. He ran his finger around his collar and then checked his tie. "Was she?" He nodded formally at Kimberly and then muttered, "Excuse me."

Kimberly stared after him as he forged through the crowd toward the attractive, forty-year-old woman near the door.

"Ginny Adams?" Kimberly asked.

"I think they make a good pair. Ginny needs someone solid and dependable like Starke. Her husband left her last year."

"Oh. I hadn't realized Starke had a, uh, romantic interest in her."

"You haven't been here enough during the past six weeks to keep track of what's been going on. Finish *Vendetta?*"

"No, but I made a lot of progress." Kimberly gulped the champagne, feeling uncomfortable and shy around her husband. Most of their conversations lately had been like this, polite but rather distant. Kimberly had told herself everything would be all right once they were married, but now she was beginning to wonder if she'd been deluding herself.

"Something wrong, Kim?"

"As a matter of fact, you can answer a question for me," she began assertively.

"A question Starke wouldn't answer? Is that why he was looking so uncomfortable when I arrived?"

"I only wanted to know what it was you two really imported and exported. A simple enough question. And don't tell me it was junk."

Cavenaugh eyed her speculatively. "A lot of it was."

"But what else was involved?"

He hesitated and then shrugged. "Occasionally Starke and I handled transactions involving information. We were sometimes in a position to acquire useful details that regular government agents couldn't get. Does that satisfy your mystery writer's curiosity?''

''Uh, yes, but tell me—''

He cut off the flow of her questions with a curious half smile. ''That's it, Kim. That's all you get from me on the subject. And I hope I never see anything close to it in one of your books.'' His expression softened briefly when he saw the disappointment in her eyes. ''I really can't talk about it.''

''Another responsibility you've assumed?''

The softness in him vanished. ''Call it whatever you like. Going to hold my silence on the subject against me along with everything else?''

Kimberly frowned. ''Of course not. I'm sure you've given your word not to talk about your former line of work. I wouldn't expect you to break it.'' Not Darius Cavenaugh. He'd see his responsibilities through to the end of his life. Kimberly drank some champagne and considered her own uncertain future.

What if she'd made a terrible mistake, Kimberly wondered with a touch of panic. Maybe everything wasn't going to be all right now. Maybe everything was going to be a total disaster.

''You must be exhausted,'' Cavenaugh said gently. ''It's been a long day.''

''I'll survive,'' she muttered.

He looked at her through faintly narrowed eyes. ''I'm not sure I will.''

She wasn't certain she'd heard him. It was the first indication of any emotion other than bland politeness she'd caught in his words for weeks. ''I beg your pardon?''

''Nothing,'' he assured her quickly, taking her arm.

"Let's go talk to your grandparents. They want to show you off a bit."

"They're delighted I've made such an excellent marriage," Kimberly said dryly.

"More delighted about it than you are, apparently."

Kimberly blinked. Again she sensed the blade of the knife beneath his words. Cavenaugh's carefully controlled temperament was fraying slightly around the edges. She wondered why.

SHE WAS STILL WONDERING two hours later, when she found herself alone in her bedroom. The last of the guests had left the estate and the various inhabitants of the house had settled down in their own rooms.

Kimberly realized she was pacing the floor in front of the bed and forced herself to stop. This wasn't exactly how she had envisioned spending her wedding night. She was alone and it was clear now that Cavenaugh would not be joining her. He had walked her upstairs, kissed her good night at the door and disappeared into his own room.

Eyes burning with tears of frustration and dismay, Kimberly sank down onto the edge of her bed and desperately tried to decide what to do next.

She was at a loss. There had been no talk of a honeymoon, not even a trip to the coast to spend some time in her beach house.

This was insane, she told herself. Here she was head over heels in love with her husband of only a few hours and he was spending the night in his own bedroom! It was beginning to appear as though he intended to live by the vow he had made the night he asked her to marry him. She would be given all the time she wanted to get to know him.

Somehow Kimberly hadn't really expected him to honor

those rash words. Especially since she had never meant
him to do so. It was ludicrous to think that they could truly
get to know each other as long as they were fencing emotionally like this.

What she wouldn't give for some genuine telepathic talent, Kimberly thought. She would sacrifice a great deal at
this moment to know what was going on in Darius Cavenaugh's head.

Slowly she stood up and unbuttoned the delicate fasten-
ings of her wedding dress. Hanging it carefully in the
closet, she pulled out the nightgown she had bought for
the occasion of her wedding night.

Grimly she stared at the frilly concoction of satin and
lace and then she put it away again. No sense wasting it,
Kimberly told herself. She might as well wear her usual
T-shirt. There would be no one sharing the bed with her
and thus no one to appreciate the horribly expensive nightgown.

Standing barefooted in front of the mirror, she brushed
her hair down around her shoulders, studying herself critically in the thigh-length T-shirt. From the beginning she
had never doubted the physical attraction between herself
and Cavenuagh. He wanted her, or at least he *had* wanted
her. She examined the thrust of her breasts against the
T-shirt and licked her lower lip uncertainly. What if even
that elemental attraction had faded?

No, she concluded, that wasn't the case. She had seen
the barely concealed possessiveness in those emerald eyes
on more than one occasion during the past six weeks. And
she was certain she'd felt him restraining himself when
he'd taken her in his arms to kiss her good-night.

Kimberly pulled the brush through her hair one last time
and threw it down on the dresser. Cavenaugh was sticking
by his plan to ''give her time.'' That was the only expla-

nation for his odd behavior. But she couldn't figure out what he expected her to do while she waited patiently for him to signal that enough time had passed between them.

It had all gone far enough, Kimberly decided with sudden resolution. She was a married woman in love with her husband. Her husband might not love her but he wanted her and he needed her. That made for a better foundation than a lot of marriages had, she assured herself.

Without pausing to think, Kimberly whirled and grabbed her old terry cloth robe out of the closet. Flinging it on she let herself out into the hall. The house was dark and quiet. She looked at the door of Cavenaugh's room and saw that there was no shaft of light under the door. He must have gone to bed.

It took almost as much courage to walk down the hall to Cavenaugh's bedroom as it had to face the punk with the silver dagger. In front of the door Kimberly lifted her hand to knock and then changed her mind. Taking a long, steadying breath she tried the doorknob.

It gave silently and the door swung open with only the smallest of sounds. She stood for a few seconds, letting her eyes adjust to the shadows. If Cavenaugh hadn't moved slightly in the darkness she wouldn't have seen him. He was sitting in a chair by the window, his legs sprawled out in front of him. There was a bottle beside him and the movement she saw was the one he made when he reached for it. She couldn't see his face.

"Cavenaugh?"

"You have a talent for it, Kim." His voice was a low growl of sound.

"A talent for what?" she whispered, daring to close the door behind her.

"For finding trouble, of course. Especially at night.

Most of your big adventures lately have taken place at night, haven't they?'' He poured the brandy with unnatural care.

Kimberly clung to the doorknob behind her back. ''Are you...are you very drunk, Cavenaugh?''

''Not yet, but I'm getting there. Don't rush me, Kim. I'm doing my damnedest not to rush you, the least you can do is return the favor.''

She still couldn't see much of him as he sprawled in the chair; only his arm was visible as he raised the brandy glass to his mouth. The arm was bare though, and Kimberly realized that all Cavenaugh was wearing was a pair of jeans.

''Is that why you haven't shown any interest in me for the past six weeks? You're trying not to rush me?'' Her voice was a thread of husky sound in the darkness. Her pulse was racing with trepidation and a strange kind of uncertain fear.

''What do you mean I haven't shown any interest in you? I married you, didn't I? A man doesn't generally marry a woman unless he's at least mildly interested in her.''

She winced. Cavenaugh was definitely beginning to sound surly. If his temper had been showing signs of fraying earlier in the evening it was ragged now.

''I can't tell you how reassuring that is,'' Kimberly managed bravely.

''Go back to your room, Kim,'' he said softly.

''Why?''

''Because if you stay here much longer, you won't be going back at all. Is that plain enough for you?''

She stepped away from the door, clutching the old terry cloth robe tightly around herself. ''I'm your wife, Cavenaugh. Maybe I don't want to go back to my bed alone. I...I have a right to be here with you.''

"Don't talk to me about rights!"

"Then let's talk about why you're afraid of rushing me," she flung back, goaded. "What are you afraid of rushing me into? Bed? I'm not trying to resist, in case you hadn't noticed!"

He set down the brandy glass with a fierce clatter and came up out of the chair with a lethally graceful movement. Nude from the waist up, his face carved in harsh, rigid lines, Cavenaugh was a formidable opponent to face in the dark. Kimberly almost lost her courage.

Placatingly she held out one hand. "Cavenaugh, how long do you think we can last in separate bedrooms?"

"Until you trust me enough to let yourself love me again," he told her with barely suppressed violence. "I don't want you in my bed until you can say you love me the way you did before I mishandled that business with your grandparents."

She stared at him. "I don't think you've been doing your usual hot job of reading my mind lately," she finally said weakly. Her hands were trembling, and she clutched at the tie of the robe in an effort to still them.

"Reading your mind has always been a fairly haphazard business," Cavenaugh rasped. "Maybe it's because you've got a rather haphazard way of thinking. A *feminine* way of thinking," he clarified accusingly.

"Is that right? And I suppose your thinking processes are more intelligible? Well, let me tell you something, Cavenaugh, I haven't been able to figure out what's going on in that…that male head of yours for weeks! I've been wondering why on earth you even bothered to marry me, for example."

"Because I love you!" he exploded. "Why else would I marry you?"

"Sex, companionship, to acquire someone who can pro-

tect you from your oversized sense of responsibility, because you felt grateful to me—all kinds of reasons!''

His eyes glittered and his voice was raw. "I married you
because I love you, Kim.''

She caught her breath. "Well, that's why I married you.
So why are we spending our wedding night in separate
bedrooms?'' she whispered achingly.

Cavenaugh moved then, gliding across the floor to scoop
her up into his arms. He swung her around with a fierce
exuberance and tossed her down on the bed. Then he was
lying heavily on top of her, pinning her to the bedclothes.

"Kim, are you sure? Are you very, very sure? I was so
afraid that I'd ruined everything.''

She speared her fingers through his hair, her heart in her
eyes. "Cavenaugh, I've never stopped loving you. I was
angry and hurt and I was sure you couldn't possibly have
loved me or you wouldn't have pulled a stunt like that, but
I never stopped loving you.''

"I only did it because I thought it was for the best, Kim.
I wanted you to be completely free of the past, free to love
me. I needed all of you.''

"I understand, darling.''

"Do you really?'' He was studying her with a burning
intensity.

Kimberly's mouth curved gently. "I didn't say I approved. I said I understood. There's a difference, I've
learned.''

"Tell me about it!'' he grated hoarsely, and then he
kissed her with rough passion. As she began to respond he
lifted his head again. "I know I'm not what you thought
you wanted in a man. But I love you so very much, sweetheart. That love is going to get us through the communication problems, I swear it.''

"You mean through all the times when you're having

trouble comprehending my 'haphazard' thinking processes?'' she teased softly. "Actually, I've been meaning to tell you that I'm thinking of changing the character of Josh Valerian slightly.''

"Is that so?''

"Umm. I'm going to make him a little more like you. Not quite so comprehensible to the heroine, but maybe a bit more interesting.''

"I love the way your mind works,'' he assured her deeply, bending his head to nibble provocatively behind her ear.

"At the moment I'm having trouble thinking at all,'' she confided, slipping her hands across his shoulders.

"Don't worry about it. I'll do all the thinking for us.'' He lifted himself slightly away and undid the tie of her robe. "You look so damn sexy in a T-shirt.''

"I would have looked even sexier in my new nightgown. But when I realized you weren't going to come to my room tonight or invite me into yours, I decided not to waste it,'' she told him sadly.

"So you just put on your usual T-shirt and this old robe and trotted down the hall to confront me, hmm?'' He was toying with the hem of the T-shirt, inching it slowly up to her waist. "Thank God you did. I was going crazy in here telling myself I had to be patient. In fact, I've been going crazy for the past six weeks convincing myself I had to give you time to learn to love me again.''

"And I've been going crazy wondering if you would ever learn to love me. Ah, Cavenaugh, we've both been fools, haven't we?''

"No. We've just been having a little trouble communicating. It won't happen again.''

"You think not?''

"Well, I suppose we're always going to have to work around the fact that you are a woman..."

"And you're a man."

"Umm. And in some ways the communication problem will always exist between us." Cavenaugh lost patience with the T-shirt and stripped it off over her head. "But I expect that's why love got invented," he stated confidently.

"To help men and woman communicate? An interesting anthropological theory, Cavenaugh." She laughed up at him with her eyes, her body warming under his. "Do you really love me?" Her hands twined around his neck.

"More than anything else on earth." He was suddenly deadly serious. "Don't ever doubt that, Kim. There will be times when I'll have my hands full with other matters and other people's problems. But there will never be a time when my heart isn't full of love for you. Do you understand?"

"Yes, Cavenaugh. I understand. And there will be times when my haphazard mind will seem full of plots and characters but there will never be a time when I am not completely in love with you."

"Good." With quick, wrenching movements he unsnapped his jeans and kicked them onto the floor. Then he turned back the quilt and tucked Kimberly underneath.

She went into his arms with a new, serene confidence, her body flowing along his. "I love you, Cavenaugh."

"You couldn't love me any more than I love you. You've been mine since the first time I made love to you. But tonight you're finally home. You're finally in my bed, where you've belonged all along."

He caressed her with wonder, his fingers seeking out the hidden places of her body until she twisted gloriously beneath his touch. When he dipped his fingers tantalizingly into the hot, damp warmth between her legs she gasped.

Then, with reverent care he began to trail a line of kisses from the shadows between her breasts to the even darker shadows at the apex of her thighs. Kimberly stirred with faint, embarrassed protest but he ignored it. Gently, with undeniable insistence, he parted her legs and gave her the most intimate of kisses.

Kimberly cried out softly, lifting herself against him as the excitement rippled through her. "Cavenaugh!"

"Sweet witch." He worked his way up her body until her questing fingers found the evidence of his arousal and he groaned aloud.

"Love me, Cavenaugh. Please love me!"

"Always."

It was a vow, and Kimberly knew in the deepest recesses of her mind that she could rely on it. Cavenaugh was that kind of man. She would be able to trust in him and in his love for the rest of her life.

He brought his body into hers, possessing and possessed, and Kimberly clung to him. The witchcraft that swirled in the darkened room was a very ancient kind, and it wrapped the two lovers in the softest of spells. Kimberly and her beloved Cavenaugh gave themselves up to it with delight, united in a passionate comprehension of each other that went beyond words.

LAST CHANCE CAFÉ
Amanda Stevens

CHAPTER ONE

"THEY SAY HE'S Gabe Foster's boy, but I know for a fact that Gabe's only son got himself shot in Mexico several years ago." There was nothing Darlene Butler loved more than a juicy piece of gossip, and a stranger in town was a particularly succulent morsel. "He can't be Gabe's son unless he's found a way to return from the dead."

"Just what every ghost town needs," Leni Crowe said dryly as she wiped down the counter in the rundown café she'd inherited from her father, along with the general store next door. "A real, live ghost."

But Rio Rancho, located off a lonely stretch of I-10 in West Texas, wasn't technically a ghost town. Not all the locals had followed the exodus to greener pastures when a five-year drought had bankrupted area ranchers and closed down most of the businesses. There were still some oldtimers who clung to their shriveled land and a dying way of life—and a few newcomers who were hiding out from their pasts and maybe even from the law.

Then there were folks like Leni, who had left Rio Rancho a long time ago only to slink back years later, tails tucked between their legs, when the outside world hadn't treated them any too kindly.

"So what do you think he's up to, out there on that old broken-down ranch all by his lonesome?" Darlene persisted. "Think he's a drug smuggler? A criminal? A sex fiend?" she added hopefully.

''Maybe he's just looking for a little peace and quiet.''
Leni wasn't much in the mood for her friend's gossip. A
sudden storm had forced a lot of truckers off the road, not
to mention some agents from a special DPS unit who were
in town investigating the death of a local rancher, and Leni
was exhausted. She waited and bussed tables while her
cook, Luis, fried burgers over a red-hot grill. He wasn't
complaining, but Leni knew he was anxious to get away
as well. He was young, it was Saturday night, and the
Mexican border was only a few miles away.

As for Leni, all she wanted to do was get home to a hot
bath, but unfortunately, the storm showed no sign of letting
up, and neither did Darlene.

''Now, Leni, you can't tell me you're not the least bit
curious about that stranger,'' she needled. ''You may live
in Rio Rancho, but you ain't dead, girl.''

Just the next thing to it, Leni thought.

''Curious about who?'' Glen Riordan sauntered over,
hitching up the khaki trousers of his deputy sheriff's uniform before straddling the barstool next to Darlene. ''Y'all
talkin' 'bout that feller who bought the old Foster place?''
he drawled.

Leni cringed. It wasn't that she didn't like Glen. What
was not to like? He was a nice-looking, soft-spoken, salt-
of-the-earth-type guy who would have made some girl a
great husband, but unfortunately, he'd set his sights on
Leni. He didn't know that her heart had been broken so
badly she had no intention of allowing him, or anyone else,
to pick up the pieces.

Everyone in Rio Rancho assumed her widowhood was
the reason she was so gun-shy about relationships, but
Leni's pain went back farther than the tragic death of her
husband. It went all the way back to the slow decline of
her marriage, the dissolution of all her dreams, and it had

culminated on the night she'd asked her husband, Danny, for a divorce. The same night he'd died in a fiery car crash that Leni still had nightmares about.

Danny was the reason Leni wasn't interested in Glen Riordan, or any man. She never would be. If her marriage to a man she'd loved with all her heart and soul had failed, what hope could there be with someone else?

She started to turn and check on her orders, but the front door opened, and a gust of cold, wet air swept through the café. A man stood silhouetted in the doorway, a hat pulled low over his eyes and a black rain poncho billowing out behind him.

He hardly seemed more than a shadow at first, but then he lifted his head and his gaze met Leni's. The hair on the back of her neck stood on end, and an icy chill shot through her as the stranger stepped inside the Last Chance Café.

CHAPTER TWO

AS THE STRANGER'S GAZE clung to Leni's, the chill inside her deepened. Something about the man's eyes, the way he looked at her, stirred emotions she thought were long dead. Had wanted to be dead.

Or maybe it was the scars on his face, the pain in his eyes that intrigued her even as something about him almost frightened her.

He wasn't handsome. In fact, on another man, his features might have been considered homely, but on the stranger, the battered face, the nose that had obviously been broken and not all that successfully repaired, the mouth that gave an odd little twist at one of the corners, were almost mesmerizing.

He was big, at least six feet two inches, with broad shoulders and a toughness about him that was formidable.

Leni found she'd been holding her breath. She let it out slowly as the stranger removed the rain poncho and hung it on a rack near the door. He took off his hat and coat, too, but he left on his gloves. Moving with a slight limp which, oddly enough, did nothing to impair his grace, he took a booth in a far corner, away from the main flow of traffic in the café, and waited for Leni.

"Oh, my *gawd*," Darlene said beneath her breath. She placed her hand over her heart and sighed. "Now, *that* is what I call a real man. How do you suppose he got his face messed up like that? Fighting over a woman, I bet."

"What makes you think that?" Leni asked, hardly able to tear her gaze from the stranger.

"Because a man like that always has a woman in his past." Darlene picked up a menu and shoved it toward Leni. "Hurry up. Go take his order. Strike up a conversation. Find out what you can about him and report back to me."

Leni snatched the menu from Darlene and gave her an exasperated look. "Yes, ma'am!"

Glen caught Leni's arm as she walked by him. "Be careful, Leni. I don't like the looks of that guy. His kind usually spells trouble."

"His kind?"

Glen shrugged. "He's been around. You can tell that just by looking in his eyes. Almost gives a body the willies," he murmured, then caught himself, squaring his shoulders in a manly gesture. "Just be careful, that's all. Lot of dope smugglers around here."

Glen meant well, he always did, but his warning irritated Leni for some reason. It wasn't like he had a claim on her or anything, and it sure wasn't like she didn't know how to take care of herself. She'd been married to a cop, hadn't she? A narc, no less. She knew about drug trafficking, and yes, it was always a danger this close to the border. But it wasn't like every stranger in town was a smuggler.

Still, there had been a lot of activity in the area lately, more than usual, and everyone in Rio Rancho was a little on edge since Ned Barnes, one of the old-timers, had been found shot dead on his ranch a few days ago. That, of course, was why agents from the Texas Confidential, a highly specialized division of the Department of Public Safety, were hanging around, although they'd never admit it. They were here undercover. No one in town besides Leni knew their true identities.

To the outside world, they worked as ranch hands on a nearby spread, but Leni had been made privy to the organization a year ago when they'd needed her café as a cover for a drug sting. She and Brady Morgan, one of the agents, had gone to the same college, and later, Brady and her husband had been cops together in Dallas. When Brady had asked for her help, Leni hadn't hesitated, and since then, she'd established a close friendship with all the agents.

Their presence now, however, filled her with foreboding. Poor old Ned had been shot because he'd seen something he shouldn't have. But what?

And now a stranger was in town. He'd bought the Foster place, a rundown ranch in a remote area of the county. Just what was he doing out there all alone? Leni wondered.

Filling a glass with ice water, she headed toward the booth in the back. The stranger watched her approach. His eyes were cool, gray, and very distant. His other features—the crooked nose, the scars, the thick, dark hair—Leni hardly noticed. But his eyes…

The water glass trembled in her hand. Her breath left her in a painful rush. Oh, my God, she thought in shock.

His eyes reminded her of Danny's.

CHAPTER THREE

LENI'S REACTION WAS not unexpected. Cade Walker was used to the stares, the shocked expressions. The way people almost always turned away from his face.

The scars caught people off guard. Repulsed them. He understood. It had been a long time after the accident before he'd been able to look at himself in the mirror.

He understood, but he'd been hoping for more from her.

Which was crazy. He hadn't come to Rio Rancho to strike up a relationship. He'd come to Rio Rancho because after three years of drifting, it had seemed like the only place on earth he could find a measure of peace.

Despite his appearance, he was still human. And the woman who stood staring down at him was gorgeous. Tall, graceful, with fiery red hair and provocative green eyes, she'd undoubtedly fueled more than one trucker's fantasies.

Not to mention the deputy sheriff who'd been hanging all over her.

But in the few moments Cade had been inside the café, it seemed to him that all the customers, mostly male, treated her with the utmost respect. She had the air of a woman who would not put up with anything less, and that made her even more appealing.

She set the glass on the table in front of him, sloshing water over the rim. "Sorry," she muttered, wiping almost frantically at the spill.

"No problem." His voice was low and raspy, still unfamiliar to him after all this time. With an effort, he resisted touching the scar at his throat.

She glanced down at him nervously. "What can I get you? Cup of coffee to start?"

"Sounds good." Cade noticed that her hands were trembling a little. Had she been that affected by his face, or was she upset for some other reason? Dare he hope she might even be a little attracted to him?

Yeah, sure. If she was partial to horror movies.

"It's a cold night," he said.

"Not fit for man nor beast," she agreed, and then her expression turned horrified. Her gaze slipped over his face. "I mean, it's cold and rainy and...wet," she stammered.

He almost smiled at her embarrassment. She wasn't used to being rattled, he thought, and her discomfort made her cling to the menu as if it were a lifeline.

"Any recommendations?"

"Oh, sorry." She handed him the menu. "Luis makes a great burger if you like them well-done. If not, I'd stick with the chili."

"Chili it is." He gave her back the menu without opening it, then glanced around the café. "Looks like you've had a busy night, Leni."

Her mouth dropped. "How did you know—"

His gaze fell on the name embroidered on her uniform. "Unusual name," he murmured.

"It's short for Lynnea."

Old-fashioned, but it suited her. "Cade Walker," he said, but he didn't extend his hand.

She nodded and started to turn away, then glanced back down at him. "Not that it's any of my business, but what brings you to Rio Rancho? I guess you've noticed we're not exactly the garden capital of world. Especially this time of year."

He shrugged. "Seemed as good a place as any to settle down."

"I guess that depends on your perspective," she said with a wry smile. "You have folks here?"

He hesitated. "No. Not anymore."

She shook her head. "Hard to imagine anyone picking this place for the climate. Or the view, for that matter."

"If it's so bad, why do you stay?"

She frowned down at him. "That should be pretty obvious, even for a stranger. I'm here for the same reason everyone else in this godforsaken town is. I don't have anywhere else to go."

CHAPTER FOUR

BY MIDNIGHT, the Last Chance Café was finally clearing out. Most of the truckers had either decided to gamble on the wet road, or else they'd gone out to their rigs to catch a few badly needed winks. Glancing around the café, Leni wondered if she should shoo the stragglers out into the cold night. The only people left besides her and Luis were the three undercover Texas Confidential agents and the stranger.

Cade Walker.

He'd finished his chili and a second cup of coffee thirty minutes ago, but he seemed in no hurry to leave. He didn't smoke, so he wasn't lingering over a cigarette. He wasn't drinking, so he wasn't waiting for last call.

Just what the heck was he doing? Waiting to catch Leni alone?

Okay, she thought. *Now he's giving me the willies.* And that wasn't a feeling she particularly liked. Normally, she wasn't the nervous type.

She walked over to the table of agents and handed them their bill. "Why don't you fellas take this party on down the road."

"Trying to get rid of us, Leni?" Cody Gannon, the youngest at the table, asked with a grin. He was an ex-rodeo star who had one of the most disarming smiles Leni had ever come across. Good thing she was several years his senior and immune to good-looking men to boot.

"Matter of fact, I am," she said bluntly.

"What do you say I get rid of these two losers and stick around while you lock up?" Rafe Alvarez had a smile, too, but it wasn't disarming like Cody's. It was downright dangerous, and he knew it.

"Tell you what," Leni said. "You close up for me, Rafe, and I'll go on home, slip into my best flannel nightie and my sexy wool socks and I'll be waiting for you in front of the TV."

Rafe winced. "Flannel nightie? Wool socks? Don't take this the wrong way, Leni, but I think I'll pass."

"I thought you might."

They all tossed money on the table and stood, gathering coats, gloves, and hats. As Cody and Rafe left the café, the oldest of the group, Jake Cantrell, stayed behind. He cast a wary glance toward the booth in the back, where the stranger sat waiting. But for what?

"I don't like leaving you here alone while that guy's still hanging around," Jake said in a low voice. "Do you know him?"

"No, but don't worry. Luis is still here." Although they both knew Luis would be no match for the stranger. The cook had a reputation across the border as a fiery, passionate lover—or so he said—but he wasn't much bigger than a minute.

Trying to diffuse Jake's concern, she said brightly, "Hey, I saw Brady the other day. He came in just after dawn with some woman." It was a small world, Leni sometimes thought, the way she and Brady had both ended up in West Texas, what some people considered the ends of the earth. "The woman was a real looker," she said. "Sort of the Shania Twain type."

Something flickered in Jake's eyes before the shutters came down, confirming Leni's suspicion that Brady's involvement with the woman was more than just personal. But before she had time to question Jake further, she saw the stranger rise from the booth and walk toward her.

Turning to face him, she felt Jake's hand on her back, as if to reassure her he was still there. But the moment her gaze collided with Cade Walker's, Leni forgot all about Jake's presence, Cody Gannon's smile, and Rafe Alvarez's charm. She forgot about Brady Morgan and his female companion.

And for a moment, she even forgot about Danny...

CHAPTER FIVE

CADE WALKER RETURNED to the Last Chance Café the next night.

And the next.

Leni's heart bounced like a Ping-Pong ball off the wall of her chest as she watched him remove his hat and coat and head toward the back booth. Like always, he'd left on his gloves. She couldn't help wondering why. Were his hands scarred, too? Or was he worried about leaving his fingerprints around?

Chiding herself for her wild imagination, she picked up a menu. It was a Monday night. The café wasn't particularly busy, but there were a couple of locals sitting at the bar chewing the fat, and the Texas Confidential agents, still in town investigating Ned Barnes's death, were gathered around a corner table. No one would suspect they were anything more than three friends, having a cup of coffee together and shooting the breeze.

Leni still couldn't shake a dark premonition that something sinister was going on in Rio Rancho. She could feel it, and she couldn't help wondering if her sense of foreboding was somehow tied to Cade Walker.

Ignoring a sudden chill down her back, she filled a water glass and headed for the back booth. ''Evening,'' she greeted him, annoyed that her voice sounded so breathless.

He looked up at her with those eyes. Gray. Piercing. Soulful.

So like Danny's.

Stop it! Leni admonished herself. This man was nothing like Danny. Danny was dead. He wasn't coming back. She had to stop seeing him every time she looked into Cade Walker's eyes. Because if she didn't...

If she didn't, she might find it a little too easy to forget that Cade Walker was a stranger.

"Another cold night," he said softly.

Leni shivered at the sound of his voice. "I guess spring's still a long way off."

"Yeah, but it always comes. Sooner or later."

His words seemed prophetic to Leni. For a long time now she'd been living in a perpetual winter. But Cade Walker made her think of warmer days. And even warmer nights.

She mentally shook herself and handed him the menu. "Need a few minutes to decide what you want?"

"No. I already know what I want."

As his gaze met hers, a thrill of excitement shot through Leni, but she tried to keep her voice even. "What'll it be then?"

He hesitated only fractionally. "I think I'll try one of Luis's burgers tonight."

She arched a brow. "You must like to live danger-ously."

"Don't you?"

"No," she said frankly. "I don't have an adventurous bone in my body. I'm more the hearth and home type."

"Then why aren't you married?" His voice was low and raspy. Intimate.

"Actually...I was married," Leni confessed.

"What happened?" If possible, his gaze grew even darker.

"He died." Her tone was matter of fact, but her insides

trembled, as they always did, when she thought about Danny.

"I'm sorry." Something flickered in Cade's eyes, a look of regret, as if he truly were sorry for her loss. Somehow Leni thought that he was.

"It was a long time ago," she said sadly. "And the marriage was already over."

"I'm sorry," he said again. And then without warning, he reached out and touched her hand. He'd taken off his gloves, and Leni could see that the back of his right hand was crisscrossed with thin, jagged lines.

Something horrible had happened to him in the past, she thought. Something had scarred him terribly, but she had a feeling the wounds on the outside were nothing compared to those on the inside.

Her eyes stung with sudden tears, and for no reason Leni could explain, she wanted to lift his marred hand to her face, to trace each and every scar with her lips, to soothe away his pain—and maybe her own—even for a little while.

Instead, she took a step back from Cade Walker. He dropped his hand from hers, and the moment was over.

"I'd better see to your order," she murmured, then turned and fled toward the kitchen.

CHAPTER SIX

CADE SMELLED an ambush.

He'd left the café a few minutes ago, heading for his truck, but he knew he'd been followed out. He turned and saw one of the three men who had been sitting at the corner table start across the street toward him. Cade didn't see the other two, but he knew they were around, just as he knew all three of them were the law. He'd known it the moment he first laid eyes on them in the café on Saturday night.

They weren't cops, though. At least not local boys. Not like the deputy sheriff Cade had seen sniffing around Leni that first night. In another few years, the deputy would have the same physique as the Pillsbury Doughboy if he wasn't careful. These guys were in top shape, which told him they trained. They were pros.

He waited beside his truck for the man to catch up to him. When he drew even with Cade, they eyed each other in the darkness. Finally the man stuck out his hand. "Jake Cantrell."

"Cade Walker." They shook hands, sizing one another up.

"I hear you bought the old Foster place," Cantrell remarked casually. But Cade wasn't fooled. There was nothing offhand about the question. "What brings you to West Texas?"

Cade started to tell him it was none of his damn busi-

ness, but trouble with the law, especially this man's kind
of law, he didn't need. "I like the peace and quiet."

"Plenty of quiet out here all right," Jake said. "It's not
too peaceful, though. There was a murder a few days ago—
a rancher named Ned Barnes."

"Is that right?" Cade said carefully.

"He was a harmless old man, shot dead with a high-
caliber rifle. As a matter of fact, his ranch borders yours
up near the foothills."

Cade became extremely wary. A murder. A stranger in
town. He didn't like the way Jake Cantrell appeared to be
adding things up.

"We think he may have seen something he shouldn't
have," Jake said. "Lot of drugs coming across the border
around here. They need places to hide the stuff until the
shipments can be dispersed to points east and north."

"You sound like a cop," Cade said.

Jake laughed, a low sound, not menacing exactly, but
none too friendly. "I'm not a cop. I work on a spread not
too far from here. We don't like drugs coming across the
border, and when someone gets murdered, we're all concerned."

Yeah, Cade thought. There was concern, and there was
concern.

"Just thought I'd give you a friendly warning," Jake
said. "So you can be on the lookout for anything out of
the ordinary."

Cade had seen some strange things already, but he
wasn't going to admit it. He'd come here to start a new
life, not to get dragged back into his old one. "I haven't
been here long enough to know if something is out of the
ordinary or not."

Jake nodded. "Fair enough. But if you do see anything

suspicious, we'd appreciate it if you'd get in touch with the authorities.''

Cade turned to leave, but Jake said quietly, "One other thing, Walker."

"Yeah?"

"I can't help noticing you've been hanging around Leni's place since you got to town."

Cade shrugged. "I'm not much of a cook. I have to eat somewhere."

"Leni have anything to do with your choice?"

"Not particularly," Cade said, but a spark of anger ignited inside him. What business was this of Jake Cantrell's? "Why? Do you have a claim on her?"

"No claim," Jake said easily. "She's a friend, and she hasn't had an easy time trying to make a go of this place. We all look out for her, that's all."

Cade's gaze went back to the window, where he could see Leni silhouetted in the light. Even going about the menial task of cleaning up the café, she looked strong and capable. A woman in charge. A woman who didn't need a man to look out for her.

But then again, it might depend on the man.

CHAPTER SEVEN

LUIS HAD LEFT a while ago, and Leni was alone in the café. The tables were all wiped clean, the floors mopped, the salt and pepper shakers replenished. It was finally time to lock up.

But Leni lingered, not anxious to go home to a cold, empty house. A lonely house. Sighing, she moved to the tiny office in the back and changed from her uniform into a pair of jeans, a thick wool sweater, and boots. Even though it only took her a few minutes to get to her house, she'd freeze in this weather if she didn't bundle up.

Fighting off a growing melancholy, she walked over and lowered the shade at the door and turned the sign to read Closed. She was just about to turn out the lights when a knock on the door caused her to jump.

Normally, she wouldn't have been so skittish, but Ned Barnes's murder had made everyone in town a little edgy.

The knock sounded again, and cautiously Leni drew back the shade on the door. The neon sign was still on, and Cade Walker's battered features stood out starkly in the garish, flickering light.

"Sorry to bother you, but I forgot my gloves," he said through the glass.

Leni hesitated. It was never a good idea to let a stranger into the café this time of night when she was all alone, especially one who seemed as mysterious as Cade Walker. But the weather was brutal outside. He'd need his gloves.

"Look," Cade said, as if sensing her trepidation. "I don't have to come in. I'll go stand next to the windows, where you can see me, and you just slip the gloves outside."

Leni couldn't find an objection with that. She nodded.

Locating the gloves in the back booth where he'd left them, she headed back toward the door. She could see his towering silhouette outside the front windows, and for a moment, she paused, staring out at him. Her heart thudded against her chest in spite of herself. She didn't want to be drawn to Cade Walker, but she was. She didn't want to find his beaten features attractive, but she did. And she certainly knew better than to let him come inside the café. But she wanted to.

She opened the front door and stepped out into the cold night.

"Cade?" When he didn't answer, she took a few steps away from the door. "Cade? I found your gloves."

Too late, she realized he was no longer by the windows. He'd come up behind her, blocking her path to the door. She started to scream, started to run, but she could do neither because he grabbed her roughly, wrapping his arm around her throat as he shoved a gun barrel against her temple.

"Scream and you die," he said in her ear.

CHAPTER EIGHT

CADE LAY FACEDOWN in the icy mud. He wasn't sure why the men who had jumped him hadn't killed him, but maybe they hadn't wanted to risk the sound of a gunshot bringing the law. Or maybe they thought they *had* killed him. Maybe they'd thought if the butt of a rifle crashing against the back of his skull didn't do him in, then he'd die of hypothermia before morning.

Whatever the reason, Cade was pretty certain they hadn't counted on his instinct for survival, honed even more sharply after three years of looking over his shoulder.

They hadn't counted on the fact that he'd recognized one of them, either. Out of the corner of his eye, before he'd gone down, Cade had caught a glimpse of one of his attackers. And though the heavy coat disguised the man's size, the white hair hanging down his back and the paleness of his skin had been unmistakable.

Cade had seen him a few days ago, on the northern edge of his property. The man had been on foot, heavily bundled up against the weather, except for his head which had been left bare. The wind had whipped his white hair straight back, exposing a face that seemed eerily devoid of color. He'd been carrying a rifle. To the casual observer, he might have been taken for a hunter, but through his binoculars, Cade had noted the way the man's gaze darted about the landscape, the stealthy but purposeful way he made his way over the craggy terrain.

He'd been up to no good. Cade had realized that immediately, but he'd kept out of sight because he hadn't wanted any trouble. He hadn't wanted to get involved in something that was no longer his business.

He hadn't known then that Ned Barnes had been murdered. Or that the white-haired man might pose a threat to Leni.

Leni.

The thought of her spurred Cade to his feet. Tentatively, he probed the knot at the back of his head. He'd bled some, and the pain was pretty intense. Cade knew he probably needed stitches, but there was no time for that. Besides, he'd learned a long time ago how to handle pain. He gritted his teeth and staggered toward the café.

The lights were off, but the front door was open. Cade backtracked and got his gun out of his truck before entering the darkened restaurant. He waited several long minutes in the doorway, listening to the dark, before he moved inside and turned on the lights.

There was no sign of a struggle, no evidence of foul play. It seemed as if Leni might have just gone home for the evening, but Cade knew that she hadn't. She was a careful person. She would never have left her front door unlocked.

He walked over to the cash register. It hadn't been touched, but there was a tissue lying on the floor. It was dotted with blood.

Leni's blood?

CHAPTER NINE

NESTLED IN THE FOOTHILLS of the mountains, the abandoned mine was hidden from view by an outcropping of rock, and the one road that led to it was hardly more than a rutted-out trail, accessible only by horseback or four-wheel drive. No one would ever think to look for her here, Leni thought as she got out of the truck.

She still had no idea why she'd been kidnapped, but she knew her predicament was dire. Before they'd left town, her two captors had forced her to open up the general store next to the café, and they'd loaded up with medical supplies, food, and blankets. Leni prayed they'd let her go once they had what they wanted, but instead, she'd been taken hostage.

Her split lip ached where the white-haired man had hit her. The pain made her angry, but she was scared, too, and she knew she had to control her temper. She was no match for two armed men. All she could do for now was bide her time.

The inside of the mine was dimly lit by a lantern hanging from a wooden rafter. The light stirred in a draft, and huge shadows danced across the cavern. But even in the faulty light, Leni had no trouble seeing a third man lying on the floor. His face was blanched, and he was shivering uncontrollably.

The white-haired man, who seemed to be the leader,

thrust the bag of medical supplies toward her. "Here," he said. "See what you can do for him."

Leni glanced at him in shock. "Me? I'm no doctor!"

"Maybe not." His pale eyes were like red flames in the lantern light. "But you're the closest thing we got."

He shoved her toward the man on the floor, and Leni sank to her knees. Up close, the man looked in even worse shape than she'd first thought. Gingerly she pulled back the blanket that was spread over him. The man's clothing was covered in blood. She recoiled in horror.

"He needs to be in a hospital!" she said on a gasp. "There's nothing I can do for him!"

The white-haired man walked over and placed his gun against her temple, cocking the trigger. "You got my brother sent to prison last year. You and those agents you work for. Nothing I'd like more than to put a bullet in you right now, but I'm giving you a fighting chance. You save this man's life, I'll let you go."

Leni looked up into those cold blues eyes and shivered. *I'm a dead woman,* she thought. *He's never going to let me go.*

CADE KNEW WHERE they'd gone. Even if he hadn't recognized the white-haired man, he would have had a pretty good idea, because in spite of what he'd told Jake Cantrell, he *had* been seeing some unusual activity the last few days. Strange vehicles using an obscure road on the border of his property. Lights moving around in the foothills of the mountains.

Cade had become suspicious, so he'd gone to investigate. He'd traveled every square inch of his property, the need to know his surroundings inside and out a deeply ingrained compulsion.

When he'd come across the abandoned mine, he'd

known immediately that it was the perfect hideout. The perfect place to stash drug shipments coming across the border. It was remote, well hidden, and extremely difficult to get to.

He'd explored the tunnel just far enough so that he knew another way in and another way out. In his old life, learning where all the exits were located could have meant life or death, and although he'd left that persona behind him three years ago, old habits died hard.

He'd been a fool, Cade realized now. He thought he could shut his eyes to whatever was going on in that mine. He thought he could leave behind a way of life that had robbed him of everything. But he'd been wrong. Ned Barnes had been killed, and now Leni was missing. There was no way he could ignore that.

He felt emotions stirring to life he'd long ago tried to bury. This time, he didn't try to suppress them. Cade closed his eyes for a moment, letting the emotions rise to the surface. Letting his instincts take over because he knew that was the only way he could save Leni.

CHAPTER TEN

LENI WAS ALONE with the dying man. The white-haired man had gone out a few minutes earlier, armed with a high-powered rifle—the one that had killed Ned Barnes, Leni very much feared—and the second man stood guard just outside the entrance to the mine. Every now and then, he'd come back inside to get warmed up and to make sure Leni was doing her job.

She'd done the best she could with the medical supplies, but she knew the wounded man was going to die if they didn't get him to a hospital. She also knew his friends had no intention of doing that. They were drug runners, associated with the group the Texas Confidential agents had brought down last year. Because of her participation in the sting, they thought she was an agent, too. She hadn't been kidnapped for her nursing skills so much as for revenge.

She gazed down at the wounded man. Apparently, he'd been shot by a rival drug cartel while crossing the border. Leni had heard the men talking. They couldn't move their hideout because a major shipment was due anytime. Nor could they risk detection by taking their comrade to a doctor. Bullet wounds had to be reported to the authorities.

Thinking of the police made Leni think of Glen. Maybe if he drove by the café, he'd realize something was wrong. But why would he? The lights were off. He'd think she was closed.

How long before anyone missed her? Not until Luis got

to work tomorrow morning. And even if the Texas Confidential agents got involved, it could take several hours to ascertain what had happened and to form a search party. By then, the trail would be cold. No one would know where to look for her. She could be dead before anyone figured out where she'd been taken.

And Cade Walker? What had happened to him? She'd known the moment she heard the white-haired man speak that he wasn't Cade, but why had Cade disappeared so suddenly before her attack? Was he in with these men? Had he left his gloves in the café to purposefully draw her outside?

Leni still had the gloves. She pulled them out of her pocket and slipped them on as she leaned against the wall. They were warm inside, as if he'd just withdrawn his hands from them. She lifted them to her face, imagining for a moment the way Cade might touch her. The way he might kiss her…

She jerked herself out of the fantasy with a cold dash of reality. It was stupid to fantasize about a stranger, especially when she had more pressing concerns to worry about. Like getting the hell out of here.

The main cavern was fairly large, but the tunnel narrowed as it ran back into the mountain. There was no way of knowing how far back it went. Leni debated on whether to take her chances in the tunnel or to try and subdue the guard. On the one hand, she was no match for an armed killer, unless she could catch him by surprise. On the other hand, for all she knew, the tunnel only went back for a few yards before it dead-ended, in which case she would be trapped.

Then again, the mine could go on for miles. She could end up getting hopelessly lost. She could fall into a pit, break a leg or something. She might even starve to death.

But she had to do something.

She gazed around for a weapon. If she could knock the guard out or disarm him, she might be able to get away before the white-haired man returned.

Outside, she heard the guard stir. He coughed, then all fell silent. She started to inch toward the entrance, but something moved in the far recesses of the tunnel. Leni whirled.

Someone—or something—had materialized from the shadows. Leni started to scream, but he was on her before she could utter a sound.

"Don't move," he whispered against her ear. "Don't make a sound."

And this time the voice did belong to Cade Walker....

CHAPTER ELEVEN

LENI STRUGGLED, but only for a moment. Cade was holding her tightly, but not the way the white-haired man had held her. His touch was protective, not threatening.

"It's okay. I'm going to get you out of here," he whispered. "Understand?" When Leni nodded, he lifted his hand from her mouth. "You okay?"

She nodded again and swallowed, never so glad to see anyone in her life—especially now that she knew he wasn't one of the bad guys. She'd never really believed that, Leni realized, and she had to fight the urge to throw her arms around him. "How did you know where to find me?"

He put a gentle finger to her hurt lip, and Leni winced. Cade's eyes darkened in the lantern light. "No time for that now. We've got to get moving." He glanced around the mine, his gaze falling on the wounded man. "Where are the others?"

"One is just outside," Leni whispered. "The other one…I'm not sure. But they're both armed."

Cade nodded grimly. "I figured that. Come on." He pulled her toward the tunnel, but before they'd taken more than a few steps, Leni heard a sound behind her. She glanced back and froze.

The blast of the white-haired man's rifle was almost deafening in the mine.

The rock wall beside Leni exploded, and she screamed.

Cade dove for the deepest shadows, dragging her with him.

"Run!" he yelled, spinning to fire as Leni's captors opened up on them.

Leni ran.

Away from the lantern, the tunnel was pitch black and narrow. The walls in places brushed both of her shoulders, but she hurried as fast as she could. She was getting farther and farther into the mine, going deeper and deeper with each step. A mountain of stone and dirt lay over her, and she tried to fight off a claustrophobic panic.

Cade caught up with her as another volley of gunfire shattered rock nearby.

"Hurry!" he urged her.

The tunnel forked ahead of them, and Cade guided her to the right. Leni could see the night sky through a hole in the roof. A rope was suspended from above, and she hurried toward it.

But suddenly everything started to tremble. The floor beneath her shook, and she lost her balance. She tumbled to the ground, not knowing what was happening at first, but then in a flash, she realized she was trapped in a miner's worst nightmare.

A cave-in!

Somehow Cade managed to reach her, and he pulled her to her feet, dragging her back from the rope. Rock and debris bombarded them from above as the hole caved in, and a heavy dust filled the air, making it impossible to breathe. There was no way out, Leni thought in panic. She and Cade would be buried alive.

He hugged her tightly to the wall. His arms covered her head, and for what seemed an eternity, the mine collapsed all around them.

Then the tremors stopped. The dust cleared.

Cade and Leni were both coughing, bruised and battered, but they were alive. Yet for the longest moment, he still held her. As if he never wanted to let her go.

And Leni realized in the aftermath of near death, she was in no hurry to move from the protection of Cade Walker's arms...

CHAPTER TWELVE

CADE HAD SOMEHOW managed to hang on to his flashlight. He shined the beam upward, where the hole in the roof had once been. It was completely filled, and a wall of rock blocked the way back to the tunnel's entrance. He and Leni were cut off from both exits.

No way they could move all that rock, he thought grimly. They'd starve to death first. Or run out of air.

He moved the beam over Leni. She appeared to be all right, although stunned. Scared. Panicky.

Who could blame her?

But when she spoke, her voice was surprisingly calm. "Can we move the rock?"

Not in a million years, he thought, but he shrugged. "Maybe. It would take a while though. I think our best bet is to keeping going, see if we can find another way out of the mine."

"Or we may find another cave-in," she said.

"That's possible. Are you okay?"

She brushed off her clothing, but her face and hair were coated with dust. "I'll live, I guess. How about you?"

"A few bruises, nothing serious. Let's get moving."

Using the light, they crept through the shaft, mindful that any sudden move or noise might bring down another onslaught of rock and dirt.

"What caused the cave-in?" Leni asked quietly. "The gunfire?"

Cade shrugged. "Who knows? This place has probably been here for years. The braces are rotting, so it didn't take much to bring it down. These old mines are all over the mountains."

"You know this area?" she asked in surprise. "I thought you were new in town."

"I am."

They were moving steadily deeper, and signs of the cave-in grew sparser. At first, they were constantly having to clear the tunnel of rubble, but for the last several minutes, the way had been clear, making it a little easier— and safer—to carry on a conversation.

"Earlier when I asked if you had family here, you said 'No, not anymore.' Which suggests you used to have family here," Leni said.

"I don't have family anywhere."

"Then why come to Rio Rancho?"

"I told you. It seemed as good a place as any to settle down."

She stopped behind him, forcing him to do the same so he wouldn't get too far ahead of her. The flashlight beam was still strong, but Cade knew it wouldn't last forever. Once the batteries were gone, they would be completely in the dark, and moving through the tunnel would be even more dangerous. He took her arm and tried to urge her forward. "We need to keep moving while we still have light."

Her gaze dropped to the flashlight, and he saw a flicker of what might have been fear cross her features. But still she lingered. "Before we go any farther, I need to know something."

He braced himself. "What?"

"How did you know where to find me?"

He shrugged. "I stumbled across this mine a few days

ago while I was exploring the ranch. I saw signs it was being used. I don't know.'' He shrugged again. ''I had a hunch they'd brought you here.''

She gazed up at him for a very long time. ''That's funny,'' she said slowly. ''Because my husband used to get hunches like that, too.''

CHAPTER THIRTEEN

"MY HUSBAND WAS a cop," Leni said. "Sometimes his hunches were almost like a sixth sense. Are you a cop, Cade?" She said his name tentatively, testing the feel of it on her tongue.

He stared down at her, his battered face enigmatic in the flashlight beam. "I'm not a cop."

"Then what?"

"Does it matter?" He sounded impatient. "The only thing we need to worry about is finding a way out of here."

"I know, but—"

"What?"

Leni drew a breath. "Why did you come for me? You don't even know me."

If possible, his expression grew even harsher. "You ask a lot of questions."

"And you don't seem to have the answers," she countered. "At least none you're willing to share with me."

"Maybe you wouldn't like my answers." He started walking along the tunnel in front of her.

Leni followed the beam of light. "Maybe I wouldn't," she said. "Maybe the fact is, you didn't come for me at all. Maybe you came to get what those men have been hiding in this mine."

When he didn't respond, she moved up behind him. "Is that it? Is that why you came? Were you after the drugs?"

Without warning, he spun and grabbed her arms, hauling

her up against him. The flashlight was angled downward, but the beam bounced off the floor, casting a sinister shadow over his features. Leni realized that she might have gone too far. If he *had* come looking for drugs, it probably wasn't a good idea to force his hand. But that was exactly what she'd done.

Not too smart, Leni, girl, she could almost hear Pop admonishing her.

"I came to get *you*," Cade said in a low, dangerous voice. "Don't you get it?"

And then, still holding her, he lowered his mouth to hers.

HE HADN'T WANTED to kiss her. Hadn't meant to touch her at all, but there she was, gazing up at him. Looking for all the world as if she wanted to be kissed.

And even with a fine coating of dust still lingering on her skin and in her hair, she was the most beautiful woman he'd ever known. Beautiful inside and out. Brave. Strong. Capable.

Leni.

With a shock, he realized he'd groaned her name out loud. He hadn't meant to do that, either, but he had no control all of a sudden. Didn't want to be in control. He wanted Leni to fill his mind, take away the emptiness of the last three years.

He knew that he should draw away, but Leni's mouth opened beneath his. She wound her arms around his neck, pressing her body close to his, and even though they both wore coats, Cade imagined the warmth of her skin, the rhythm of her heartbeat beneath the heavy layer of clothing.

"Leni." He whispered her name again, caressing the smoothness of her cheek with his hand. She felt incredible, and it had been so long. So very long…

He broke the kiss, resting his forehead against hers. Neither of them said anything for a long moment, but remained almost motionless in one another's arms.

Finally Leni took a step back. "I don't know what came over me."

He almost smiled at that. "That's a cliché, Leni. We both know what came over us."

He couldn't see her expression clearly in the dim light, but he thought she might be blushing. Not something she would want him to see, he thought. She pulled a hand through her tangled hair. "Okay," she said with a sigh. "Then what's your take? Adrenaline rush? A reaction to danger?"

Yes, he thought. All of the above and something more. Something she didn't want to admit. Something she didn't want to recognize.

Something that Cade had no intention of telling her...

CHAPTER FOURTEEN

"YOU'RE BEING QUIET." Cade glanced over his shoulder. Leni hadn't said anything for the longest time, but instead had trudged silently behind him. He wondered if she was thinking about their kiss. If she was regretting it.

"I don't think we're going to get out of here," she said wearily.

"Sure we are. There's bound to be another opening somewhere. We just have to keep going." But Cade wasn't as certain as he sounded. The flashlight beam was almost gone. If they didn't find an opening soon, it might be better to turn around and go back, take their chances on clearing the tunnel near the mine's entrance.

"Look," Cade said. They'd rounded a corner in the shaft, and a large cavern-like room opened up before them. He played the light over the walls, probing the corners. There was a bedroll on the floor and candles scattered about.

"Someone's been here," Leni whispered, as if that same someone might still be lurking nearby.

"Sometimes the miners would spend days at a time underground, especially if they'd struck a rich vein, or thought they were getting close. This stuff's probably been here for years." Cade walked over and kicked the bedroll. A cloud of dust drifted upward.

With a match, he lit the wick of one of the candles, and the light flickered to life. Quickly he extinguished the flashlight, preserving what little was left of the batteries. Then he stuffed some of the other candles in his pocket, in case they didn't find a way out anytime soon.

"Let's take a breather." He shook out the bedroll, stirring up another dust storm. "Come to think of it, the ground might be preferable," he said, coughing.

Leni walked over and sat down beside him. "Do you really think we're going to find a way out of here?"

Cade shrugged. "I've been in tighter situations than this."

"Such as?"

He hesitated. "Let's just say, I've faced death a few times and lived to tell about it."

"I don't know if that makes me feel better or not," Leni murmured. Her gaze was on his face, on the scars. Without warning, she reached out and touched the one at the corner of his mouth.

He caught her hand. "Sure you want to do that?"

"Do what?" she asked softly.

His gaze was dark and mysterious as he stared down at her. "Start something you might not want to finish."

LENI WASN'T CERTAIN how long she'd been sleeping, but she awakened suddenly with the realization that she was lying on the ground and her head was pillowed in Cade's lap. He stroked her hair gently, almost lovingly, and a shiver coursed through her. She couldn't remember the last time a man's touch had affected her so deeply.

In candlelight, the tunnel was even spookier. It should have been frightening, but it wasn't. It should have been cold, but it wasn't. Leni felt cozy, almost content, and she sighed, reaching for Cade's hand.

Like a blind woman, she explored his callused palm, tested lightly the jagged ridge that ran across the back.

Another scar. She moved to his fingers, brushing them with her own until she came to the smooth metal band on the third finger of his left hand.

And then she froze.

CHAPTER FIFTEEN

"YOU'RE MARRIED?" Leni sat up on the floor and stared at him in the flickering candlelight.

"I was," Cade said carefully. "I lost my wife several years ago."

Something flashed across her face. Not pity, Cade thought, but compassion. Empathy. "I'm sorry," she said. "I know what it's like to lose someone you love."

"But you said your marriage was over before your husband died," he reminded her.

"That didn't mean I didn't love him." She grew surprisingly defensive. "Even through the worst of times, I never stopped loving him."

Cade's heart gave a funny little twist. "Then he was a very lucky man."

"I'm not sure he felt that way." She hesitated for a moment, then said, "How did your wife die?" Before he had time to answer, she shook her head. "I'm sorry. I shouldn't have asked that. It's none of my business. It's just…" She trailed off as her gaze moved over the scars on his face.

"The accident came later," he said softly.

"A car accident?" When he nodded, she turned to stare at the candle flame, hugging her knees to her chest. "My husband died in a car crash."

Cade didn't know what to say, so he remained silent, wondering how much more of herself she would reveal to him. Wondering if it was fair to listen. And yet how could he not? He wanted to know what her life had been like. He wanted to know everything about her. He especially wanted to know if there was a chance she was still in love with her husband.

"He worked Narcotics," Leni said. "Undercover. Sometimes deep cover. The assignments were dangerous, and the least little slip-up could have meant his life. He always said the only way to pull off an undercover job was to become the cover. To live it and breathe it. And he did. He did it very well. He did it so well that I don't think he even knew who he was anymore. I know I didn't."

She drew a long breath, her gaze still watching the flame. "Foul play was suspected in his death. He'd penetrated a very powerful drug ring, and his cover was blown. They put out a hit on him, but it wasn't so much for what he knew as for revenge, the police said. And to use him as an example. His car was forced off an overpass one night. It exploded on impact, and he was trapped inside."

Cade closed his eyes, her words conjuring powerful images.

"Sometimes I still have nightmares about it," she said. "Sometimes I can see him in that car, calling out to me for help. But I can't get to him. I can't do anything but watch him die."

The anguish in her voice tore at Cade's resolve. "Leni, don't. It wasn't your fault."

She turned in surprise. "I'm…sorry. I didn't mean to sound so maudlin. It's just…I've never told anyone about this before. I guess I needed to open up to someone, and it may sound crazy, but I feel as if I know you. Maybe because of the danger we're in. Maybe because we're trapped in here together." She shrugged. "I don't know. I just feel as if I can trust you."

"Maybe you shouldn't," he said darkly. "Trust me, I mean."

"Why not?" Her eyes deepened in the candlelight, and it seemed to Cade that he could lose himself in those eyes, if he wasn't careful.

The only way to pull off an undercover job is to become the cover.

He glanced away from her probing gaze. "I'm not the man you think I am, Leni."

CHAPTER SIXTEEN

LENI COULDN'T BELIEVE what had just happened. She'd laid bare her soul to a man she didn't even know, and he was the one who'd had to remind her that she shouldn't go around trusting strangers.

"Then who are you?" she demanded.

"That may not be something you really want to know." Candlelight flickered over Cade's face, making him seem even more mysterious. Even more dangerous. "I'm a wanted man, Leni."

She caught her breath. "That's why you came to Rio Rancho. You're hiding from the law."

"We're all hiding from something," he said grimly. "Even you."

She started to deny it, but couldn't. It was true. She was hiding out in Rio Rancho. Hiding from her past, yes, but even worse, she was hiding from a future.

"What did you do?" she asked hesitantly, not certain she really wanted to know.

"It's not what you think. I'm not a criminal. But there are people who want me dead."

"Those men who kidnapped me...are they looking for you?" Leni asked. Or was she their only target?

"No. If they'd been looking for me, I'd be dead right now." Cade gave her an enigmatic glance. "You don't seem frightened. After what I just told you, you should be running scared."

Leni glanced around the tunnel. "In case you hadn't noticed, there's nowhere to run to. We're stuck here together, and no, I'm not afraid. Not of you."

He gave her a long, measured look. "You're a brave woman, Leni."

"Or stupid."

He smiled at that, and Leni's gaze fell on his mouth, remembering what it was like to have those lips on hers. To have his hands moving through her hair, against her skin. She wondered what it would be like to lie with him in bed, sated from his lovemaking and yet still hungry. Still wanting more.

She lifted her gaze to his. *He knows what I'm thinking.* She could tell by the dark glow in his eyes, and before she could stop him, he reached out a hand to touch her face.

His knuckles skimmed along her jawline. His thumb traced her mouth, moving gently over the cut. "What happened to your lip?"

"It doesn't matter."

"Oh, it matters," he said in a voice Leni hardly recognized. "It matters very much."

And then he kissed her, softly at first, pulling back to gaze down at her. "I don't want to hurt you."

"You won't." She cupped his neck and pulled him toward her.

He resisted for only a moment before his arms came around her, and he drew her to him, kissing her almost fiercely. Almost desperately. He broke apart only long enough to whisper her name, and then he was kissing her again. And again. Until Leni grew dizzy with need.

She'd never wanted a man the way she wanted Cade Walker.

No, a voice inside her insisted. She'd wanted Danny this

way. She'd loved Danny with her heart and soul. She still loved him.

But Danny was dead. And Cade was...Cade...

It took her a moment to realize he was no longer kissing her. His arms around her had stiffened, and he was holding her as if he wanted to push her aside.

Leni tried to draw back to see his face, but his grasp on her tightened.

And then, through the lingering haze of passion, she heard a sound that chilled her blood. The unmistakable clatter of a rattlesnake coiled to spring.

CHAPTER SEVENTEEN

CADE WATCHED the snake. It had slithered out of a pile of rocks near the old bedroll and was coiled at Leni's feet, ready to strike if she made one false move.

He tightened his grip on her arms and whispered in her ear, "When I give the word, I want you to lunge away from me. As fast as you can. Okay?"

She barely nodded. He saw her swallow hard as she steadied her nerves.

"Now!"

As she sprang forward, Cade grabbed the rotting bedroll and threw it over the rattler. The snake struck at him, but not in time. Cade wadded up the cover and tossed it to the far corner of the cavern. The snake slithered out, unharmed.

He grabbed Leni's hand. "Come on. Let's get out of here."

Obviously, the rattler was using the mine to hibernate for the winter, and Leni and Cade had disturbed its rest. Where there was one, there was apt to be others. Dozens. Maybe hundreds.

Cade suppressed a shudder. He hated snakes, especially the kind with fangs. He'd been badly bitten as a kid, and the venom had almost killed him.

He reached for the candle and used it to light their way along the tunnel.

"You think there're more snakes in here?" Leni asked,

as if reading his mind. Her voice was steady. She didn't seem nearly as affected by the incident as he was, but then, she hadn't seen the size of that rattler.

Cade shrugged. "Who knows? Maybe that one was a loner. But I don't want to stick around long enough to find out."

Behind him Leni laughed suddenly.

He turned at the sound and held up the candle to see her face. "What's so funny?"

"I don't know. This whole thing." She laughed again, as if she couldn't help herself. "You were in a gun battle with drug smugglers. You're hiding out from someone who wants to kill you. And yet the only thing that's rattled you—no pun intended—is a snake."

He arched a brow, irritated. "And your point is?"

"I guess you're human, after all."

That took him aback. Stung him more than he cared to admit. "My appearance to the contrary," he muttered.

He started to turn away, but Leni grabbed his arm. Her expression was completely sober now. "I didn't mean it that way. I meant…you're vulnerable. I like that," she said softly. "I like the way you look, too."

"Right."

"I'm serious. You're a very attractive man, Cade."

"I've seen a mirror, Leni. I know what I look like."

"The scars don't matter," she insisted. "You've got something…powerful. I don't know how to explain it. It's…magnetism, I guess." She trailed off, gazing up at his face. A curious expression came over her features. "My husband was a very handsome man," she said slowly. "But that wasn't what first attracted me to him. He had the same quality as you. The same allure."

"I'm not sure I want to be compared to Danny Crowe," he said grimly.

Leni stiffened as she gazed up at him. "How did you know his name?"

CHAPTER EIGHTEEN

LENI'S HEART WAS BEATING so quickly she could hardly breathe. "How did you know my husband's name?" she asked again.

Cade shrugged, but his expression darkened. "I don't know. You must have mentioned it."

"No, I didn't."

"Then someone else—"

"I don't think so." Leni started backing away from him. He put out a hand, but she slapped it away. "Don't touch me."

"Leni, come on. We've got to get out of here—"

She shook her head. "I'm not going anywhere until you tell me who you are. How you knew my husband's name. Why you have his eyes."

Cade glanced away, as if no longer able to meet her gaze.

Leni put a shaking hand to her mouth. "You get hunches just like Danny did. You're afraid of snakes just like he was. You reminded me of him the first time I laid eyes on you. Oh, my God."

"Leni—"

She shook her head, refusing to believe what her instincts were telling her. "It can't be. It isn't possible."

He said nothing, but this time, he didn't turn away from her. He stared down at her for the longest moment as a thousand emotions crashed over Leni.

"Who are you?" she asked in a desperate whisper.

"You know who I am, Leni. You've always known."

"DANNY?" A look of joyous disbelief transformed her features, and for one crazy moment, Cade thought it was going to be okay. She took a step toward him, and then she was in his arms, and he was holding her close. So close it was hard to breathe, but Cade didn't care. He never wanted to let her go. His eyes filled with tears, and he squeezed them closed. He had never thought to feel this way again. Had never thought he would hold Leni like this again.

Wiping away her own tears, she drew back and searched his face. "It is you," she whispered in wonder. "I can't believe it. I don't understand. How—"

"Shush." He knew she needed an explanation and he would have to give her one, but not now. Not yet. The truth would bring a whole new set of problems, but for now, for one moment in time, he had his wife back.

He pulled her into his arms, but something had changed. Leni wasn't quite as pliant, wasn't quite as joyful as she had been a moment ago. She hung back, still studying his face. "Why?"

The word was softly spoken, but there was an edge of anger in her voice.

"I can explain," he said, just as softly.

"Can you? You can explain why you let me think you were dead all this time? Why you let me grieve for you? Why you let me live with the almost unbearable guilt of having asked you for a divorce on the night I thought you were killed?

"You can explain why for three years, you left me in a living hell while you...while *you*..." She seemed overcome with fury all of a sudden. She tore her hands through her hair. "While you were doing *what?*"

"Leni, please calm down—"

"Calm down?" she all but screamed at him. "Don't you think I have a right to be upset? Oh, God, when I think of all the nights—"

Cade felt the tremors at the same moment she did. He was watching her face and saw her eyes widen as they both glanced at the roof of the tunnel. Dirt sifted down over them.

Cade threw down the candle, and grabbed Leni's hand. "Come on!"

He managed to flip on the flashlight as they raced through the narrow passage. An avalanche of rock and dirt tumbled into the tunnel behind them. The air grew thick with dust, but they kept going, running as fast as they could away from the collapse.

Finally, as the air began to clear, Cade slowed their pace. But if he thought the new crisis had bought him a reprieve, he was dead wrong. When he turned back to Leni, the look on her face told him everything. Told him just what the last three years had cost her. Told him that there was a very good chance he'd lost her forever this time.

"Why?" was all she said before she slid down the wall and began to cry.

CHAPTER NINETEEN

"OH, GOD, I HATE to cry," Leni blubbered. "I never cry. Not even at Danny's funeral—" She broke off and sobbed even harder. She couldn't seem to stop.

Danny was alive! A part of her had never felt such intense elation, but even in that first moment of wonder, the sense of betrayal had already set in. He'd let her think he was dead, and Leni didn't think she could ever forgive him for that.

Still, even in her anger, she found it difficult to keep her distance from him. She felt the need to touch him, to reassure herself he was real and this wasn't some kind of crazy dream. But if she touched him...if she let herself want him again...

Cade tried to put his arms around her, but she pushed him away. "Don't touch me!"

"I'm sorry." He rose and gazed around in frustration, as if not having a clue what to do or say. "I'd like to tell you what happened," he finally said.

She sniffed, wiping her nose on a tissue she found in her pocket. "I can't wait to hear it."

He came back and sat down beside her. "Everything the police told you was true. My cover was blown, and a hit was put out on me. My car did go over an overpass that night, but I somehow managed to climb out of the wreckage before the explosion. When I came to in the hospital, I knew I was going to be a wanted man for the rest of my life, and worse, your life could be in danger as well. When the feds offered me a deal, a new identity in exchange for what I knew, I took it. I had no choice. I was moved to a series of safe houses the first year, and then I was let go, with a new identity, but very little else. I settled in Denver for a while, then L.A., then Montana. For three years, I've been drifting, because the one place I wanted to be was the only place I couldn't go.''

''Why didn't you tell me?'' Leni cried, caught up in the urgency of his story in spite of herself. ''Why make *me* think you were dead?''

''Because it was the only way to convince them I was dead. These people are ruthless, Leni. If they'd suspected I was still alive, they might have come after you to get to me. I couldn't take that chance.''

''Might have,'' she said slowly. ''But you didn't know for sure they'd come after me. You let me think you were dead because of what *might* have happened.''

''You wanted a divorce, remember?'' he asked grimly. ''You didn't want to be married to me anymore. I thought it was the best way of setting you free. Letting you get on with your life. At least if I was dead, you'd have my pension. The city had to give it to you, because it would have looked suspicious if they hadn't. It was the only way I had of taking care of you.''

''You thought I'd want money that came from your death?'' she asked incredulously. ''I haven't touched a cent of it.''

''I guess I should have known it. That sounds like you.'' His gaze was suddenly tender, but Leni didn't trust it.

She turned away. ''You can't imagine what my life has been like for the last three years. The hell I've been through.''

''I have some idea, believe me.'' His voice grew harsh

again. "Besides, I thought that's what you wanted. I thought you wanted to be on your own."

"What I wanted was my husband back. I didn't want to be married to a stranger, a man who was hardly ever home, and when he was..." Leni trailed off, the pain of remembering almost too much to bear. "You changed so much."

"I know. I lost sight of who I was. What I was. I got so caught up in living a lie, I didn't know what the truth was anymore."

"Why did you come to Rio Rancho?" she asked him. "To finally tell me you were alive?"

He shook his head. "I didn't think you'd recognize me with all the surgeries I've had since the accident. Even my voice has changed." He touched his throat. "I didn't plan to interfere in your life. I just wanted to be near you. Even if you were with someone else. I told myself I could deal with that, but seeing you that first night with that deputy. And then Cantrell—"

"Jake Cantrell? He's just a friend. So is Glen Reardon."

"Are you saying there's no one in your life?"

Leni's gaze met his. "There's no one," she said. "And that's the way I intend to keep it."

CHAPTER TWENTY

THE FLASHLIGHT BLINKED once, twice, and then went out altogether. Cade shook it viciously, but he couldn't get so much as a flicker.

They'd moved on, and for the last several moments, Leni hadn't spoken a word. Cade couldn't blame her. She was probably still in shock. Probably still angry and hurt, and he wanted to believe that she would come around in time. She would understand why he'd done what he had. Why he'd had no choice. But Leni was a proud woman, and she could be stubborn as hell. Besides the hurt, he'd abused her trust in him, and that wasn't something that could easily be repaired.

He stopped for a moment, and lit one of the candles he'd stuffed in his coat pocket earlier. The wick caught, the flame danced to life, then went out. Cade struck another match. It went out before he had time to light the candle.

He glanced around. The air in the tunnel was colder. A draft was getting in from somewhere.

"I feel cold air," he said.

"So do I." Leni moved up beside him.

He wanted to take her hand and pull her forward, but he knew she wouldn't welcome the contact. "Let's keep moving. Maybe there's another hole somewhere ahead of us."

Thirty or forty feet ahead, the air grew almost frigid. The tunnel had collapsed again, and a wall of rock blocked their way. But toward the top of the boulders, the night sky glimmered with stars.

"Look!" Leni started to hurry toward the opening, but Cade held her back.

"We need to be careful," he warned. "We could start another cave-in if we loosen the wrong rock."

Leni nodded. "What should we do?"

"We'll have to climb up. There's no other way. But we'll do it one at a time. You go first. You're lighter than I am," he said when she started to protest. "If my weight shifts the rock, then we'll both be trapped in here."

As carefully as she could, Leni began to climb. The boulders at the bottom were stable, but toward the top, the rocks were smaller, and once or twice she unwittingly sent a shower of dirt and gravel tumbling down on Cade.

With something of a shock, Leni realized that she thought of him as Cade, not Danny. He was the same man, and yet he wasn't. The last three years had been torture, and she wasn't certain she could ever forgive him for that. But at the same time, she'd seen the evidence of his own pain, and not just physically. He'd suffered, too. He'd been lonely, too. It was possible he'd been through an even darker hell than she had.

But she wouldn't think about that now. She had to concentrate on climbing toward that opening. Pulling herself up and out of the tunnel.

She was almost there!

The cold night wind blasted against her face as she struggled through the opening. Leni lay on the ground for a moment, unable to believe she was finally out. She was finally free.

But Cade was still trapped inside.

She rolled over and peered down the hole. "Cade?"

He'd left the candle on the floor of the tunnel, and Leni

could see him as he climbed toward her. At the sound of his name, he glanced up.

And the rock shifted beneath his feet.

Leni gasped as she saw him fall, and she reached down to try and grab him. But he was too far away. And before she could lean down any farther, the pile of rocks came crashing down on him.

LENI HEARD the telltale snap of a dead twig a split second before a voice spoke from behind her. She whirled as the white-haired man stepped carefully out of the shadow of a boulder, his rifle at his side. But it was the other man who held his gun on Leni. He cocked the trigger as he eased over the rocky terrain toward her. "You didn't think you could get away from us that easily, did you, Red?"

"Where's the other one?" the white-haired man demanded.

It took all of Leni's willpower not to glance at the hole. "He's dead. He was buried in the cave-in."

He pointed to the opening with the barrel of his rifle. "See if you can spot him down there," he said to his partner.

The other man knelt at the opening and shined his flashlight inside. "He's not moving. I think he's dead."

A fist of dread closed over Leni's heart. No! Not again! She couldn't lose him again!

"Go down there and make sure," the white-haired man ordered. "That fool rancher almost got away, thanks to you. Don't make the same mistake with these two."

The second man took a coil of rope from his shoulder, fastened one end to a boulder, then dropped the other end into the hole. Within seconds, he'd disappeared into the abyss.

"Cade, watch out!" Leni screamed. She tried to run to

the opening, but the white-haired man grabbed her arm and threw her to the ground. In the next instant, a gunshot sounded from below, and for a second, Leni felt as if her own heart had stopped beating.

Terror surged through her, and then a dark rage came over her. "No!" She lunged toward the white-haired man, but he stopped her with a rifle butt against her shoulder. She fell hard against the frozen ground, the breath knocked out of her.

She was going to die. Leni knew there was no way out of this, but she almost didn't care. Cade was dead. What did she have to live for?

Revenge, a little voice whispered inside her.

The white-haired man smiled down at her, as if he'd read her mind. "You let my friend die back there. Now it's time to pay up." He lifted the rifle. "I'm going to enjoy this."

Leni didn't close her eyes, but gazed at him steadily, almost defiantly. "You won't get away with this. There are men in town right now looking for you."

"They won't find me. They never do."

Leni watched, breathless, as the man's finger squeezed the trigger. She heard the sound as it echoed down the mountain, and for a moment, after he'd fired, she wondered why she felt no pain.

And then, as if in slow motion, he tumbled backward as a hand closed around his ankle and jerked.

Using the rope, Cade pulled himself up out of the hole. But before he could get to his feet, the white-haired man had regained his balance. He swung the rifle around as Cade sprang toward him, and the two went crashing to the ground.

The rifle between them, they fought viciously. To the death. Then suddenly, the ground shifted beneath them as they rolled toward the opening into the tunnel. The white-haired man clung to Cade for a moment, then screamed as he fell. Leni rushed toward Cade. Dropping to her knees, she grabbed his arms and helped him over the edge a split second before dirt and rock collapsed inward, sealing the opening—and the white-haired man's fate.

Breathless, Leni and Cade found their way into each other's arms.

"Leni, I'm sorry. I'm so sorry," he muttered, over and over. "I didn't think I had a choice."

She closed her eyes. "I didn't think I could ever forgive you. I didn't think I'd ever be able to trust you, but when I thought you were dead…again…" She trembled uncontrollably. "I don't want to lose you a second time. I couldn't stand it."

"I've changed," he warned her. "I'm not the man who lost his way from you, but I'm not the man you married, either. Danny Crowe is dead. He has to be."

"I know. And a part of me will always miss him. He was my first love, but—"

Cade lifted a brow. "But?"

"You'll be my last."

And then, after a long moment, they rose to their feet. Cade took Leni's hand, and with nothing but moonlight to guide them, they started down the mountain together.

BAYOU REUNION

Rebecca York

CHAPTER ONE

CHASE MELANCON FELT his chest tighten as he pulled to a stop at the wrought-iron gate to Belle Vista plantation. Contrary to the name, the view wasn't very impressive. The gate hung crookedly on rusted hinges. And tall stands of cane had encroached on the access road, making it look more like a trail through the swamp than the entrance to a grand estate.

Before climbing out of the van to move the barrier aside, Chase swept his dark gaze over the cypress and oak trees that blocked out most of the light. Then he picked up the automatic pistol that lay on the passenger seat and stuffed it in his belt. No use getting shot before he got a chance to inspect his property.

"My property," he said aloud as he brushed back the thick dark hair that had fallen over his brow.

The reality of ownership struck him as he closed his strong hands around the rusted metal, and he went very still. Belle Vista plantation was *his*. Defying convention and his grasping relatives, old man Rousseau had left the house and surrounding land to Chase Melancon.

He shook his head, still hardly able to believe the turn of events. The Melancon family had been servants on this plantation—at the beck and call of the Rousseaus. And now a Melancon was the top dog. If he lived long enough to establish his claim.

After climbing back into the van, Chase drove slowly

up the rutted drive, holding his breath as he came around the final curve and saw the house. From a distance, in the rays of the late afternoon sun, it looked just the same as he remembered. The wide galleries. The raised porch. The white columns. However, the closer he came to the edifice, the more he took in the state of disrepair. Some of the columns sagged. And mold discolored the corners of the white siding.

Well, he was going to put it all right. Turn the house and grounds into a showplace. And he had the skills to do it. Before he'd left to enlist in the army, his father had taught him everything he knew about repairs and restoration. Some of Chase's tools were in the trunk. He'd bring the rest from Lafayette later.

Again he drew his gun as he stepped onto the circular drive. Again he scanned the underbrush, looking for one of the Rousseau men, Hugo or Wyatt. Either of them would drop him in his tracks as soon as speak to him.

He was cautious, too, of the weathered boards under his feet as he climbed the wide front steps. They needed replacing. So did much of the porch surface.

Mr. Gaylord, the lawyer who had informed him of the legacy, had given him the key. He inserted it in the lock, pushed the door open, and stepped into the front hall.

Instantly he knew that something wasn't right. The scurry of footsteps caught his ears. One of the bastards had gotten here first after all.

"Hold it right there."

The intruder ignored him.

In a rush of movement, Chase pounded down the hall, gun drawn, in time to catch up with a fleeing figure disappearing through the kitchen door. He got a quick impression of a black T-shirt, black sweat pants. A baseball cap.

He grabbed an arm, whipped the intruder around. The baseball cap flew off, and long blond hair cascaded into view.

He drew in a quick, shocked breath as he found himself staring into the wide blue eyes of Julienne Rousseau....

CHAPTER TWO

CHASE FELT JULIENNE tremble, saw her sink against the wall, her ivory skin blotched by fear. Then he watched in fascination as she pulled herself together, straightened, lifted her chin as though her family still owned this place and he was the trespasser.

She'd been beautiful as a child, more so as an adolescent. But now...she was stunning. The pale skin, the wide blue eyes, and the wild golden hair creating a vision that called to him with a familiar, forbidden longing. For an instant he wondered if this was really her or some dream from his subconscious come to life.

Her gaze flicked from his face to the pistol in his hand.

"Are you going to shoot me, Chase?" she asked in the musical voice that he remembered so well—the voice that still had the power to stir his senses.

He pulled himself together. "Why shouldn't I? You're trespassing on my property."

Doubt kindled in her eyes. "I know. But we were... friends. I thought you'd..."

"I'd what?"

She gave a small shrug, but he was still dealing with her previous statement.

"Friends." He threw the word back at her. "I was the hired help. You were the little princess who wound your father—and everybody else—around your fingers."

"My father's dead now." She said it with deep sorrow.

"I'm sorry," he murmured before he remembered that he owed her nothing. They had played together as children. And when they had reached adolescence, he had longed for more than friendship. He'd even been foolish enough to think she returned his feelings—until the night he'd found out she was just toying with him.

He gave a small shake of his head. She'd dashed his hopes in the cruelest way possible, and he had left the next day to enlist in the army.

His eyes must have given him away, because he saw her cringe. Well, she was going to find out that he had a long memory.

"How did you get in here?" he demanded.

"It wasn't difficult. I opened a window."

He made his voice flat and hard. "What—did your brothers send you on ahead to try to persuade me to leave? Or are you supposed to get me to let down my guard so they can kill me?"

"My brothers don't know I'm here."

"I'll bet."

"It's the truth."

Julienne stared into his dark eyes, seeing the new anger and the old hurt. A wave of sadness swept over her. She'd come here in desperation. Now she realized her mistake—and she was terrified.

But she wouldn't let him see that, couldn't let him see.

"I knew Grandfather left you the plantation," she whispered. "I was happy for you when I heard."

"Why should I believe that—or any other lie you have to tell me?"

She tried to push past the harsh words, past the rigid way he held his body. Once his good looks had been boyish. Now he was all grown up and truly magnificent with a strong face and well-developed muscles. Even the dark hair that was a little too long and a little too shaggy added to the picture of defiant masculinity.

"Why should I believe you?" he said again.

She felt her eyes grow moist and struggled against the sudden surge of pain and fear.

"Because if you don't, then I'm in even worse trouble than I thought," she whispered.

CHAPTER THREE

CHASE WATCHED JULIENNE standing there with her breath shallow in her chest. He could throw her out right now. This house where she had grown up was his by the terms of her grandfather's will. But something stopped him. Maybe the ghost of their old friendship.

"This place was a mess," she said softly. "I cleaned it. I can help you fix it up. And I can cook." Before he could comment, she went on quickly, "You only remember the girl I was. I'm a lot different now."

He could see it. In her eyes. In the tight lines of her face.

"What are you really doing here?" he demanded.

"I knew you were coming home, and I needed a place to stay."

"Yeah? Well, let's be logical. You expect me to believe your brothers don't know you're here?"

"My brothers are in New Orleans. I went to them when I needed…help. And they turned me away. I haven't seen them since."

He felt his jaw drop open. "They turned you away? Why?"

She bent her head, spoke in a barely audible voice. "That's between me and them."

He took in her defeated posture and her low tone, and suddenly he didn't have the heart to keep jabbing at her. If she needed a place to crash, well, she could make herself useful around here for a couple of days. Then...she'd better leave, for both their sakes. Because if Hugo or Wyatt found her hanging out with Chase Melancon, they'd kill them both. And that would solve a big problem for the Rousseau brothers—because if the present owner died without heirs, this place reverted to the Rousseau family.

Julienne broke in to his thoughts, and he could see she was making an effort to change the subject. "The electricity and the gas aren't turned on. But I have a cooler and a camp stove. I made Creole gumbo yesterday. Are you hungry?"

He realized suddenly that he was.

He followed her into the kitchen, silently acknowledging that she had told the truth about one thing, at least. The room sparkled. She'd cleaned the countertops, the old appliances, the floor.

"I've got some of the old hurricane lamps out of the cellar. For when it gets dark," she said.

"Okay. Tomorrow I can check the electrical system, see if it's safe to turn it on."

"You know how to do that?"

"Yeah." Pulling out a chair, he sat down, stretching out his legs as he watched her efficiently prepare a meal on her makeshift equipment.

As the gumbo warmed, it filled the room with a wonderful aroma. She set a plate in front of him. And a cup of strong, chicory-laced coffee.

"Aren't you going to eat?"

"I had lunch a little while ago." She propped her hips against the counter, keeping several yards of space between them.

He forked up a bite of the seafood stew. It was rich and flavorful—the way he liked it.

She'd gone to a lot of trouble to please him, it seemed.

Yet he found it was impossible to stifle the kernel of resentment that he'd carried inside himself all these years.
Tipping his head to one side, he peered at her. "This is
good. My compliments to the chef—and to your house-
keeping."

Her cheeks colored, but her eyes turned suddenly wary.
"Thank you," she said in a thin voice.

His eyes traveled over her. She was wearing a shapeless
man's shirt and baggy chino pants, clothing that almost but
not quite hid her feminine curves. "What if cooking and
cleaning aren't enough to earn your keep?"

He saw her swallow before asking carefully, "What do
you mean, exactly?"

"I think you know what I mean. I might require a little
more of you than just household help."

Her skin color changed from pink to white. "No."

"So even though I own this place now, I'm still not
good enough for you?" he pressed.

She knitted her hands together in front of her. "I...
can't."

The broken way she said it sent a ripple of cold skim-
ming over his skin. Instinctively he knew that his words
had cut her more deeply than he'd believed possible.
"Julienne?"

He started to rise, started to go to her. But she was
already darting out of his reach. She fled from the kitchen
and he stared at the door flapping back and forth behind
her long after she'd disappeared.

CHAPTER FOUR

JULIENNE FLED FROM CHASE—fled up the wide front stairs, then along the upper hall to the small room she'd taken for herself. Without thinking, she rushed across the room and threw herself into the closet, pulling the door closed behind her. In the dark, she huddled against the wall, her knees drawn up against her chest and her head bent.

She'd been a fool to think that this could work, a fool to assume that Julienne Rousseau could just walk back into Chase Melancon's life—and everything would be all right between them. Not after the way it had all ended seven years ago.

Her cheeks were wet, and she swiped at them with the back of her hand, struggling to get control of her roiling emotions, angry with herself and with him.

She might as well pack up and leave, she thought, wondering where she was going to go.

When she heard footsteps in the hall, she went rigid.

"Julienne?" It was Chase, his voice soft but urgent.

She didn't answer.

"Julienne, that was a dumb thing for me to say. I'm sorry. Really sorry. You can trust me to act like a gentleman."

There was a long pause, during which her heart started to pound wildly in her chest. Did he mean that? Or was he just saying it because it was what he thought she wanted to hear?

"Don't do anything as stupid as I did. Don't run away from me. Please," he added, and she heard his contrite, strained tone.

He sounded almost as upset as she felt, but her throat was too clogged for her to answer. And even if she could have spoken, she wasn't sure what she would have said.

"I'm going to bring some stuff in from the van. Then I'm going down to the den. I'd…like it if you came down, too."

Chase stood in the hall, his breath shallow in his chest. It took all his formidable will to stop himself from tearing down the hall, tearing through the rooms to find her.

The wounded, vulnerable look on her face when she'd fled the kitchen haunted him.

Something had happened to her. Something bad. He knew that from the violence of her reaction—knew it as surely as he knew the pain he felt inside himself now. And he was deathly afraid that he might know what it was.

He wanted to call out to her again. *Chère, trust me. Just trust me enough to tell me what happened to you.*

Trust him!

After the insult he'd flung at her? Cursing himself, he turned and stalked down the stairs, forcing himself to tread lightly in his heavy boots.

Shadows gathered like ghosts around him in the darkened hallway. Outside, he stood for a moment in the waning sunlight, dragging in air and expelling it in great gusts. Then he slammed open the door of the van and began pulling out heavy equipment, straining his muscles, the exertion calming him a little.

But only a little. Because he knew he had screwed up badly. And the worst part was that he didn't know if she would give him a second chance.

CHAPTER FIVE

JULIENNE STEPPED QUIETLY out of her room. There was no electricity or running water in the house, but she'd used some of the water she'd hauled from the cistern to wash her face and hands.

Although the sun had almost set, there was a glow at the end of the hall, and she saw that Chase had left a lighted hurricane lamp for her. Picking it up, she found her hand was trembling.

By the time she reached the den, she felt as if her heart was going to pound its way through the wall of her chest.

Chase was slumped in one of the armchairs. Hardly making a sound, she glided into the room and took an identical chair a few feet away.

"Thank you for coming back," he said.

"I guess I had to."

"Why?"

"I've waited seven years to tell you what happened the night you left."

He made a low, strangled sound in his throat. "You don't owe me any explanations. We were just kids back then."

Ignoring him, she swallowed hard and went on. "I know you thought I chickened out. Or decided you weren't good enough for me, and I changed my mind about...about making love with you." She said it in a rush, glad that the darkness hid her suddenly hot cheeks. "I was coming to meet you, like we planned. Then I realized my brother, Wyatt, was following me. I knew if he caught us together, he'd...hurt you.''

"I could take care of myself.''

"Chase, he had a gun. I saw it.''

He cursed softly.

She had more to say, but now it was impossible for her to speak above a whisper. "I was coming to find you the next morning. But you...you'd cleared out.''

Her hands twisted together in her lap as she said, "I know you were never sure of what I felt for you. Is that why you didn't stick around?''

She thought he wasn't going to answer. Then his voice cut across the darkness. "That was part of it. Back then, I wasn't all that sure of myself.''

Silence stretched between them until she said, "I heard later that you'd joined the army. How was it?''

"Okay. I did my hitch. Then I moved to Lafayette and put the skills I learned from my dad to work. Doing remodeling jobs and restorations of old houses. Like this one.''

She was eager to hear more. It sounded as though he'd made a success of his life, and she was so happy for him.

But when he spoke again, it was to change the subject abruptly. "What happened to you after I left?''

"I got a job with an accounting firm.''

"And then?''

A simple question. She gave him as simple an answer. "I quit. Then I came back here.''

She knew he was waiting for her to elaborate, but she sat with her head bowed.

"Someone...hurt you,'' he finally said, and she felt a shiver cross her skin.

"Yes,'' she whispered, wishing her previous behavior

hadn't given her away. But then, Chase had always been perceptive.

"Can you tell me about it?" he asked softly.

She sucked in a couple of ragged breaths and let them out. Before she could change her mind, she blurted. "I was working late. This guy…this guy…broke into the building. I guess he came to steal stuff. And I was in the wrong place at the wrong time. He had a gun. He…uh…he dragged me into the boss's office. Pulled me down on the rug…and he…" Her voice hitched and she stopped speaking.

"Did he rape you?"

The ugly word hung between them like a razor-sharp sword.

She couldn't speak, only nod as she slid lower in her chair.

"And I was dumb enough to come on to you in the kitchen."

"You didn't know," she managed.

"That doesn't matter. I should have treated you better."

"Chase, it's not you. It's me. I ran away from you because I don't know if I can let a man touch me."

CHAPTER SIX

CHASE FELT HIS HEART twist inside his chest as he heard Julienne's broken voice. She had said that she didn't know if she could let a man touch her. But her next words humbled him.

"I came here because I wanted to be near you. Maybe that's not fair of me. But here I am."

She looked so fragile. So lovely. He wanted to go to her then, take her in his arms. "*Chère,* I want to be closer to you," he said. "If I come over there, will I frighten you?"

"No," she answered, but he heard the quaver in her voice.

Carefully he eased himself up, then moved to the floor beside her chair. He touched the back of her hand and felt her jump. Then she seemed to relax as he folded his fingers around hers. He held her hand for long moments, then brought her fingers to his lips and kissed them.

"*Chère,*" he murmured, his lips moving against her flesh, "I give you my word, anything you and I do together, it will be because it's what we both want. Okay?"

"Okay," she answered, her voice still uneven, her eyes telling him she couldn't believe how much he was offering her. She looked quickly away, and took her lower lip between her teeth, but he sensed that there was still something she wanted to say.

"What?" he asked softly, stroking his thumb across her knuckles.

She swallowed, then whispered, "You mean you still might want...me, after what I told you?"

His chest felt so tight that he could hardly breathe. "How can you even ask that question?"

"Because Hugo and Wyatt..." She gulped. "They said I was looking for trouble. That I never should have been at the office that late." Again she came to a halt.

He felt a surge of anger at the two men who couldn't even stand up for their sister in a time of trouble. But then, Hugo and Wyatt had never impressed him as being interested in helping anyone besides themselves. "You mean those no-good bastards blamed *you?*"

"People were talking about me. My brothers didn't like it. I can understand why."

He swore under his breath. "You get attacked and those jerks feel as if their honor's been tarnished. I'd like to kill them."

"That won't do either one of us any good."

He nodded tightly.

"I had to get away. Then I knew you were coming back, and I was hoping you'd let me stay here. Until I get on my feet."

"That's all you want? To stay here for a little while?"

"I...want more than that," she said in a small voice. "But I don't dare let myself think about how much I want."

"You can dare anything! You always had guts. You got together with me when we were teenagers—when you knew your grandfather would whip your hide if he found us together."

"It didn't work out, did it?"

"It will," he said with conviction.

"How can it? I told you I can't stand being touched."

"I'm touching you now."

He saw her eyes widen. "You are. I guess because it's you, and I didn't even think about it."

He squeezed her hand, but he didn't ask for anything more. Not yet. "So what about your brothers?" he asked. "What are their plans?"

"They didn't confide in me. I think they'll try to take this place away from you."

"I'll be ready for them."

"I hope so. But they're...dangerous."

"I know. I'm not going to get careless." Before she could continue with the subject, he said, "You should get some sleep." His hand moved to stroke her beautiful golden hair, but he thought better of it and pulled back at the last minute. "Things will look better in the morning."

"They already look better."

"Good."

He left the oil lamp where it was and switched on the nine-volt flashlight he'd brought. It wasn't as charming as the lamplight, but it was more practical for moving around in the dark. He'd come back later and put out the lamps.

Stepping into the hall, he followed Julienne toward the stairs. He was only a few paces behind her when he heard her scream....

CHAPTER SEVEN

JULIENNE'S SCREAM SENT Chase pounding after her. In the darkened hallway ahead of him, he saw her arms flail, her body teeter, then drop several feet as her legs disappeared through the floor. Tossing the flashlight aside with a clatter, he sprang forward and grabbed her under the arms before she could fall to the basement below.

The flashlight had landed with its beam pointing in the wrong direction. But he could just make out what had happened. A section of the old flooring had given way beneath her. And he could feel the damaged boards bowing under his own weight. If he wasn't careful, they were both going to crash through and land on the cellar floor.

"*Chère*, don't move," he cautioned. "Hold perfectly still."

She gulped. "Okay."

The boards under him groaned. Praying he could get her out in time, he lay down on his stomach and stretched out his legs to distribute his weight over as wide an area as possible.

Still, the surface made a cracking noise. Then some of the wood fell away, crashing onto the cement floor below them.

Julienne made a strangled sound.

"It's going to be fine. You're doing great," he said as he gently pulled her up, moving backward as he eased her legs through the broken area.

She cried out as a board tore across her pant leg, and he stopped abruptly. Then the floor shifted under him, and he knew he had to move quickly. Jerking backward, he took Julienne with him. She choked out a sob as they tumbled together onto a section of the floor where the surface felt stable.

He felt her shoulders shaking, heard her gasp of relief as he clasped her in his arms.

He lay on his back. She was sprawled across him, both of them breathing hard.

"Are you all right?" he asked, between gulps of air.

"Yes. Oh, God, Chase, the floor..."

"You're safe now. I've got you."

He squeezed his eyes shut, relief flooding through him like morning sunlight. He clung to her, stroking his hands across her shoulders, over her hair, feeling her trembling subside as her body relaxed against his.

At first all he could think about was what might have happened if he hadn't gotten there in time. He pressed her close, feeling the way her slender body molded itself to his.

His hand stroked up and down her back, comforting her, as well as himself. It had been an eternity since he had held her in his arms. Yet the time they'd been apart suddenly seemed of no importance.

She'd been a teenager back then. Now her body was more mature, more feminine. He could feel the soft mounds of her breasts, which had flattened themselves against his chest, her hips pressing against his middle. The narrow indentation of her waist, where his free hand curved to steady her.

Without conscious thought, the stroking of his hands changed, becoming more sensual as long-buried needs rose

to the surface of his mind. His body hardened, and he made
a low sound in his throat as he gathered her closer. For a
moment ripe with promise, she seemed to melt against him.

Then, in an instant, the sensual spell shattered.

CHAPTER EIGHT

ONE MOMENT CHASE WAS holding a warm and pliant woman in his arms. In the next, she was gasping in fear, pushing herself away from him. Frantically she levered her body off his and scooted across the floor, putting the width of the hall between them.

When he saw the wild, panicked look in her eyes, he called out gently, "Don't run away from me." At the same time he slowly pushed himself to a sitting position.

Julienne stayed where she was, her back pressed to the wall.

Slowly he turned to face her, but made no move to come any closer. As he stared at her, he felt a wave of tender emotions surge through him. He had been afraid to admit his vulnerability, even to himself. But he had never stopped loving this woman. Never—no matter how hard he had tried to put her out of his mind.

And now here they were, facing each other across four feet of charged space that might as well have been the width of the earth.

"*Chère,* it's all right. I won't hurt you."

"You...you got hard," she whispered. "I could feel it—pressing against my leg."

His heart was thudding inside his chest, but he kept his gaze steady, kept his voice even. "That's right. I couldn't keep myself from wanting you. Not when you were lying on top of me."

Her next words shook him to the core. "You think I was trying to turn you on?"

"Of course not!"

He saw her swallow and knew that what she had been through—with the rapist and then with her damn fool brothers—had affected her thinking on every level. He knew, too, that he could lose her if he wasn't careful. "*Chère,* I'm not blaming you for anything," he said softly.

"Why not?" she pressed.

"You were frightened, and you were clinging to me because I'd just pulled you out of that hole in the floor. And I was frightened, too. At first all I thought about was holding on to you—making sure you were safe. Then…when I knew you were all right, I started feeling how soft and feminine you were in my arms. There's nothing wrong with any of that."

He watched her moisten her lips, give a small nod.

He could see she was hanging on to every word as he added, "Please, don't be afraid of me. I would never do anything to you that you didn't want me to do. Do you understand that?"

"I want to believe you."

"*Chère,* I would never lie to you."

Julienne looked into his eyes, longing with every fiber of her being to believe him—to believe that the two of them could win back everything they'd both lost. She had come here with that hope blazing in her mind—in her soul.

With a small nod, she pushed herself up straighter. "I knew this wasn't going to be easy," she murmured.

"But you came here. You came to me."

"Yes."

"Can you talk about why?"

I came here because I love you. Because I knew you were the only man in the world who could help me. The

words trembled inside her, but they were still too dangerous to speak. Instead, she gave him a quick shake of her
head.

She breathed a sigh of relief when he didn't press her.
Suddenly aware that they were still sitting on the floor in
the hall, she started to push herself up and gave a small
gasp....

CHAPTER NINE

WHAT? WHAT'S WRONG? Are you hurt?" Chase asked urgently.

Julienne pulled up her pant leg, inspected her ankle. Where her foot had plunged through the floorboards, the skin was raw and scraped.

"You're bleeding," he said, and she realized that he had instinctively moved closer to her.

"I'll be fine."

"You can get a nasty infection—unless we clean that up."

She might have protested, but she knew he was right. So she let him lead her back down the hall to the den.

Sinking into the chair where she'd been sitting previously, she leaned her head back and closed her eyes, trying to hold herself together.

She heard stamping noises out in the hallway, and thought Chase was probably testing the floor to make sure there wouldn't be any other nasty surprises.

When she heard his footsteps returning, her eyes snapped open. He was carrying the camp flashlight, a bowl of water, paper towels, and a first aid kit.

He set the light on the floor where it could shine on her leg. Then he hunkered down beside her chair.

"*Chère,* I'm going to wash the wound, then put on antiseptic. Okay?"

"Okay," she agreed, struggling to keep her voice steady.

She watched as he dipped the towel into the water.

When his fingers touched her ankle, she sucked in a small breath, held herself rigid.

His ministrations were gentle as he cleaned her injured flesh, then brought the flashlight closer so he could inspect the wound.

"I don't see any splinters. Do you feel any?"

"I don't think so."

"Good."

He swabbed on the antiseptic, and she couldn't hold back a small sound as she felt the sting.

"I'm sorry."

"It's not your fault."

She watched him retrieve a roll of gauze, watched him slip off her shoe so he could wind the bandage under her heel and around her ankle. As his fingers moved against her skin, she shivered, but she didn't draw away. After he'd tied the end of the gauze, he kept hold of her.

"I'd forgotten how small your feet are," he murmured, stroking his finger under her arch.

She remembered long ago when he'd held her foot like this. "You used to tease me about them. You told me they looked like they belonged to a little kid."

"You remember that?" he asked with a laugh.

"Mmm-hmm."

"Now I think they're very feminine," he said, clasping her flesh more tightly.

He stared up at her, simply stroking her foot, his fingers playing with her heel, her instep. His touch felt good, so good that she ached to forget her fears. But they were still there, in the background, ready to overwhelm her if she thought he was going to make demands she couldn't meet.

He must have sensed her uncertainty, because he gently

slid her slipper back on and stood, wiping his hands across the knees of his pants.

She pushed herself out of the chair, tested the injured ankle.

"All right?" he asked.

"Yes."

"Then we should go to bed," he said. "And in the morning, I'm going to take a good look at that floor."

The suddenly sharp tone of his voice made her heartbeat quicken.

"What are you saying?" she asked.

"The boards didn't break by themselves. Someone cut through them."

CHAPTER TEN

JULIENNE LOOKED STUNNED. "Someone cut the floor-boards?" she asked. "But who?"

"Three guesses. Or rather two," Chase answered, his voice coming out more sharply than he intended.

"You think my brothers were here?" She gulped. "Doing things?"

"Yeah, that's exactly what I think."

Her head jerked up. "I didn't see them."

"Maybe they came for a visit before you arrived."

"Maybe? You think I saw them here, and I didn't say anything about it?"

"No. Of course not," he answered quickly, wondering exactly what he *had* been thinking.

Picking up the flashlight, she started for the hall.

When he grabbed her arm, she went rigid.

He let his own hand drop back to his side. "Wait. I don't want you getting hurt again. Stay on the left side of the hall, away from the hole."

"I was planning to do that," she clipped out.

As he watched her walk rapidly up the stairs, he cursed softly under his breath. He hadn't meant to accuse her of anything. But it seemed she'd taken it that way.

He squeezed his hands into fists, wishing he could close them around the neck of the man who had raped her—and then do the same with her damn brothers. The Julienne he remembered had been so confident, so sure of herself. The rapist had made her afraid of men. It seemed her brothers had done their best to pound her self-esteem into the ground.

With a sigh, he waited until he heard her door close. Then he went back for the oil lamp and started up the stairs to the room where he'd put his luggage.

Chase kicked off his shoes and socks and lay down on the bed in his jeans and T-shirt. It seemed to take aeons for him to fall asleep. Then it felt like only moments later when suddenly a sound jerked him awake. Grabbing the gun he'd shoved under his pillow, he leaped out of bed and stood listening intently.

The sound came again. A moan. From Julienne's room.

The gun at the ready, he ran down the hall and threw open her door.

He had expected to find someone in the room with her, but she was alone, her head thrashing on the pillow.

"No," she whimpered in her sleep.

She was dressed in a long T-shirt that would have skimmed her thighs if it hadn't ridden up, revealing the silky fabric of the panties she wore underneath, and her long, lovely legs.

The gun was still in his hand as he crossed the room.

Then her eyes snapped open and focused on him- focused on the weapon. The scream that tore from her throat made his whole body go rigid. She sprang back, her shoulders hitting the wall.

"*Chère,* no! It's all right. I didn't mean to frighten you. I thought someone was attacking you. But you were having a bad dream." As he spoke, he set the gun down on the dresser.

She stared at him, her back still wedged against the wall as though she needed the support to hold herself upright.

"I'm sorry I scared you," he repeated. "I'll leave if you want," he added, waiting for her answer with his breath frozen in his lungs.

CHAPTER ELEVEN

JULIENNE WET her parched lips. "What if I wanted you to stay here? What if I wanted you to hold me...but I was pretty sure I couldn't give you any more than that?"

Her whole body tensed as she waited to hear his answer to that. It came swiftly.

"You don't have to give me anything, *chère*. You only have to let me shield you from your nightmares."

His eyes were fixed on her as he took a step toward her and then another. Each step closed a little more of the space between them until he was standing beside the bed.

He towered over her, and for a moment she felt her chest tighten.

"Can I sit down?"

"Yes," she managed.

She was vividly conscious of his weight making the mattress shift. Then he scooted across the bed and joined her, sitting with his back against the wall.

Lazily he stretched out his legs and leaned comfortably back.

She stayed where she was for long moments—watching him, wondering if she could really handle this. Then, before she could change her mind, she closed the distance between them, pressing her shoulder against his.

Slowly, giving her time to escape, he turned toward her. When she stayed where she was, he opened his arms, and she moved into them, moved so that she was pressed against the solid wall of his chest. With a small sigh, she let her eyes drift closed and her head fall to his shoulder. She breathed in his scent, snuggled into the warmth of his body. The strong arms that circled her shoulders were like a refuge.

"Oh, Chase," she murmured. "I missed you so much."

His hand stroked over her hair. "Did you?"

"Yes." She paused. "I wouldn't lie to you about that. Or anything else."

"I know."

She dragged in a breath and let it out in a rush. "But downstairs, when you asked if I'd seen my brothers here—"

He cut her off before she could finish the sentence. "I wasn't accusing you of anything. I was just frustrated, and I guess I was taking it out on you. I'm sorry. I won't do that again."

She nodded against his shoulder.

"And you won't run away from me. Deal?"

"Yes," she breathed.

"Because I've missed you, too."

"Did you? Why?"

"Are you fishing for compliments?"

"Maybe."

"You don't need to fish. I'll give them freely. You're more beautiful than the last time I saw you, and you're so brave."

"I'm a coward."

"If you were a coward, you wouldn't be here in my arms." He turned his head, stroked his lips against her cheek, her hair. "I'll hold you as long as you want me," he whispered.

Forever, she thought dreamily. If she could just stay in his arms forever, she would be content.

He made no demands on her, only held her and stroked her, and after a time she realized she wanted more.

"Chase?"

"Umm?"

"I want to kiss you."

"You don't have to ask permission."

"I know. But I want...you to understand...." She stopped, swallowed. "I mean...I don't think I can go any further than that. But I want to try. So much."

CHAPTER TWELVE

THEY WERE SITTING sideways across the bed, Chase's back pressed against the wall and Julienne in his arms.

Now he shifted her slightly so that his eyes could meet hers.

"I told you I wasn't going to push you into anything you're not ready for."

She could hear her own uneven breath rushing in and out of her lungs. "I want to kiss you," she repeated. "But what if…what if…you're not satisfied with that?"

"A kiss isn't going to turn me into a savage beast, if that's what you're worried about."

Despite herself, she laughed, and the laughter broke some of the tension. Without giving herself time to draw back, she slid her hand possessively across his broad shoulders.

"Oh, Chase." She sighed. "I dreamed of seeing you again. And now I don't know what I can give you."

"*Chère,* I'm here to give *you* anything you want. As little or as much."

Anything she wanted. With hands that trembled slightly, she reached up, tunneling her fingers through his dark hair so that she could bring his face within reach.

The first touch of his lips on hers was sweet and warm, like a familiar memory wafting on a spring breeze.

Chase. This was Chase, and she knew her instincts had been right all along. Coming to him was the right thing to do. His mouth melted against hers, and she made a little exclamation of pleasure. There was so much she wanted to say to him. So much locked inside her.

She was still afraid to speak the words, but she could show him what she was feeling. Eyes closed, she shut out everything but him, the taste of him, the feel of him. He sent her senses on overload as memories melded with present reality. She was aware of so many details. The silky texture of his hair slipping against her fingers, the hard muscles of his shoulders, the scent of soap and water and man.

"Julienne." Her name sighed out of him like a prayer of thanks.

Craving more, she eased his lips apart so that she could taste him more fully, drink him in.

And though his mouth moved hungrily over hers, she knew he was holding back—clamping down on the strength of his response.

When she finally lifted her head, they were both breathing hard. Her whole body felt hot and tingly. Her breasts ached. And her brain felt as if it were on fire.

She knew what she had always known. She wanted this man—needed him. Yet there were other remembered sensations, too. The panic that came from a man's heavy weight pressing her down into the carpet. The terror of helplessness. The fear of having all control taken away.

Chase must have seen the sudden panic racing through her because he drew back so that his chest was no longer pressed against her breasts.

"Chère?"

"I...can't. Not yet."

"I understand."

"But you want me," she answered, her gaze falling to

his lap. There was no way to hide the truth of what they both knew.

"And you want me. I know that as surely as you can see the state I'm in."

She gulped. "Yes."

"Then everything's going to be okay."

She wanted that to be true. More than anything she'd ever wanted in her life. Yet fear still kept her from reaching for her heart's desire.

CHAPTER THIRTEEN

CHASE GAZED INTO the troubled eyes of the woman he loved. "We can work things out, *chère,* because I'm willing to wait for you. For as long as it takes."

"And what if I...never can...give myself to you?"

"I think you will, because what we both want is stronger than your fear. But I'm not going to make demands. I told you that."

She gave him a tiny nod.

"If I leave you, will you be all right? Will the nightmares come back?"

"I don't know," she answered. "But we'd both better try to get some sleep."

"Okay."

In fact he lay awake long into the night—aroused and angry with the bastards who had torn Julienne's life to shreds.

Downstairs the next morning, he assessed the extent of the damage to the hall floor. Someone had made tiny cuts in the old wood-cuts that had allowed the boards to give way under Julienne's weight. He was pretty sure her low-life brothers had been in the house.

Last night she'd been worried that he'd think she was involved. No way! At least he could thank the Lord it hadn't happened when she was here alone, he thought as he got out a hammer, chisel, and crowbar and began removing rotten wood.

He had pulled up most of the damaged boards when he heard her footsteps above him—moving around the upper part of the house.

His breath stilled as he silently acknowledged that he'd been listening for her all along.

It seemed to take forever for her to reach the hall. Then, looking up, he saw her coming down the stairs. Her hair fell around her shoulders in a golden cloud. And she'd changed from jeans and a shirt into a soft pink-and-green shift that flowed around her legs, accenting her slender beauty. In the morning light she looked different. More relaxed. Younger. Freer.

As he stared at her, he saw color come into her cheeks.

"Hi," she said, her voice low and throaty. Then, "The nightmare didn't come back, and this morning...I woke up feeling...better."

"I'm glad."

"I mean better than I have in weeks. You make me feel strong," she added. "Strong enough to fight for what I want."

He thought he understood what she was telling him, and joy leaped inside him. He might have gone to her then and folded her into his arms, but he didn't want her to think he was pushing to satisfy his own needs.

Before he could respond, she gestured toward the pile of boards and went on quickly, "You must have been up early."

"I wanted to get this fixed as soon as possible."

"Have you eaten breakfast?"

"Just coffee." He picked up some wood and loaded it into the wheelbarrow that he'd brought into the hall. "It's pretty dark in here. I should put a barrier up so nobody falls into this hole."

"Not on my account. I'm not going to forget it's there."

"I guess not."

"Can I help you?"

"I'm fine."

"Then I'll fix you something to eat. How does old-fashioned Cajun-style French toast sound?"

"*Pain perdu?* Wonderful."

He wheeled the load of refuse down the hall, through the kitchen and out onto the back porch, where he dumped it into a canvas carrier.

From the top of the steps he stood looking out at the overgrown foliage in back of the house—the water oaks draped with Spanish moss. The thicket of cane had grown to twice the size he remembered. Here in the bayou country plants grew quickly, and in the time that the property had been neglected, unruly nature had invaded the once-manicured garden.

Back beyond the cane thicket was an area that his father had used as a dumping ground. He could stow the wood there—along with the other debris that he hauled out of the house.

The path to the place was almost obliterated, but he could just make it out from his vantage point on the porch. Slinging the carrier over his shoulder, he started into greenery—then froze as he heard the sound of steel jaws snapping shut....

CHAPTER FOURTEEN

JULIENNE HUMMED an old Cajun dance tune to herself as she cracked eggs into a bowl. Outside, the sultry warmth of another day was building. She had heard people complain about the steamy Louisiana heat. But she loved it. Loved being back at Belle Vista.

Then the morning calm was shattered by a shout.

She knew instantly that it was Chase. And it sounded as though he was in some kind of trouble out in the swampy area beyond the house.

Lord, she'd been feeling so at home. Now she remembered the dangers of this place. What if he'd come upon a gator or a poisonous snake, or even a bear? All of them had been known to venture near the house at one time or another.

Flinging open the kitchen door, she looked wildly around, but didn't spot him immediately.

"Chase?"

"I'm fine. Don't come out here."

Ignoring the warning, she crossed the porch, shading her eyes as she followed the sound of his voice. Finally she spotted his head and shoulders through a screen of foliage about fifty feet away. With no thought for her own safety, she pounded across the porch, then sprinted down the back steps. Crossing the yard at a dead run, she made for the tangle of greenery beyond the house.

He shot her a warning look. "Get back."

"No." Plowing ahead, she found him hunkered down in the dirt.

As she drew up beside him, he looked down toward the ground. When she followed his gaze, she saw that the toe of his work boot was caught in the massive jaws of a steel animal trap.

On a gasp, she knelt beside him, staring in dumb-eyed horror at the wicked-looking teeth that bit into the leather. "Chase! Are you all right?"

"Yeah. But I'd be better if you went back to the house."

"Not until I know your foot is all right."

He sighed. "It is. But I'm damn lucky I have on these steel-toed shoes—or this thing would be embedded in my foot right now." His features were set in grim lines as he studied the mechanism. Then he sprang the catch and began to ease the saw-toothed jaws open. Once his boot was free, he untied the lace and eased it off, carefully inspecting his foot.

Julienne held her breath until she saw that the sharp points had missed his flesh.

"Let's get out of here," he grated. "There could be other traps like this one out here—and Lord knows what else. I don't want you outside again until I make sure the area is secure."

Despite the heat, she shivered. She'd already walked around the house several times, inspecting the state of the property. It was only by dumb luck that she hadn't come this way.

When he slung his arm around her shoulder as he led her back to the house, she pressed herself tightly to his side.

They climbed the porch together, and he carefully shut the door, then turned to face her.

"Will you promise me you'll stay inside until I check the rest of the property?"

"I can't hide in here."

"Do you know how I'd feel if something happened to you?" He stopped and swallowed. "Like I'd lost a major part of myself."

"Oh, Chase. That's the way I feel. If something happened to you, I'd lose everything."

"I'm here. I'm fine! I'll be here for as long as you want me."

Though the words were uttered with an underlying passion, he stood unmoving.

CHAPTER FIFTEEN

"CHASE." Julienne whispered his name, because he filled her universe. She had been dead inside for months. Scared. Unsure of how she was going to face life. Now she knew. If she had the guts to reach for what she wanted.

And she understood she was the one who must do the reaching. Because he'd said he wasn't going to push her into anything she didn't want. And he meant to keep that promise.

When she couldn't stand the uncertainty any longer, she raised her face toward his. Still, he held himself rigid.

Last night she had told him she wanted to kiss him. What she'd really wanted was to make love with him. But she'd been afraid to act on her desire. She wasn't going to let fear stand in her way again.

With a heady feeling of power, she took a step closer and brushed her lips against his. It was only the barest contact, but all the good things she'd felt the night before came swirling back over her like a shower of stars raining down from a black velvet sky.

Slowly she experimented with the pleasure of it, rubbing her mouth back and forth against his, increasing the pressure, nibbling, taking his lip between her teeth, then easing up.

"Do I have to do all the work?" she asked, her mouth millimeters from his.

"No," he answered in a strangled voice, just before his mouth took command and his arms tightened around her.

The kiss went from warm to white-hot in the space of a heartbeat. He angled his head, his mouth skilled and hungry, so that her knees weakened—she needed to anchor her hands against his shoulders.

When he silently asked her to open her lips, she did his bidding—then shivered with delight as his tongue swept into her mouth, stroking, arousing.

This was what she'd craved from him all along, she thought with the last shreds of coherence her brain possessed, the two of them caught in the eye of a storm, so that the only hope of survival lay in clinging together. At the same time, a tiny grain of fear wavered at the edge of her consciousness.

She had asked for this. She wanted this. But the idea of giving up control was still daunting.

He must have sensed her uncertainty, because he raised his head.

"*Chère*," he murmured gently, "I asked you to tell me if I was going too fast for you. I mean it."

"You're not."

"I think I am. I think we'd better slow down a little."

He stepped back so that several inches of space separated them. With his body heat gone, a chill swept over her, and she cupped her hands convulsively around her shoulders.

"Chase—don't stop."

He had been looking at her. Now his eyes were fixed on some point outside the window.

As she watched, his expression changed from passionate to angry.

"Chase, what is it?"

Instead of answering her, he swore....

CHAPTER SIXTEEN

"CHASE, WHAT'S WRONG?" Julienne repeated.

"I saw somebody outside the house!"

"But..."

"One of your brothers. Hugo or Wyatt. I haven't seen them in a long time, so I don't know which it was. But I recognized the profile—the big beak of a nose. The jutting jaw."

She shook her head in denial. But even as she tried to tell herself it couldn't be true, she was turning toward the window, scanning the foliage behind the house. The scene was just as she had remembered it—the water oaks draped with Spanish moss. The cypress trees beyond them. The cane thicket. Yet now she wondered who might be lurking in the dappled shade.

"I'm going up to get my gun," Chase said. "You stay here—away from the windows."

She didn't want him to leave her, but she didn't protest as he strode toward the hall. Before she could draw in a dozen shallow breaths, he was back beside her, the gun in his hand.

"What are we going to do?" she asked.

"I'm going out there. You stay inside. Promise me that!"

She nodded.

"Promise! Say it."

"Okay. I promise to stay inside." As soon as the words

were out of her mouth, she closed her fingers around his arm. "You should stay inside, too."

"I'm not going to hide in here—waiting for them to do Lord knows what. Suppose they decide to set the house on fire?"

"Would they do something like that?"

"I don't know. If they're crazy enough to set traps, they're crazy enough to do anything."

Unwillingly, she nodded. Then her heart was in her throat as Chase opened the back door. Crouching low, he sprinted across the yard. As he did, she heard the unmistakable sound of a gunshot break the morning silence.

One of her brothers was shooting at him!

"Chase! Chase, are you all right?" she called out.

"Stay in there," he shouted.

The gun sounded again, and she knew she had made a terrible mistake. She'd forced him to call out to her, and that meant he'd given away his location.

Cursing herself for a fool, she looked around the kitchen, wondering what she could use for a weapon.

Hysterical laughter bubbled in her throat when she thought about attacking one of her brothers with a saucepan or a skillet.

Then she sobered. She and Chase needed help—real help.

But from whom?

This morning she'd stopped in his room to make his bed, because she'd wanted to touch the sheets where he'd slept.

Now, as she recalled the room, she remembered a cell phone lying on the old dresser.

Which meant that she could call the police. There was no hesitation on her part. The enemy out there might be her own flesh and blood, but her brothers had severed their ties with her weeks ago. She'd come to them in her hour of greatest need—when she'd had nowhere else to go. And they'd turned her away with a coldness that had cut her to the bone.

Quickly she sprinted for the steps, taking them two at a time. Then she was pounding down the hall to Chase's room.

The phone was on the dresser where she'd seen it. Snatching it up, she pressed the on button. The screen came to life, and she started to punch in 911.

Before she could finish dialing, the display flickered and dimmed, and she saw, to her horror, that the battery indicator on the lower right corner of the screen was showing almost no power left.

CHAPTER SEVENTEEN

WITH A SICK FEELING, Julienne put the cell phone where she'd found it on the dresser. It was out of power—probably because the electricity in the house wasn't turned on yet, and there was nowhere for Chase to recharge the battery.

So there was no way she could summon help. Not unless she drove into town. And that would probably be too late to help Chase.

No, the two of them were on their own.

As she stood in the middle of the room trying to decide what to do, she heard two more shots outside.

Chase? One of her brothers?

She pressed the flat of her hand to her lips. She didn't know what to do, but she knew she couldn't stay up here.

Feeling sick and shaky, she started down the stairs. It wasn't until she reached the bottom riser that she saw the figure standing just inside the hall.

It was Hugo, his dark eyes fixed on her and a gun in his hand.

As she stared at him, her heart started to pound so wildly in her chest that she could barely breathe.

Going very still, she tried to calm herself, tried to think. Then as she raised her chin, she asked, "What are you doing here?"

"Making sure Rousseau property doesn't end up in the wrong hands—Melancon hands."

"It's not Rousseau property. Grandfather left it to Chase."

"Chase Melancon is scum. He's stolen what's rightfully ours."

"He hasn't stolen anything. It was a gift, because Grandfather knew he'd take care of Belle Vista, cherish it, and you and Wyatt would just sell it to support your dissolute lifestyle."

Hugo made a snorting sound. "Well, aren't you high-and-mighty. Gotten over that incident at the office, have you?"

Her temper flared. "How dare you talk to me like that."

He laughed. "I see Melancon's made you feel a lot better about yourself. It was never any use warning you about him—was it? You were hot for him when you were just a kid. Now you've come back to be his whore. A clever way to get a piece of the pie."

"How can you be so coarse?"

He laughed in her face, and she saw all the bitterness he'd built up over the years. She'd always been her grandfather's favorite. And she'd always known her brothers hated her for it. She'd also known that they were grasping and manipulative. It was only recently that she'd realized how truly rotten they were. But how far would they go? Would Hugo shoot his own sister?

Before she could answer that question, a bloodcurdling scream from outside split the air.

Then men were shouting. It sounded like more than two voices, but she couldn't be sure what was happening or who was out there. Maybe her brothers had brought reinforcements.

Hugo whirled toward the door, and Julienne took that opportunity to escape. Clearing the stairs, she dashed down the hall—keeping to the right side, where the wood was intact. As soon as she passed the hole where Chase had removed the damaged boards, she angled to the left, hugging the wall as she went.

"Come back here!" Hugo shouted, taking off after her.

Praying that the light was too dim for Hugo to see exactly where he was going, she sprinted for the kitchen.

"Stop or I'll shoot," he warned, and she braced for the impact of a bullet in her back....

CHAPTER EIGHTEEN

THE GUN NEVER FIRED. Instead, Julienne heard a terrible scream as Hugo reached the hole in the floor and plunged through.

She heard him scream again. "My leg. It's my leg."

Then he was silent. She found the flashlight that Chase had been using and crept to the hole. Hugo held up his hand to her, then let it drop back.

"I'm hurt bad," he moaned.

"Just lie still," she told him. "We'll get you medical help—then call the police."

"I'm your brother. You can't turn me over to the police," he gasped.

"You're no brother of mine. Not after what you've done. You and Wyatt are a disgrace to the Rousseau name."

She saw a shadow in the hall and looked up to find a man standing in the doorway. It wasn't Chase.

When she cringed away from him, he called her name. "Julienne, it's all right. I'm Chase's friend, Tyler Belton. It looks as though I picked a good time to pay you a visit." He looked inside the hole at the injured Hugo.

"I met up with Chase and some trouble outside. Chase asked me to come inside to tell you he's okay, and to help you. But it looks as if you have the situation in here under control."

She stared at Tyler Belton, remembering his name from

long ago. One summer Chase had gotten into some trouble and been sent to a camp for delinquent boys. The experience had toughened him. But he'd also come home talking about the friends he'd made—Tyler Belton and two others boys whom she'd probably remember if she heard their names.

"What—what are you doing here?" she stammered.

"It's a long story. I'm a federal agent, but no one knows I'm here because of an undercover assignment that went bad." Tyler shrugged. "So I can't stick around, but I called the police for you." He moved toward the open door.

"Wait."

Tyler turned to face her. "I can't. I'll be back when I can."

Then he was gone, and she wondered whether she'd only dreamed him.

Hours later Julienne lay on her bed, her mind still trying to cope with the events of the past few hours. The police had carted her no-good brothers away. Chase had told her what had happened outside.

Tyler had shown up, and the two of them had closed in on Wyatt, giving him no choice but to flee into the swamp—where he'd stumbled into one of the traps he'd set. That was the scream she'd heard outside—the trap springing on his foot. Only, *his* shoes hadn't been sturdy enough to stop the metal teeth from digging into his flesh.

Now everybody was gone, and all she felt was relief that her brothers wouldn't be able to hurt her or Chase.

She looked up and found him standing in the doorway, watching her.

"Are you all right?" he asked, taking a step inside the room. "I mean, after everything that's happened?"

She sat up and held out her arms, and he came to her, clasping her tightly.

"Now I'm fine," she murmured.

"You need to rest."

"I *was* resting. Now I need to pick up where we left off before we were so rudely interrupted." Before he could protest again, she pressed her lips to his. At the first contact of his mouth on hers, she felt time fold back on itself. They were where they'd been before the shooting had started. Back into the eye of the hurricane.

Only, now her feelings were sharper—sweeter. Because in the hours since Chase had held her, she knew she'd almost lost him. "Chase, make love to me," she whispered.

"You're sure that's what you want?"

"Don't you?"

"It doesn't matter what I want."

"Yes, it does."

She found his hand and brought it to her breast.

He sucked in a sharp breath as he cupped his palm around her, then gently stroked his fingers back and forth across her hardened nipple.

She sighed with pleasure. "Oh, that's so good."

"Oh, yes."

"Chase, I want everything—everything a man and a woman can give each other."

"I want that, too. Because I love you."

"Oh, Chase. I love you so much!"

He searched her eyes, saw that she spoke the truth. "Tell me what you need. Tell me how to make this perfect for you."

It was hard to say the words, but she knew she had to tell him what would work for her when they made love....

CHAPTER NINETEEN

"I WANT TO MAKE LOVE with you so much. But maybe it would be better if we don't lie down. If I don't have to worry about your weight pressing over me, I won't be frightened," Julienne whispered.

Chase nodded, then slipped off his shoes and scooted back, propping his shoulders against the wall as he had the night before, and she came into his arms. He folded her close, then turned to kiss her cheek, her hair, her eyebrows, murmuring loving words.

When she stayed where she was, he locked his eyes with hers and slowly lowered the zipper of her shift. Slipping his hands inside, he splayed them against her flesh.

His hands played with her back, then slid up and down her ribs, touching the sides of her breasts. She sighed with pleasure, then whispered, "I want more."

"All you have to do is tell me how much—and when."

She nodded, knowing she had to convince him that she was ready for this. So she angled away from him, then boldly pulled her dress over her head and unhooked her bra.

When she'd tossed them both away, she raised her eyes to his again.

His gaze was dark and heated and worshipful. "Lord, I knew you'd be beautiful," he murmured, reaching to gently touch her. "I didn't know you'd be stunning."

He gave her tiny, provocative kisses as he caressed her

breasts, then discarded his own shirt and pulled her into his arms—the touch of his naked skin against hers setting off shocks of pleasure along her nerve endings.

He seemed to know what would feel good, what would drive her higher and yet higher, so that there was only the joy of being with him like this.

Nothing with him felt forced or false. It was all so tender, so natural, so thrilling that she wondered why she had ever been afraid of giving herself into his care.

His hands moved over her body, finding what gave her the most pleasure. And as he touched her and whispered words of love, he healed the pain in her heart and in her spirit.

When they were both naked and he had made her ready for him, he urged her onto his lap, facing him, her legs straddling his.

She felt a moment of hesitation then.

He gave her a soft kiss. "*Chère,* we don't have to go any further. Not tonight. There's plenty of time for everything."

"This is the time, Chase. Our time."

She raised her hips, then lowered them, bringing him inside her, a high sound escaping from her throat as his body joined with hers.

He went absolutely still, and she knew he was still offering her the chance to stop. Instead she gave him a tremulous smile, and the smile turned to triumph as she took him more deeply inside her. For a trembling moment she felt overwhelmed. Then she began to move again, slowly at first.

His lips were at her ear, telling her how wonderful she felt, clasping him so tightly. And his hands stroked her breasts, stroked her most sensitive flesh, building her need to heights she had never imagined. The rhythm became fast and frantic. She gasped, clutched his shoulders, feeling her body clench and release in a cascade of ecstasy.

And then her joy was complete as she heard his shout of satisfaction and knew that he had followed her into paradise.

Luxuriously limp, she sagged against him.

"Oh, Chase," she murmured. "That was beautiful."

"Oh, yes," he agreed, kissing her lips and then her cheek.

CHAPTER TWENTY

JULIENNE STILL FLOATED on a current of pleasure as Chase stretched her out beside him, pulled the sheet over them, and gathered her in his arms.

"How are you?" he whispered as his lips skimmed the tender place where her hair met her cheek.

"Wonderful. Chase, you healed me. You knew how to make me whole again."

His arm tightened around her. "I only did what I've been wanting to do for years."

"You did it very well," she whispered, snuggling against him.

No woman had ever been so cherished or so loved, she thought as she relaxed in his embrace, relaxed into the most satisfying sleep she'd had in months.

Some time later, she felt his lips graze her cheek. "Want to get up and have breakfast?"

"Breakfast! We never did have it, did we?"

"We can cook it together," he said, climbing out of bed, giving her a view of his magnificent body as he found the jeans he'd discarded and pulled them on.

He probably knew she was feeling a little shy, because he left before she slipped out of bed.

By the time she'd dressed in her shift again and come downstairs to the kitchen, he was already expertly frying the toast.

"I see you didn't need my help."

He grinned. "I can do the easy stuff."

She set the table, then ducked outside and gathered some blue chicory flowers that had rooted at the side of the house, placing them in one of her grandfather's best cut-glass vases.

"Nice," Chase complimented her, leaning down to nuzzle her neck.

"Next time I'll find something fancy."

"I don't need fancy. I like homey."

A few minutes later, as they sat across the table from each other, he rubbed his bare foot against her leg and said, "I haven't told you my plans for Belle Vista."

"I'd like to hear them," she answered, leaning eagerly toward him.

"I want to fix up the house—and the garden. Then I'm going to turn it into a B and B."

"That sounds like a fine idea."

He reached across the table and clasped her hand. "Do you want to do it with me? Do the decorating—then help me run the place?"

She raised her eyes and stared at him.

She saw a smile flicker on his lips. "I guess I'm really asking if you want to marry me."

Taken by surprise, she heard her fork clatter to her plate.

His expression turned wary. "You don't like the idea?"

She turned her palm up, gripped his hand more tightly. "I love the idea," she answered. "I've wanted to be with you for so long. But I thought it was just a dream that was never going to come true."

"It was like that for me, too," he agreed. She saw him swallow before continuing. "Then when I came back here and found you waiting for me, I was too shocked to admit what I was really feeling."

She kept her gaze steady on his. "Chase, I didn't come

here by accident. Before Grandfather died, he told me about his will. He told me to come back here—to you. He said he'd realized that you and I belonged together. He wanted to give this place to both of us, and that was the only way he could do it. Because he knew if he left it to me, you'd be too proud to come back here and accept 'charity' from a Rousseau.''

It was Chase's turn to look stunned. "He said all that?"

She nodded. "I was afraid to trust his judgment. Afraid you wouldn't want me. Then I knew that coming back to you was the only way to…to make myself whole again."

"It took courage to come here."

She gave a little shake of her head. "I was scared. But wanting to be with you was stronger than my fear."

"Thank the Lord," he murmured.

"And now I'm so happy," she whispered around the lump in her throat. "I never thought I'd be happy again. But here we are having this meal together, like it's the most natural thing in the world—and at the same time, the most astonishing, magical thing."

"It is," he answered, his voice thick with emotion. "All of that."

She smiled at him through her tears, clasping him more tightly, their locked hands the link to the past and their present and the rich future that waited for them.

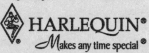

HARLEQUIN®
INTRIGUE®

LOOKING FOR BREATHTAKING ROMANTIC SUSPENSE?

HARLEQUIN HAS A SPECIAL OFFER FOR YOU....

During March, April and May 2003, present this coupon
at any of your favorite retailers and save 50¢ off
your next purchase of a Harlequin Intrigue® book!

SAVE 50¢

off the purchase of one book
from Harlequin Intrigue®.

52604528

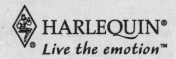

HARLEQUIN®
Live the emotion™

HARLEQUIN®
INTRIGUE®

LOOKING FOR BREATHTAKING ROMANTIC SUSPENSE?

HARLEQUIN HAS A SPECIAL OFFER FOR YOU....

During March, April and May 2003, present this coupon at any of your favorite retailers and save 50¢ off your next purchase of a Harlequin Intrigue® book!

SAVE 50¢
off the purchase of one book from Harlequin Intrigue®.

5 65373 00050 2   (8100) 0 11045

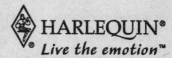

HARLEQUIN®
Live the emotion™